THE WARRIOR TRAINER

"Russell, the winner of *RT*'s American Title II contest last year, debuts with an action-packed, emotion-driven story that immediately captures your attention. Readers yearning for strong heroines and masterful men will find them here, along with a carefully plotted story. Russell's fresh voice secures her a place on the to-buy list."

—*Romantic Times BOOKreviews*

"*The Warrior Trainer* is a romantic, action-packed story. Scotia is as hard as stone, except when it comes to those she loves. The characters are lovely and the story line will keep you coming back for more. I highly recommend this debut novel from talented new author Gerri Russell."

—Fresh Fiction

"*The Warrior Trainer* is an intelligent, heart-wrenching historical romance that convincingly and seamlessly weaves actual history and mythical fiction together in a work of literary craftsmanship. Gerri Russell has succeeded in rendering emotions, both ecstatic and agonizing, onto the written page. Pangs of joy and grief will linger long after the read is done. *The Warrior Trainer* is a wonderful gift from a very talented author."

—Romance Junkies

"Gerri Russell provides a strong fictional twist to the authentic history. The story line is action-packed from the start. Fans of medieval romance with a wee bit of a whimsical legend (anchored in history) will enjoy this fine tale of a daring skillful heroine and the laird who loves her."

—Book Crossing

THE WARRIOR'S RETURN

Rhiannon shut the door of her bedchamber behind her. She leaned against the wood, trying to steady herself. Her breath came in short, sharp bursts, not because she'd run through the castle to get to her room, but because of the magnitude of what she'd almost revealed to Camden.

Her physical response to his presence had been immediate. The heat had moved through her body in mindless, melting waves. She had wanted to touch him, to greet his return in a very different sort of way. She wanted to touch him still.

"Rhiannon."

A shock of desire moved through her.

"Open the door." His voice sounded thick.

"I can't," she whispered.

"You can't or you won't?"

Silence followed.

He'd gone. Rhiannon leaned back against the door, grateful that he'd left and yet disappointed all the same.

A moment later he stood in the door that separated her room from Violet's. She could see the tension in his body as he slowly moved toward her.

"Camden."

"We need to finish what we started below."

Other *Leisure* books by Gerri Russell:

WARRIOR'S BRIDE
THE WARRIOR TRAINER

GERRI RUSSELL

Warrior's LADY

LEISURE BOOKS NEW YORK CITY

A LEISURE BOOK®

October 2008

Published by

Dorchester Publishing Co., Inc.
200 Madison Avenue
New York, NY 10016

ISBN 10: 0-8439-6111-2
ISBN 13: 978-0-8439-6111-9

The name "Leisure Books" and the stylized "L" with design are
trademarks of Dorchester Publishing Co., Inc.

Printed in the United States of America.

10 9 8 7 6 5 4 3 2 1

Visit us on the web at www.dorchesterpub.com.

"Each man stands with his face in the light of his own drawn sword. Ready to do what a hero can."
—Elizabeth Barrett Browning

Thank you always to my editor, Leah Hultenschmidt, and my agent, Pamela Ahearn. You both light my way and smooth the path.

Also, thank you to my four "angels": Tammy Fleis, Mary Queitzsch, Dorothy Summerill, and Kristy Szablya. Your care and kindness kept me going during one of the most difficult times of my life.

And to my husband, Chuck; after twenty-three years, no matter the obstacles, the magic is still there.

Warrior's
LADY

Prologue

Scotland, 1377

She was not a witch. When had healing people become a crime?

Clara Lockhart's breath formed a white shroud in the air, lingering but a moment before vanishing into nothingness. The hazy gray light of the approaching dawn crept through the small barred opening cut into the heavy wooden door of her prison cell, heralding the birth of a new day. Her last day on this earth, unless a miracle saved her.

Through the opening she could hear the muffled voices of men milling about, preparing for the day.

Heaven help me. Clara grasped the bars that lined the window, the solid, cold metal a stark reminder of her situation. She'd be hanged by the first light of morning, all for the sake of a stone.

Soft footsteps padded toward her. A moment later the gentle face of Mother Agnes appeared, framed by her black wimple as she peered through the door's opening. "Clara?"

"I am here." Hope blossomed inside her.

"Open this door, young man," the nun demanded.

The rattling of keys preceded the soft creaking of the door opening. Mother Agnes slipped inside.

The nun stepped forward and clasped Clara's hands in her bony ones. "My dear Clara, what have they done to you?"

"I am charged with witchcraft." Speaking the words opened the dam of emotion trapped inside since her capture and imprisonment. Tears escaped their confines, racing down her cheeks unheeded.

"Oh, my heavens." The nun pulled Clara to her, pressing Clara's head against her shoulder.

"I always knew it was a possibility, yet I had hoped for something more," Clara sobbed, burying her face in the rough wool of Mother Agnes's habit. She had married into the Lockhart family. And with her husband's love she had accepted the burden the family carried: to heal the sick, whether human or beast.

"The Charm Stone," Mother Agnes whispered into the still air of the dawn.

Clara straightened, then reached down to pull up the hem of her heavy damask gown. Slowly, she unwound a length of linen she had tied to her upper thigh. She pressed the bundle into Mother Agnes's hands. "Along with Robert the Bruce's heart, the Lockharts carried the Charm Stone back from the Holy Land. 'Twas the one good thing that came out of the Crusades. This Stone is not a source of witchcraft as the bishop claims."

Mother Agnes's gaze snapped to the closed doorway, as fear drove the color from her face. "If he finds the Stone—"

"Make certain he doesn't," Clara whispered, increasing her grip on the nun's hands. "If I must die for a crime I did not commit, I beg you to protect the Stone for my daughter."

Mother Agnes's eyes widened. "What of the danger to such a young child?"

Pain clutched Clara's chest at the thought of what she risked. "If I cannot protect Violet, then maybe the Stone can. It will give her the ability to heal herself and survive to adulthood."

"When so many die young, that is worth the risk." Mother Agnes nodded. "Where is Violet?"

"Hidden at the castle. You must retrieve her. You know

where." Clara's gaze met the nun's, searching for under-standing.

Mother Agnes inclined her head slightly, indicating with-out words that she knew where to look. "When I know it is safe to do so, I will send her to her uncle."

"My thanks," Clara said, as a sense of peace came over her. This was not how she wanted to end her life, but it eased her mind knowing that Mother Agnes' care would in-crease the odds of Violet surviving to carry on the tradition of the Lockhart clan.

With wooden movements, Mother Agnes slid the bundle containing the Charm Stone into the folds of her habit.

The rhythmic beat of a hammer pierced the silence, and any peace Clara might have imagined vanished. Her knees grew weak. She reached a hand toward the cold stone wall of the prison to steady herself and squeezed her eyelids shut against the growing light of day. But even the self-imposed darkness did not block the knowledge that men were preparing the platform where she would take her final breath.

She opened her eyes. Her other hand crept up to her neck. "Is there any hope of reprieve, Mother Agnes? Or am I a fool to ask?"

"I have tried, my dear." Sorrow shadowed the lines etched into the old nun's face. "The bishop's decree is binding. All I can offer is my presence and my prayers."

Cold spread through Clara's limbs, taking with it any hope of rescue. There was no one to intervene. Not her husband James, who had been murdered the night of her capture. Not her brother-in-law Camden. He might be strong enough to defy the bishop's decree, but she would be dead before word of her situation ever reached him.

Heavy footfalls sounded outside. Mother Agnes clasped Clara's hands within her own. The door to her cell creaked open. A swath of morning light streaked across the dirt floor. Clara blinked against the sudden brightness. She ducked her head as her eyes adjusted to the new source of light. She returned her gaze to the door.

Her accuser.

The bishop entered the chamber, his ornate cape fluttering to a stop as he filled the open doorway. He bowed his head, bearing its tall triangular hat, in greeting. The man looked more like the harbinger of death than a shepherd to his people.

"Bishop Berwick." Mother Agnes glared at the supposed holy man with burning, reproachful eyes. "Healing the sick has never been an act of witchcraft."

"Good day to you both, Mother Agnes, Lady Lockhart. The charges stand." He signaled for the guard at the door to enter. "Escort Mother Agnes to her horse cart."

The guard clasped the nun's arm. Mother Agnes jerked away. "I will not abandon Clara in her time of need."

The bishop's dark eyes grew stormy. "Stay until she swings if you must. But you *will* leave us alone while I take the woman's confession."

The guard reached for the nun's arm once more, his grip solid despite her attempts to break free. Over her objections, he wrestled her from the prison cell.

As Mother Agnes's voice faded in the distance, the bishop's gaze filled with contempt. "Now that your little savior is gone, I'll ask you one last time: Where is the Charm Stone?"

Clara looked away. A long, heavy silence ensued as she struggled with her thoughts. She knew the bishop would never drop the charges of sorcery, that she would face her death whether she revealed the location of the Stone or not. And yet some part of her hoped, prayed, that he might be merciful.

She inhaled a shaky breath, knowing what her response must be. She met his hard, unyielding gaze. "I can give you no knowledge of the Stone."

"The widow Clarence said in her confession that you healed her phlegmatic chest. She was quite willing to call your work a miracle. But we both know that cannot be true." He narrowed his eyes. "Miracles are not performed by mere commoners. Therefore, you must be a witch."

"You would violate your sacred privilege in taking the woman's confession for your own gain?" Shock caused the words to wedge in her throat.

His gaze hardened. "I'll do what I must to get that Stone. Tell me where it is or I'll be forced to wrest that information from your daughter."

"Leave Violet alone." Anger deepened her voice.

"For the last time, where is the Stone?"

Clara clamped her jaw tight. He'd get nothing from her. *"Fool."*

Clara kept her shoulders straight. Her daughter and the Stone would be safe.

The bishop shot her a withering glance. "So be it." He signaled, and two more guards appeared at the doorway. "Take her to the gallows."

Her anger faded and fear permeated her mind, but she allowed only courage to reflect in her gaze. Clara strode toward the men with grim purpose. At the bishop's side, she hesitated. "I go to my death with a clear conscience and a pure heart. Will the same be said of you?" She caught his gaze with her own. In his eyes, she saw a flicker of fear before rage swamped it.

"Who are you to judge me?" His hand snaked out.

Stinging pain blossomed across her cheek. "An innocent woman."

"God will judge innocence, but here on Earth your death will serve as a warning to the clan of Lockhart. One of you will surrender that Stone or all of you will meet a violent end."

Violet. Clara hoped her own sacrifice would be enough

to protect her daughter. Let the bishop's threats be hollow.

Clara looked in the man's eyes again and fought to keep despair from rising anew at the cold determination in his eyes.

Chapter One

As the sun slowly rose over the horizon, the weary Lockhart clansmen rode through the gates of Lee Castle. They had ridden hard most of the night, eager to return home. Their latest battle against the English invaders had been a triumph. But who knew how long it would be before King Edward III sent another army to take their place? Until then, Camden Lockhart intended to enjoy the fleeting moments of peace.

He led his men through the grassy expanse of the outer bailey. *Home.* His haven. He owed so much to his brother for granting him Lee Castle. His brother had known how much this place meant to Camden after the nightmare of his youth.

And even though he was home, the relief he expected at the sight of the familiar walls did not come. Instead, an odd tingling crept across the back of his neck, as if warning him that all was not as it seemed.

The closer they came to the gate leading into the inner bailey, the tauter his nerves became. His instincts warned of danger. He drew his sword and charged forward. His men did the same.

Camden burst into the courtyard. His heart stilled. His fist tightened on the hilt of his sword. Silence descended.

Seven warriors lay dead. Their bodies were strewn across the courtyard, the violence of their deaths obvious from the agony etched into their faces.

But it was not the men who captured Camden's gaze. Nay, his gaze swept across the carnage to the tall, freshly

cut cross, driven into the soil at the base of the stairs to the
keep—a cross that bore the body of his brother. James's
dark eyes stared down at Camden, frozen in a rictus of
agony. His brother's body had been disemboweled, the
sword still protruding from his gut.

James. Camden's sword fell from his hand, hitting the
ground with a thump. The sound echoed through the palpable silence.

A sudden cold sickness clenched Camden's stomach. He
dismounted, then raced forward, wrenching the sword from
James's flesh. Rivulets of his brother's blood trickled down
the blade, engulfed his hand. Not James! Camden squeezed
the hilt of the murderous weapon until the pain in his hand
matched the pain in his soul. He let loose an inhuman
sound that filled the silence, reverberating through the
Highland hills the unbridled sorrow that swamped him.

Orrin, his lifelong friend and man-at-arms, appeared at
his side. Gently, he tried to pry the weapon from Camden's hand.

"I'll cut him down, milord, if you'll loosen your grip,"
Orrin pleaded.

The words barely sank through the turmoil that crowded
Camden's mind. From somewhere outside himself he
watched his men dismount with a speed that belied their
weariness, and race forward to assist Orrin. With the ut-
most care, they lowered James's mutilated body from the
cross.

Camden released the pin from his cloak and laid it upon
the ground, cradling James in the softness of the wool.

"Why would someone do such a thing to Lord Lockhart and his men?" asked Hamish, the youngest warrior of
the group, his tone barely above a whisper.

Why? Camden's mind screamed the same question as he
balled his fists, fighting back the rage that threatened—a
rage that had been building for the last ten years. 'Twas a

rage he'd never given in to—a part of him that once un-leashed might consume him and devour those he loved.

The feel of James's cold blood trickling down his arm brought him back to the moment. Camden forced himself to relax, to breathe the sweet Highland air—air free of the tang of salt and the grit of sand. He had to put his own emotions aside. He had to be strong, brave, dependable. His men, and his brother, deserved that much and more.

"Who would do such a thing?" asked Kyle, another of the younger warriors in the group of twelve men who surrounded Camden and James.

"I can tell you who," Orrin said, his gaze fixed on the sword in his hands. "This blade bears the markings of clan Ruthven."

"Ruthven?" Titus, a warrior who had been with the Lockharts for years, reared back, his eyes wide. "The traitors have betrayed their countrymen yet again."

"What shall we do?" Kyle asked.

Hamish drew his sword. "I am prepared to fight."

Camden could not answer past the constriction in his throat. A wave of hatred, black and burning like acid, boiled up from some hidden depth of his soul, pulsing through his blood and cramping the muscles in his gut. He had somehow known the Ruthvens were involved.

"'Twas Dougall Ruthven and a band of Englishmen that attacked us." A weak voice came from the stairs.

Camden's gaze shot to his steward's. The aging retainer clung to the wooden railing near the stairs. His garments were slashed to tatters. Fresh blood oozed from wounds on his shoulder, thigh, and abdomen. Bertie's face was a translucent white, and it looked as though it took every ounce of his strength to remain upright. "That vile Ruthven betrayed your brother. He betrayed us all." On unsteady legs, Bertie struggled down the stairs.

Camden surged forward to help his servant, his friend.

"Damn the Ruthvens." The words squeezed through taut white lips. "Dougall Ruthven set us up, drawing me away to Glasgow, then luring James and his men here, knowing they'd be a small contingent and unprepared for battle."

Orrin raced to Bertie's side as well, helping Camden guide the aging servant down the stairs of the keep. Orrin's face filled with barely concealed violence. "Shall I prepare the men?"

Fighting his desire to agree, Camden shook his head. He had to remain logical and in control of his emotions. "We have to bury James and his men. Then we must go to Lady Lockhart and Lady Violet." Camden sent up a silent prayer that his sister-in-law and niece had somehow been spared.

Working in silence, Camden and his men dug graves in the churchyard for the warriors. Then Camden methodically wrapped strips of linen around his brother's body and set it in the Lockhart family plot. He carefully placed James next to their father's final resting place, then smoothed the soft earth back into place. As soon as he was able, Camden would commission a tombstone to be created in James's honor here at Lee Castle.

And even though Lee Castle was the lesser seat of the Lockhart family, it had been their family home long before James had commissioned Lockhart Castle to be built. It seemed right that James had ended up here, with Camden and all the others who had loved him so well.

Camden braced himself against the ache of sentimentality. He could think on such things later, after he made certain his sister-in-law and niece were safe. Yet even as the thought formed, he realized no Lockhart would ever be safe as long as the Ruthvens still roamed the land. His own life was proof of that.

He brushed the dirt on his hands against the soft wool of his tartan. What they'd done to him . . . what he'd had to survive . . . Camden forced the thoughts away. Nay, he would not go back there. He would never give the Ruthvens that kind of control over him again.

"Bring me a fresh horse," Camden called to the men near the stable.

"What do you intend to do?" Orrin asked, his body tensed, awaiting orders.

Camden bent down to retrieve the Ruthven crested sword. With methodical care, he wiped the blade clean of James's blood, then slipped the weapon into the sheath at his back. "Lady Lockhart and Lady Violet should be my first priority." He stood. "But James deserves a swift revenge." And he knew what to do. A quick and violent end was more than the Ruthvens deserved.

"You are right to think that Lady Lockhart and Lady Violet could be in trouble." Orrin met Camden's gaze, his concern palpable.

"That's why you will take the men and head to Lockhart Castle. As soon as I put my plan in motion, I shall join you there."

"Revenge?"

Camden gave a savage nod. "Justice. This time the Ruthvens will suffer. They have murdered too many Scots, collaborated with the English, and tormented this family for far too long." Fury coiled within him, vibrating with intensity. "It will end here and now, until they no longer walk these lands in human form."

Orrin frowned. "Revenge has a way of coming back at you."

"Not this time."

Camden strode through the darkened streets of Glasgow, toward the alley where the blacksmith on the green near the River Clyde had directed him. The glare of the torch in his hand caused eerie shadows to play across red stone walls wet with brackish slime. Mist from the river hung heavy on the air, seeped through his cloak, while the stench of sewage clotted in his nostrils.

And despite the dreary, ghostly facade the night cast upon this dangerous part of town, Camden found himself smiling. 'Twas the perfect part of town to find what he needed.

His boot heels beat a sharp tattoo on the cobbled street. A figure moved out of the shadows and into the light of the torch.

The glare from the flame made cruel work of the man's haggard and pinched face, and exposed an arsenal of weapons. Three lethal daggers nestled beneath a harness over his chest, and a sword lay strapped to his back. The man waited, hands on hips. "Ye lookin' for trouble?"

"The smithy said you were looking for work." Camden strode closer.

The man relaxed his hands. "What kind o' work ye got?"

"The lethal kind."

The man smiled, revealing brown, uneven teeth. "Murder?"

Camden lowered his voice. "Find and kill all the remaining Ruthvens."

The man's smile slipped. "All o' them?"

"Aye."

"It's gonna cost ye."

Camden's pulse beat thick and urgent in his veins as he unhooked a heavy bag of gold from his belt and tossed it to the ground at the man's feet. "There's half. You'll get the other half when your deed is done."

A soft jingle shattered the silence of the night as the stranger scooped up the bag. He opened the pouch. His expression grew serious. "Should I send ye word when they're dead?"

"The blacksmith will release the other half of your payment when you prove the remaining Ruthvens are dead."

The man nodded, then stepped back into the shadows. A moment later he was gone.

"The Ruthvens will rue the day they betrayed the Lockharts or any of their countrymen," Camden whispered into the night. He expected to feel a sense of satisfaction at the thought. He did not.

For the last ten years he had dreamed of nothing but his revenge against the Ruthvens. He'd plotted how he would make each and every one of the last remaining males pay for their part in his own torture and imprisonment. He had wanted them to suffer as he had suffered. And yet, now that the moment was at hand, it seemed less than heroic to hire a mercenary to destroy his enemy.

Clara and Violet need you. The thought steadied him, brought his focus back to the tasks that remained yet undone.

He strode back through the alley to his horse. He mounted, then kicked his horse into a gallop. Duty to his family forced his hand. He had no choice but to leave things as they were. Let the stranger execute his revenge.

His kin needed him more.

Chapter Two

Rhiannon Ruthven stopped. She forced her mind to quiet as she concentrated on the blade of soft green grass between her forefinger and her thumb. She held her breath and willed the beat of her heart to slow. The wind whispered through the field in which she lay flat on her back, trying for just a few moments to escape her troubles.

One blade of grass. Pliant yet strong. Simple yet part of a larger whole. And when one blade of grass went bad the others grew up around it, strangling it out. That's the way it should be. Not one bad blade of grass causing all the other blades of grass to be seen as bad for all eternity.

Rhiannon released a heartfelt sigh and flicked her grass among the others surrounding her head. "Why can't people be as simple as nature?"

The moment she gave voice to the words she regretted them. Her thoughts turned to Mother Agnes's lecture when Rhiannon had arrived at Taturn Abbey two weeks ago. It'd had something to do with apples and seeds—she being the bad seed, of course.

If her father were an apple, she wanted to be a pear.

Rhiannon squeezed her eyes shut, forcing back tears of pain and guilt. She'd loved her father, she supposed. Why else would she feel so empty at the thought of his death?

His brutal murder had turned her life upside down. And yet now that he was gone, why did she feel a sense of peace? Whether or not they liked her, Rhiannon had company in the other nuns at the abbey. She was no longer isolated and alone as she always had been, even in her own home. There she'd been separated from her brothers, spending days, weeks, even months without seeing or speaking to anyone. At least here at the abbey, they spoke to her. And while no one had been overly friendly, they had not been cruel either.

Rhiannon drew a breath. The air held just the hint of heather mixed with the earthier scent of grass. She extended her arms away from her sides and moved them through the supple spring grass. The blades bent beneath her assault, then bounced back into place as though nothing had ever disturbed them.

She'd come to the abbey two weeks ago because she'd had nowhere else to go. Her brothers, Dougall and Cory, cared nothing for her, having never known her. She'd had no kin to turn to. No one to turn to except God.

And Mother Agnes had called even that relationship into question. Rhiannon frowned at the clear sky overhead. She had come to the abbey, hoping to leave her life as a Ruthven behind. She'd wanted a fresh start, a new beginning. But even though Mother Agnes had taken her in, she'd refused to accept her as a novice, saying Rhiannon's calling was elsewhere. *Because even God had no need for a Ruthven.*

No matter how much she tried to convince Mother Agnes she was not her father's daughter, no matter what she did to show the abbess she could change, she would always be Rhiannon Ruthven. The bad seed.

"There you are," came a voice from over her head. Rhiannon looked up to see Sister Bernadette peering down. "I've been looking all over for you. Mother Agnes wants to see you," Sister Bernadette whispered, her eyes wide with trepidation.

Rhiannon sat up and twisted toward the only friend she'd made since coming to the abbey. "Me? Why?" A summons from the abbess usually boded trouble, and involved penance and often sacrifice for the summonee.

Rhiannon frowned. "Any idea why?"

Sister Bernadette shook her head. "She hasn't stopped pacing or praying since she returned from her trip to Lock-hart Castle."

Rhiannon jumped to her feet. "What has any of that to do with me?"

"I don't know." Sister Bernadette bit her lip. "But you best hurry to find out."

With a sense of impending doom, Rhiannon raced across the open grass back toward the abbey. She pushed the wrought-iron gates of the abbey's entrance aside and hurried down the long open breezeway that led to the abbess's office.

At the overly large wooden door, Rhiannon paused, taking a deep breath to compose herself. It would do her no good to stumble into the room in chaos. That would only reinforce what Mother Agnes and the others already thought of her. She reached up and quickly tucked the escaped ends of her hair beneath her wimple and veil. When she regained her composure, she pushed the heavy door open and stepped inside the golden glow of the room.

Despite the fact that it was the middle of the day, the room was blanketed in hazy darkness as three braces of candles at the front of the room struggled valiantly to force the shadows away.

Mother Agnes paced slowly back and forth in front of her small wooden desk, a worried frown tugging at the corners of her mouth.

"You asked to see me, Mother?"

The abbess's gaze swung to the doorway. "Rhiannon, my child. Come in. Sit down." She gestured toward a chair in the darkest corner. No doubt the place where "bad seeds" could not harm others. Rhiannon sat.

The abbess continued to pace. "I know what you think,

child. That I have been harsh with you." The abbess hesitated before her. "Perhaps I have."

Rhiannon's heart stumbled. "Does this mean that I may take my vows? Oh, thank you, Mother Agnes. I will not let you down. I will be the best—"

"Stop, child," she interrupted. "God has shown me a different path for you. You will leave here today."

Shock and bewilderment blanketed Rhiannon as effectively as the darkened shadows. "I can't go—"

"I know this is unexpected." The abbess stopped pacing. "True callings usually are."

Her words jarred Rhiannon from her stupor of disbelief. "What calling is that?" she asked, rising from her chair, entering the golden glow of the candlelight to stand before Mother Agnes. She needed to see the abbess's face, needed to read her expressions to understand why she was being cast out of the safety of the abbey and into the unknown.

A serene peace reflected on the abbess's face. "As of this moment, you are now a nursemaid to a young girl who desperately needs you." The abbess came forward. "It will not be an easy task. It is rough territory, and there will be many dangers. But I sense in you a deep strength."

"What kind of dangers?" Rhiannon asked cautiously.

"There are others—besides her family—who are looking for young Lady Violet. And not everyone would care for her well-being. I must caution you, Rhiannon, never to let Bishop Berwick anywhere near this child. Her life could be in danger if you do."

Before Rhiannon could react to the strange words, the abbess reached into the folds of her habit and produced a small bundle of linen, then handed it to Rhiannon. "Take this. Protect it with your life until you deliver it safely to Violet's uncle, Camden Lockhart. He'll know what to do with it."

The abbess gripped Rhiannon's hands firmly in her own.

"A few last words of advice I must impart to you. Whatever happens to you from this moment forward, you must fill your heart with forgiveness."

Rhiannon frowned. What did that mean? Before she could ask for an explanation, the abbess turned away to open the door to the room. Framed by the doorway stood a girl of no more than six, her gaze cast to the floor, her shoulders slumped forward. Golden hair fell in knotted clumps down to her waist. Her simple dress was shredded and dirty, as though she'd lived through some horrific trauma.

"Oh, my," was all Rhiannon could think to say. But those words brought the girl's gaze to her own. And Rhiannon forgot to breathe. Pain, loneliness, and uncertainty echoed in the depths of the child's soft blue eyes—emotions she herself had been familiar with from the time she was a child.

"You will leave with Lady Violet immediately," Mother Agnes announced. "Gather your belongings and meet us at the horse cart."

As much as Rhiannon wanted to protest, she knew she could not. She had seen too much of herself in the young girl's eyes. She wanted to ask where she was headed or why the abbess had chosen her, but in that moment, her own worries seemed so small and insignificant.

That girl needed someone as much as Rhiannon herself did.

After half a day's ride, Orrin and the other warriors found the gates of Lockhart Castle open wide. A sense of unease came over Orrin as they entered the grounds unchallenged.

As they rode through the bailey, men and women dressed all in black stopped their activities to watch the warriors' progression. The blacksmith halted his mallet midblow. The women milking the cows ceased their undulating rhythms. The women at the quern stone stopped grinding the wheat into flour as the warriors approached the keep.

The residents were all dressed in black—the color of mourning. A chill crept up Orrin's spine. How could they possibly know about Lord Lockhart's death? The news could not have traveled that quickly in these Highland hills. Unless it was not the lord's death they grieved. . . .

Orrin dismounted and handed the reins to a stable boy who raced out to greet them. "Where might I find Lady Lockhart?" Orrin asked.

The young boy's gaze shifted to the ground, but not before Orrin noted how the color drained from his cheeks. "My good sir—"

"Who are you?" a voice beckoned from behind him.

Orrin twisted toward the entrance of the keep.

The Bishop Berwick glided down the stairs. His eyes narrowed and his features sharpened with hostility as he drew closer. "You wish to see Lady Lockhart? Why?"

"Your Grace." Orrin offered the holy man a bow. "I am Orrin MacAllister, friend and loyal servant of Camden Lockhart. He sent me here to check on his sister-in-law and niece. Do you know where I might find them?"

A hint of suspicion filled the bishop's gaze as he crossed his arms over his chest. The rich brocade of his gown with its gold trimmings seemed out of place in the dusty bailey. "I had rather hoped *you* could tell *me* where I might find the girl, Lady Violet."

"Lady Violet?" Orrin asked.

"Aye, she's gone missing."

"And Lady Lockhart?" Cold dread rode through Orrin at the way the bishop's lips curled into a half-smile.

"She was hanged two days past for her crime of witch-craft."

"Witchcraft? That's absurd," Orrin spat out. "Who brought the charge against her?"

"I did." The bishop's grin held a hint of superiority. "'Twas my duty as a servant of the Church to expose her to the Church council for what she was. They found her guilty and sentenced her to death."

Orrin clenched his fists at his sides, desperate to control his growing anger. "She was the kindest of women and certainly no witch."

The bishop shrugged. "Her judgment has been made by those mightier than you or I."

Orrin shut his eyes and drew a breath. He had to stay in control. Attacking the bishop would not help him find Violet and certainly wouldn't help Camden. With his brother's death, Camden was now the clan leader. Good relations with the bishop would be critical with a weak Scottish king on the throne and the English king constantly stirring up the political climate and threatening their lives.

Like it or not, the bishop held the power, whether good or evil, over all their lives.

Orrin opened his eyes, feeling more in command of his emotions. "Where is her body? Might I at least take charge of her burial in Camden's stead?"

"No need, Orrin. I will take charge from here on out." Camden's steely voice broke into the conversation. Orrin turned to his friend, thankful that he'd returned from Glasgow to join his men. The bishop would not deny Clara's body to the new Lord Lockhart. Camden brought his horse to a stop at the bishop's feet. The bishop took a quick step back and frowned at the horse as it sniffed at the gold edging of his sleeves.

Camden's gaze, glittering with intense anger, penetrated the bishop's. "Where is Lady Lockhart's body?" His tone was as hard as his eyes. Even so, Orrin could see through the hardened exterior to the pain beneath.

Camden had lost his brother, his sister-in-law, and quite possibly his niece in the span of two days. And the strain of it showed. He sat his horse with confidence, but the flesh of his cheeks pulled taut over his high cheekbones, and the pain and sorrow mixed in his ice-blue eyes.

The bishop flinched. "I've left her mortal remains in the great hall. The servants laid her out. She'll receive no Christian burial from me."

"Then why are you here?" Camden demanded.

The bishop straightened. "I've come for the child, and for the Charm Stone. Both belong to me now."

"Lady Violet is still a Lockhart. And as I'm the leader of the clan now, that brings her under my care." Camden dismounted, then strode forward, stopping a hairsbreadth from the bishop's face. "And as for the Stone, it belongs to no one, least of all you. If I knew where it was, I'd make certain it never fell into your hands."

"Well—"

Camden moved forward, forcing the bishop back another step. "These grounds are also mine now that James and Clara have both been murdered." Camden let the emphasis fall on the last word, carefully observing the bishop's reaction.

The man paled.

Camden's face hardened. "Get out. Immediately."

"You'll regret this, Lockhart," the bishop said, the color in his face shifting from pale to mottled red.

Camden drew the sword that had been used to kill his brother and kept walking forward, maneuvering the bishop back to his horse that stood nearby.

At the sight of the sword, the bishop turned and fled. He barked orders at his man and a moment later, the horses lurched forward, heading for the gate. *You'll regret this, Lockhart.* The bishop's words hung in the air as they disappeared from sight.

"No more than the loss of my kin," Camden said so softly only Orrin could hear.

"Your orders, milord?" Orrin asked, knowing that his friend would prefer action to ruminating over what just transpired. There would be time for thought later.

Sincere gratitude reflected in Camden's eyes. He sheathed the sword at his back. "Gather Lady Lockhart's body. I want to take her back to Lee Castle with us. She deserves an eternal rest at her husband's side. And I will speak to the staff. Someone must know what happened to my niece."

Orrin watched Camden's body tense, as it did so often before they charged into battle side by side. If anyone could find Lady Violet, Camden would.

But was the girl dead or alive?

Chapter Three

Rhiannon breathed a sigh of relief when the driver of the horse cart came to a stop at the top of a ridge. The land below stretched twenty miles to the south to form a scenic panorama. Drifts of heavy snow still dotted the area, melting slowly into the streams and cataracts from the hills beyond.

"We're about a half day's journey to Lee Castle, milady," the driver announced as he swung down from the driver's seat. "We'll be heading down the ridge. I want to check the harness and the wheels before we do. You can never be too careful," he said with a cheerful wink.

Rhiannon wished she had half the man's enthusiasm, but she appreciated his caution. They'd made it this far without incident. For that she was grateful.

She cast a glance beside her. Violet sat at the far edge of the open air seat, a blanket wrapped snugly about her shoulders, and still she shivered beneath a weak spring sun.

"Would you like an extra blanket?" Rhiannon asked, breaking the silence that had stretched between them since leaving the abbey several hours ago.

A mighty shiver wracked the girl's body, but she remained silent.

Rhiannon knew she should offer the girl a kind word, or if she were any decent human being, she would pull the girl to her, offering to share her warmth, whether it was welcome or not. Still she hesitated. When she had done similar things in her youth, tried to assist an injured servant or joined in play with one of their children, they'd either flinched at her touch, or fled her company.

She'd learned long ago that no one wanted comfort from a Ruthven.

And still the child shivered.

Rhiannon dropped her gaze to the gray woolen blanket that covered Violet from shoulder to toes. She could hear the whistle of the driver as he inspected the front wheels, could feel the beat of her own heart beneath the warmth of her own blanket. She raised her gaze to the mottled gray and white sky overhead, took a deep breath, and pulled the little girl to her. Swiftly, she wrapped a second blanket around them both and she waited—waited for the refusal that was sure to come.

Instead, another powerful shiver wracked the child's body and then, she nestled against Rhiannon's side. She sighed, closed her eyes, and if Rhiannon wasn't mistaken, drifted off to sleep.

Warm tears sprang to Rhiannon's eyes. Such simple acceptance had never happened to her before. Rhiannon tightened the blanket around their two bodies, cocooning their heat. She held her body rigid, not knowing what else to do and unwilling to do anything that might make Violet move away.

Strange emotions tumbled through her. Joy and gratitude mixed with her ever-present fear of yet another rejection. "It's going to be all right, Violet," she whispered over the girl's head. She wasn't even sure if Violet heard her. But that didn't matter. The words were spoken more as a comfort for herself.

The driver finished his inspection and settled himself in the driver's seat. "Hang on," he warned. "This is going to be a steep descent."

As if obeying their master, the horses jerked forward, heading down the incline with sure and steady feet.

Rhiannon nodded, then closed her eyes as they started down the incline. Even as she kept repeating the words that they would be all right, a sense of doom nagged at her—a sensation she'd been unable to shake since her father's death. As unsettled as she felt now, she was certain the real trial would begin the moment she and Violet arrived at Lee Castle. Violet would be welcome, but what of her?

To that end, she opened her eyes and started rehearsing what she would say, how she would present herself. Perhaps she did not need to reveal who she truly was. Could she assume her mother's maiden name? Would they be more likely to accept her if she did?

So lost in thought was she that she startled when they were abruptly jerked to the left, then the right as the horse cart careened from one side of the path to the other.

Violet stiffened and turned to face Rhiannon, her eyes huge in her pale face. Still she remained silent, but Rhiannon read the plea in her gaze,

"I beg your pardon," Rhiannon called to the driver. "Could we please slow down?" Cool wind whipped past Rhiannon's cheeks as the horse cart continued to gain speed.

"Sir, please slow down." Rhiannon released her hold on Violet to slide forward on the wooden seat. She tapped him on the shoulder.

No response.

She shook him gently.

His body slumped sideways. His eyes stared vacantly back at Rhiannon.

Rhiannon gasped. Her throat locked with terror. An arrow protruded from his chest. *He was dead!*

They hit another bump, throwing Rhiannon hard against the left side of the cart. Violet shrieked. In the same instant, the reins slipped from the driver's hand, then disappeared over the front of the cart to dangle freely just above the ground behind the horses' feet.

The horses responded to the lack of restraint, picking up the pace to an even more dangerous speed. They had to slow down or they'd crash and likely be crushed to death.

Rhiannon's heart thundered in her chest. She clutched the wooden cart with white-knuckled force as she surveyed the ridge for whoever had killed their driver.

A lone horseman perched on the trail on the opposite side of the ridge, his longbow raised. A moment later, an arrow quivered in the wood above Rhiannon's hand. She threw herself back into the seat and quickly pulled Violet down into her lap.

"Violet, I need you to lie on the floorboards." Rhiannon didn't give the girl a chance to respond. She thrust the softly sobbing child out of view beneath the simple seat.

The cart careened from one side of the steep path to the other. The horses tossed their heads, their terrified cries mirroring Rhiannon's panic.

She forced her thoughts to clear and her nerves to steady. She had to stop the cart. She pushed out of the rear seat and tried to make herself as small a target as possible as she made her way to the driver's perch.

The cart slammed into the dirt wall on the left, knocking her back. Rhiannon's heart plunged, and she began muttering frantic prayers beneath her breath as she once again began to make her way to the front of the cart.

Wood creaked and splintered, no longer able to support their frantic pace. The horses, further panicked by the sound, pulled hard to the right. The right rear wheel slipped over the edge of the trail. The cart dipped crazily to the side.

As Rhiannon glanced over her shoulder to assess the damage, she saw a man on horseback racing down the path after them. His dark hair whipped around his face, a face set with determination.

Would he help them or finish the archer's job?

As Rhiannon was torn between stopping their wild ride and protecting Violet, the horseman maneuvered between the cart and the dirt wall. He grasped the harness of the horse on the left and brought the cart to a jerky stop.

The horses whimpered, and their sides heaved as they pranced in place. "Well done, my beauties," the man said to the beasts. As the horses quieted, he gently stroked the long, sleek neck of the mare beside him before he released first one horse, then the other from their harness.

That task complete, his gaze shifted. Ice-blue eyes commanded her attention. "Are you well?"

Jolted by the unexpected concern in his eyes, Rhiannon sat absolutely still. The man did not have the sinister look of a murderer, nor did he have the rugged, hungry look of a thief. Instead, he carried himself like a nobleman.

Rhiannon stared at the stranger for what seemed like half an eternity. Dark hair framed his face and fell to his shoulders—shoulders that were broad and sculpted beneath a finely tailored linen shirt.

A whistle followed by a sharp thwack ripped Rhiannon's attention from the stranger to the arrow imbedded in the seat beside her.

"Get down," the stranger commanded as he leapt from his horse and was at her side in a heartbeat. He grasped her hand.

"Nay," Rhiannon cried, pulling out of his grasp.

"You careless fool," he thundered, gripping her by the shoulders this time.

She wrestled free. Then, scooping Violet into her arms, thrust the little girl at the man. "Take her."

He accepted the bundle of arms and legs, then crouched to place her safely on the ground behind the cart.

While he did, Rhiannon stood and jumped down before the archer could get another shot at her.

Why would anyone be after her? Even as the thought

formed, she already knew the reason. She was a Ruthven. A bad seed. One her countrymen had no doubt finally decided to rid themselves of.

An arrow whizzed past her head. Rhiannon shrieked and ducked.

"Back here," the stranger commanded. Before she could take a step, he was beside her. He wrapped his arms around her shoulders, then guided her to the back of the cart.

Rhiannon could only follow his lead, so overwhelmed was she by the feeling of safety that his arms around her brought. Was that how Violet had felt earlier?

"Stay down," he commanded, as he cradled her in his arms. Rhiannon could see the archer from between the wheels of the cart. The dark rider drew another bow.

"There is nowhere for us to go." Rhiannon's breath hitched in her chest, from the stranger's nearness or from fear she did not stop to examine.

"Don't give up so easily, my sweet," he whispered beside her ear. She felt the warm caress of his breath against her skin. He smelled of musk and mint. He tucked the top of her head beneath his chin, and she felt small but safe cradled in his arms.

The archer aimed to strike, then lowered his weapon at the sound of a dozen or more horses racing toward them.

"My warriors," the stranger explained as he turned her in his arms. He smiled.

The archer put his heels to his horse's flanks and vanished over the lip of the ridge. The stranger's men followed in pursuit. " 'Tis not every day one finds a maiden in distress." His smile deepened the roguish cleft that divided his chin.

And even though he smiled, a glance into his light eyes warned her that he was not a man who followed any rules other than those of his own making. There was something raw and primitive about him. Something reckless and sinful that made her heart pound and sent her blood singing through her veins.

"My services are yours to command, milady. How may I be of help?"

The pile of blankets flipped back. Violet emerged. "Uncle Camden?"

Any warmth she'd imagined in the stranger's eyes vanished as his gaze shifted between herself and the young girl. "Violet?"

He pulled away from Rhiannon to embrace the child. "You're safe." His tone was raw.

His gaze flicked back to Rhiannon. He said nothing. He stared. Hard. Only the square ridge of his jaw betrayed the control it was taking to keep his anger in check. "How, milady, do you happen to have possession of my lost niece?"

"Your niece?" Rhiannon straightened beneath his punishing gaze. "I am but her escort, milord. And her appointed nursemaid."

"Appointed by whom?"

"Mother Agnes of Taturn Abbey."

He narrowed his gaze. "Violet, does she speak the truth?"

Rhiannon tensed. The girl would disagree, and Rhiannon would be punished. She flinched away from the pair. Was he the kind of man to take a lash to her back as her own brothers had, or would he lock her in a dark dungeon instead? Should she run and take her chances alone?

Rhiannon sat back on her heels, ready to sprint when Violet threw herself into her arms, clinging to her and nearly knocking her over.

"She saved me from the bad man. And she's my friend."

Rhiannon returned the girl's hug with stiff arms. She hadn't expected that response. Violet hadn't said a word to her since they'd left the abbey.

"I see," the stranger said, the anger clearing from his gaze. His gaze moved back to Violet. He ruffled the chaotic mess Violet's golden curls had become. "You are a brave girl." He lifted the child away from Rhiannon and into his arms, then whistled for his horse. The beast promptly reported to his master's side. "Hold on tight," he cooed to Violet as he set her atop the animal. "We will ride the rest of the way to Lee Castle on horseback."

The stranger stopped beside the horse cart, and passed his hand over the driver's face, closing his eyes. "Why, mi-lady, would someone be trying to kill you?"

Rhiannon stood. She swallowed hard. How could she possibly explain to this man who she was, who her family was, without him also judging her the way everyone else in her life did? The name of Ruthven closed people's minds.

Honesty is a virtue. Mother Agnes would disapprove of any lies. "I'm not at all certain he was after me."

The stranger frowned once more, and she could see the doubt in his eyes. "Hmmm," he responded. He stepped away from the horse cart to one of the horses that had pulled the vehicle. "Do you ride?"

"Aye." She'd spent much of her childhood on the back of a horse, riding the woods near their home, alone. It was the one thing her father never reprimanded her for. He'd even seemed pleased that she had as much, if not more, skill with the beasts as her brothers.

The stranger brought one of the horses to her side. Before he could offer her a hand up, she swung easily onto the horse's bare back.

He said nothing, but a hint of admiration shone in his eyes. Then he turned away, busying himself with securing the body of their driver to the back of the third horse. He had just completed the task when hoofbeats echoed at the top of the ridge.

His men had returned.

The stranger mounted his horse behind Violet, then secured the reins of the other horse to his saddle. They held their position until a tall, elegant man rode up beside Violet and the stranger. "Lord Lockhart," he greeted with a nod. "We lost the archer when he fled into the woods."

Lord Lockhart nodded. His gaze held a shuttered watchfulness as he studied Rhiannon. His intense scrutiny sent a shiver of fear down her spine. "The man won't return anytime soon. Besides, we have the prize he was after."

"What prize?" the slim man asked. He shifted uneasily on his horse when his gaze lit upon the driver's body, and then he stared at Rhiannon.

Lord Lockhart ignored the question clearly written on his friend's face about who she was. He playfully jostled his niece's hair. "Orrin, do you remember Lady Violet?"

Orrin's eyes went wide. "Your niece? She's grown since I saw her last. Praise the saints. But how?"

"She is safe, that is all that matters." Lord Lockhart wrapped his arms around his niece and nudged his horse forward, sparing Rhiannon not so much as a glance. "Let us return home. Once there, we can explore the issue more fully."

"Agreed," Orrin replied. He positioned his horse next to Rhiannon's on the trail, then signaled the men to fall in behind them.

As both men ignored her, Rhiannon did the only thing she could, sit quietly by and follow where they led. As the moments ticked by, the terror of her ordeal along with the biting cold seeped through what remained of Rhiannon's defenses. She started to shake uncontrollably. No matter how hard she tried to force her limbs to still, she could not stop the shudders that wracked her body. She'd almost been killed, and now she was powerless and in limbo again.

She had no illusions about why someone wanted her dead. But why now? She'd been relatively unprotected for days after her father died, as well as when she'd sought shelter at the abbey.

Why did whoever wanted her dead wait to strike just when she'd started to believe she had a chance to start over?

Rhiannon and the others rode through the iron gate of Lee Castle as the sun painted the horizon a deep scarlet. The first of the stars winked overhead and the ground reflected the creeping shadows of dusk.

Rhiannon's body ached from an untold number of bruises she'd no doubt received when she'd been slammed against the sides of the cart, and her temples throbbed in rhythm with the beat of her heart.

As they progressed through the bailey toward the keep, Lord Lockhart's mood darkened until it matched the impending nightfall.

The castle servants streamed from the door, lining up along the bottom of the stairs to the keep as if following some ritual of greeting their lord upon his return. It was something that had never happened at her father's country house.

Lord Lockhart reined to a stop before them and dismounted. An older woman, most likely his chatelaine, stepped up to his horse to receive Violet, who had fallen asleep on their journey. "Place her in the nursery," he said, "and prepare the room next to it for our guest."

The woman assessed Rhiannon without a hint of friendliness in her gray eyes.

Rhiannon held her head high, refusing to let the woman see how intimidated she was beneath the hard stare. The once fashionable gray traveling gown Rhiannon wore was covered with splatters of mud beneath the wings of a light woolen cape. Her hair was pulled back from her face and protected by a muslin cap trimmed with lace. The small gray hat that used to cover the cap had been lost at some point during the wild journey here.

Rhiannon dropped her gaze to her hands—her bare, work-roughened hands. She would have worn gloves had she had them, as a proper lady should. But when had *she* ever been a proper lady? Rhiannon swallowed thickly, certain at any moment the woman would send her away.

"Thank you, Mistress Faulkner. That will be all." Lord Lockhart's voice broke thorough the uncomfortable silence that had fallen over those assembled in the courtyard.

Without speaking a word, the woman nodded, then slipped up the stairs with Violet tucked safely in her arms.

"Milord," an older man said in a tight voice. He stepped forward from those gathered.

"Bertie." Lord Lockhart's dark mood faded, and a smile brightened his face. "You are looking much improved. Your injuries worried me when we left—"

"How could you?" the man interrupted.

Lord Lockhart's frown returned. "Explain yourself, Bertie."

"How could you bring that woman into this castle in anything but irons?"

Rhiannon felt her face pale beneath the older man's glare. Her breath stilled in her chest and the world around her wavered.

"How could you bring a Ruthven into this castle?"

Chapter Four

hat do you mean, a *Ruthven?*" Lord Lockhart erupted.

Bertie's eyes narrowed as he pointed at Rhiannon. "The lass is a Ruthven. Although she is fair where her kin are mostly dark, you can see it in her eyes and in her chin. A Ruthven stands before us, by all that is holy."

Lord Lockhart's light, penetrating gaze shifted to her. "Correct the man if he is wrong," he demanded, striding toward her. He unceremoniously gripped her ankle and yanked her from her horse, imprisoning her in his arms before she could tumble to the ground.

Rhiannon caught her breath and stared up at him.

"Explain yourself." He pulled her against the hard contours of his body. His eyes demanded her full attention, insisted on the truth. She was only dimly aware that the others had closed in around them as though protecting their master from some unknown threat. Her heartbeat thrummed in her ears. He held her too close, demanded too much.

"Are you suddenly mute? Or does your silence damn you?" he asked, his voice cracking with anger.

Rhiannon jerked out of his grasp. She took several halting steps back, creating some distance from him, but she still felt penned in by the others.

"I am Rhiannon Ruthven."

Lord Lockhart stared at her for a long, taut moment. Bewilderment flared in the depth of his gaze. "A female Ruthven?"

Rhiannon straightened beneath his regard. "The last."

"But a Ruthven nevertheless."

She tightened her jaw, prepared for the onslaught of insults certain to follow.

"The abbess knew who you were and still she entrusted you with Lady Violet's care?" His voice was low and deceptively silky.

"Not all people judge others by their name alone."

He seized her arm and pulled her tight against him once more.

She gasped and tried to break free, but to no avail.

"Some people deserve such judgment." He yanked her across the courtyard. His people scattered as he approached, then fell in behind him, their curiosity evident.

They came to a halt in the churchyard before several freshly turned graves. He released her for a moment and drew the sword from his back.

Rhiannon flinched back as he drove the blade not into her, but into the ground at her feet. "Is that your family's crest upon that sword?"

She swallowed roughly as she recognized her father's sword. "Aye."

"Dougall Ruthven. Who is he to you?"

"My oldest brother."

"All of these men died at the hands of your kin." Before the horrific image could sink into her soul, he grasped her arm and jerked her to the right, to stand before the freshly turned soil of another grave. Beside that grave lay a body wrapped in sheets of linen.

He pulled her down to her knees beside the concealed body. "I have every right to judge you, and any Ruthven, by name alone when it is your family who has murdered my own." Kneeling beside her, he grasped her chin, forcing her gaze to the fresh grave. "My brother was disemboweled by your brother."

Hot tears sprang to Rhiannon's eyes.

"And this," he said, forcing her chin toward the wrapped body. With his free hand, he pulled back the white cloth to reveal the even whiter face of a female whose features were frozen as though in a mask of pain bored into her own, accusing her, damning her, as Lord Lockhart did. "This is my sister-in-law, Lady Violet's mother, who was left unprotected because of your kin's actions. In the absence of anyone to defend her, she was charged with witchcraft and hanged."

Rhiannon squeezed her eyes shut, blocking the sight of such horror from her vision, but the images would stay with her always. The pain and desperation she could hear in Lord Lockhart's words would haunt her all of her days.

And *his* treatment of her . . . A sob escaped her. Would she never be free of abuse? Her father? Her brothers? This man? "Milord, I am sorry for your loss." She brought her gaze back to his. His face hardened to a mask of freezing rage.

Beneath the chill of his scrutiny, Rhiannon continued. "That my kin had any part in either of their deaths grieves me most desperately." She stood, praying her legs would support her. "But I am *not* my family, milord." She nearly crumpled to the ground once more at the hatred mirrored in his eyes.

"Regardless of my name, I have been appointed as Lady Violet's nursemaid by Mother Agnes. Until a suitable replacement can be found, I must remain with my charge as instructed by the abbess."

His contemptuous gaze raked her.

"That girl has already lost everything. Don't take me away from her as well." With all the courage she could muster, Rhiannon straightened and met his hard gaze. "Hate me, milord. Despise my family, but don't make Lady Violet suffer for it."

★ ★ ★

His jaw clenched in anger, Camden watched the woman stride away, her head held high, toward *his* keep. He could force her to go. Even if the abbess had designated her as Violet's nursemaid, he was the child's uncle. His gaze dipped to Clara's pale, delicate face frozen in death. He was Violet's guardian. With a final glance at James's freshly turned grave, he reminded himself that he was also the leader of the Lockhart clan.

Camden sought out Orrin in the crowd around the graves. "Get the men to dig a grave for Lady Lockhart. Call me when they're done. It will be dark soon."

"What about the woman?" Orrin asked.

A Ruthven female? He'd had no idea any daughters had been born to Malcolm Ruthven. Or he never would have given the order that sentenced her to death. "What have I done?" His words jolted him into action. "Secure the portcullis and close the gates. No one enters without my permission," he instructed the gatekeeper. "Double the guards at their posts."

The grinding of the iron chains filled the air as the heavy portcullis slipped back into place. When the heavy doors closed a moment later, relief surged though Camden. Yet even with the castle secure, unease settled in the pit of his stomach.

Camden had sentenced all the Ruthvens to death. All of them. And if the attack on the ridge told him anything, it was that the assassin he'd hired knew more about the Ruthven family than he himself did.

A woman? With a curse, Camden ran a hand through his hair. He had never considered the possibility.

Camden found her in the great hall next to the hearth. Rhiannon stood off to the side, staring into the flames while the others went about their evening duties. She twisted in her hands the lace cap she'd worn earlier. Thick, luxurious waves of gold cascaded across her shoulders—shoulders that dipped with the weight of her burdens. She looked as vulnerable as a child. All of her previous bravado had vanished.

In the moments since he'd discovered who she was, his temper had cooled. And an inexplicable irritation took its place. He was partly to blame for how discomfited she appeared now. He shouldn't have thrust James's and Clara's deaths in her face. Simply being a Ruthven didn't mean that she'd killed them.

Even so, it was difficult to accept that his enemy's spawn stood before his hearth. He balled his fists, fighting his own revulsion.

She cast a glance sideways, and he could see by the redness surrounding her eyes that she'd been crying.

She looked away. "I must apologize. I had no right to talk to you that way. You are lord and master here, and regardless of what Mother Agnes has said, you are in charge of your niece. I shall leave immediately."

She faced him. Backlit by the fire, her blonde hair turned to burnished gold, and a delicate pink tinted the pale ivory of her cheeks. Something inside him stirred. Irritated at his response, he bristled.

She paled and swallowed thickly, no doubt fearing what he would do to her now. "Before I go, I must deliver something." She reached into the folds of her gray gown and produced a small packet wrapped with linen. "Mother Agnes asked me to deliver this parcel safely into your hands." She pressed the packet against his fingers. "I am so very sorry to have troubled you."

She had taken two steps from the fire when Violet raced across the room and wrapped herself around Rhiannon's legs. "No, Rhiannon, you can't leave me," she wailed.

Rhiannon's amber eyes widened with surprise. She

stared down at Violet and drew a shaky breath. "That decision is not up to you or me." With hesitant fingers, she patted his niece's head.

Violet's blue eyes, eyes so like his own, brimmed with tears. "Uncle Camden, you can't make her leave, *please*. I want her here."

"You are with me now, Violet. Nothing will hurt you as long as I am here."

"That's what Father said. . . ." Tears spilled onto her cheeks in twin ribbons of sorrow. Camden clutched the parcel in his hand, battling his own grief.

"You will be safe, I swear it with all my heart," Camden vowed with a catch in his voice. Violet continued to sob softly against Rhiannon's body.

Two women. One melted his heart, the other fired his anger.

He would like nothing better than to toss Rhiannon Ruthven out of his castle and out of his life. But how could he when he knew an assassin lay in waiting? An assassin he had unleashed. An assassin who would surely carry out the death sentence he had set in motion.

"She can stay for now," he said more harshly than he had intended. Both Violet and Rhiannon startled at his response, fear in their eyes. "Show her to the room next to yours, Violet."

The girl nodded, her face still wreathed in grief. She grasped Rhiannon's hand and tugged her toward the stairway that led to the castle's private sleeping chambers.

What had the world come to? In the past two days his life had been turned upside down. He had gone from a warrior who protected his country to a warrior who now protected his enemy.

Camden balled his fists, suddenly remembering the packet in his right hand. He unwound the linen wrapping to reveal a silver coin held by a chain. Set into the center of the groat, the legendary Charm Stone glistened brilliantly, catching the light from the fire.

His family's legacy.

The reason Clara was dead. Camden tensed at the thought. His sister-in-law had accepted her role as healer to the Lockhart clan or anyone who came in search of her talents.

It was those very same skills and this stone that had brought Clara to the hangman's noose. A witch? Not Clara. She was merely a caring and loving woman who'd often put the needs of others above her own.

Clara had died, yet the Charm Stone remained—the very stone Bishop Berwick had demanded at Lockhart Castle. Camden frowned as he smoothed his thumb over the bloodred stone. It warmed beneath his touch. How had the healing stone gone from Clara's possession into the hands of Rhiannon Ruthven? What was her connection to all of this? What events had transpired that placed her in charge of his niece's care?

He tightened his fist around the Charm Stone. He would have answers, and determine what to do with the Ruthven girl before his niece grew any more attached to her.

But before any questions could be answered, he had to try to stop what he had begun. One task remained yet undone. Before he could leave, he had to hide the Stone.

Alone in the chapel, Camden unfurled his fist, exposing the Charm Stone. The small coin in his hand glistened beneath the silvery moonlight that shone through four tall and narrow windows near the altar. The stone in the center winked, bloodred.

Camden closed his hand around the Stone. Forty-six years ago Camden's father had taken ownership of the relic from an emir's mother in the Holy Land, a drop of his blood had sealed the transfer of power. And since then the Lockhart blood spilled for the Stone never seemed to end. James and Clara were proof of that.

They had needed him to protect them. Instead, Camden had been off fighting for a king of whom he had only been a subject for the last three years. Since his return to Scotland. Memory sparked as he stared at the Stone.

Nothing but black surrounded him. How long had he been pitched in darkness with nothing to eat and only sips of water offered twice throughout the days—days that melded one into the next as he sat on the dusty floor of his prison cell?

Camden lifted his hand to wipe the trickles of sweat from his forehead only to find his arms were shackled to the stone wall at his back. Drawing a deep breath of the heavy humid air, he turned his head slowly to the side. Orrin lay there. So still. Yet in the silence he could hear the soft rumble of Orrin's breathing. Only sleeping. At least Orrin had found respite from the horrors they'd had to endure.

Why were they not just killed? Both he and Orrin would have preferred death to the humiliation they'd suffered. They'd been stripped bare by their captors, forced to march down the center of the marketplace where their ears were nailed to the gallows, then they'd been pelted with rotten fruit.

It was not a warrior's end.

The more their captors tried to humiliate the "pale young Christians" the more defiant both he and Orrin had become. They had nothing to lose.

Then the unthinkable happened. A Saracen holy man had purchased them from the gallows. The moment their ears were freed from their torturous prison, they attempted escape, challenging the holy man's guards for their swords. Their revolt had nearly succeeded. A bold act that landed them both here, in the darkness of hell, waiting for respite or, if they were lucky, death.

Camden leaned his head back against the wall and tried to think of home, of the sweet, rolling meadows of heather, of the soft morning mist, of the family he had never bidden good-bye.

Would he spend the rest of his days in this inferno of dust and sand? He lolled his head to the side once more. At least he had Orrin. Perhaps he could bear the loss of everything else— Scotland, freedom, his family—as long as he had Orrin by his side. They'd been friends forever. And it looked as though they would die together as well.

No sooner had he finished the thought when the door of their prison cell creaked open. Camden shielded his eyes against the sharp sting of light. A moment later he turned his gaze back to the intruder to see a billow of white robes that stopped at his feet.

"My pale ones. Have you had enough of these dark days?"

Camden tried to tell the intruder to go to hell, but the dryness in his throat prevented him from releasing more than a soft choke.

The man bent down in front of Camden, just out of reach. "You are both determined fighters." He stroked his long black beard. "I have had a vision from Allah about you both. He showed me that through you I can attain untold riches—wealth I can use to drive foreigners from our lands forever. Because of that vision I have decided to make you a bargain."

Camden nudged Orrin, who startled and bolted upright, swinging his arms, only to feel the bite of the irons against his wrists. "Argh!" A moment later, he froze. "What do you want?" he asked the man.

"You are both so very young, yet strong in body and mind. I would regret killing you this day. But know that I will if you refuse the offer I am about to make."

Camden's gaze met Orrin's. He cleared his throat. "We are listening," he croaked.

"I am known as Shaykh Haashim." He bowed his turbaned head in greeting. "I am a holy man to my people—a people who are often at war with our neighbors and with those seeking to possess the Holy Land."

"What does that have to do with us?" Orrin asked.

The man smiled a terrible smile that did not quite reach his eyes. "Since you both have proven to me your skills as fighters, I am offering you a chance to put those skills to use."

"Why would we fight for you?" Camden did not hide the anger in his voice.

"Because we will make an agreement. Fight for me for the next seven years, take one-fourth of any spoils that have been gained to divide among yourselves, and when your terms of service are through, I will set you free."

Camden's gaze flew to Orrin's. Hope leapt into his friend's tired gaze. "Seven years?" Camden repeated. At the age of nineteen they could return to their own country, their families. Unless they died here first.

Hope collided with reality. And in that moment, Camden knew they could not refuse. To refuse meant death. Acceptance would at least give them hope. "We will fight for you. Become Saracens for seven years." And in that time, they would have to become the best warriors this part of the world had ever seen if they were to survive.

They *had* survived. They had returned wealthy men. Camden clutched the family relic in his hand. It too had survived the Holy Land.

Since his father's time, the Stone had become a Lockhart legacy. Only Lockharts through birth or marriage could use it to heal. As much as he respected what the Stone could do, a part of him hated the reminder of where he had spent so much of his life.

His memory of times past faded, and Camden became chillingly aware of the filtered darkness surrounding him, the smell of incense that lingered from past ceremonies. They would light the incense again, for James and for Clara, sending them both on their journey to the beyond.

He tightened his jaw. Damn his king for keeping him from his family when they had needed him. And damn the

Ruthvens for James's and Clara's demise. In a few short days, he had lost everything of importance in his life. Frustration—acid hot, bile bitter—tore through him.

No more. What remained of his family and the residents of his castle would come first from this moment on. He would protect Violet and the others with his dying breath if need be. If there was one thing he had learned in the seven years he'd spent away from Scotland, it was how to fight. But whom would he defend them from? Who posed the biggest threat? Was it the English invaders? Demands from his own king? The remaining Ruthvens? Or Bishop Berwick?

The bishop had demanded the Stone from him at Lockhart Castle. How had the man learned that James and Clara were its keepers? Had someone betrayed them, or had word of the healing miracles Clara performed with the use of the Stone reached beyond the local village? As word spread, so did the dangers of using the Stone. The bishop was proof of that. But how far would the man go to obtain the relic? There was no doubt it could prove quite valuable. "Miraculous" cures would bring pilgrims to his church and money to his coffers.

Camden unfurled his fist, revealing the Charm Stone once more. He had to keep it safe. And he knew just where to conceal something so precious.

Upstairs, Rhiannon entered her room with more fear than she'd experienced when she'd gone to Taturn Abbey seeking shelter, begging for entrance even though she had no dowry to support her. The abbess had accepted her, reluctantly. Just as Lord Lockhart had now allowed her to stay here with his niece.

Even though he'd agreed, she'd seen the resistance in the way he'd held his body. But it was his eyes that revealed his true emotion. He despised her. He would have kicked her out of the castle without hesitation if Violet had not interceded.

Should she stay regardless of his feelings? She had nowhere to go and wasn't certain the abbess would take her back if she abandoned her charge.

Nothing felt natural to Rhiannon about caring for the little girl. She'd had no experience with children. And her own upbringing certainly was not a good example of how to treat a child. But Violet expected something from her— a soft word, a kind gesture. Even now, the little girl clung to her fingers. Rhiannon had to force herself to relax, to accept a physical connection that she'd seldom experienced before.

What did a nursemaid do exactly? She'd never had one growing up. She'd learned how to act, speak, behave by mimicking the few women she'd come into contact with during her youth. She'd taught herself most of what she knew through sheer determination. She was hardly nursemaid material.

You can do this, she said to herself as she took up the burden of her new role. Her first task: to settle herself and Violet into their rooms.

Rhiannon closed her eyes and drew a steadying breath, preparing herself to gaze upon the most humble room in the castle. A Ruthven deserved no better than a lice-ridden mattress in a dark and dank room.

She opened her eyes and gasped.

"This is my favorite room in the castle. Uncle Camden brought all of these things back with him after he—" Violet's cheeks turned a deep shade of red. "He probably wouldn't like me talking about it. Do you like it?" Violet asked.

"This must be a mistake," Rhiannon said, convinced the

little girl had misunderstood her uncle's request. "I am certain your uncle had intended more humble accommodations."

"He said the room next to mine." Violet tugged on her arm, pulling Rhiannon across the luxurious crimson and gold carpet that covered most of the wooden floor.

Exotic opulence played before her eyes. A huge wardrobe, with dark unfamiliar wood, covered one wall. Opposite that stood a rosewood dressing table with a huge mirror, draped in crimson damask. More deep crimson damask covered a seat near the room's one tall and narrow window, and draped with artless elegance the enormous bed in the center of the room. She had never seen anything quite so ornate. And never expected such opulence to be part of her life, however temporarily.

Violet tugged on Rhiannon's arm again, leading her to a door on the opposite side of the room. "This is my room when I come here to stay." She opened the door to reveal a chamber that was no doubt the nursery.

Another tightly woven carpet in various shades of blue and yellow stretched across the polished wooden floor. The spacious and airy room contained four small beds that lined the far wall. Each bore a dark blue silk coverlet and elaborate bed drapes that swirled around the bedposts to appear more like an unrestrained springtime waterfall than fabric. Atop each bed perched a dozen pillows in various shapes and shades of yellow and gold.

She felt a bit dazzled by the colors all around her—blues and purples were colors that only the wealthiest could afford. And these were whole rooms decorated in the rich and rare colors.

A hand-carved cradle in a dark, highly polished wood sat between the room's two tall and narrow windows. Windows. Another luxury. An ornate wardrobe hugged the wall closest to the door.

"Oh my," was all Rhiannon could say. Both rooms were breathtaking, elaborately decorated with furnishings, woods, and colors that Rhiannon had never seen before. And the carpets. She dug her thin slippers into the decadently thick weave. Had she ever experienced anything more luxurious?

"Your uncle lives well," Rhiannon commented more to herself than to converse, which is why she startled when Violet answered.

"It wasn't always that way." She pulled her hand out of Rhiannon's.

Curiosity flared, but Rhiannon resisted the temptation to ask the girl to explain. So the man had secrets. Didn't they all?

Rhiannon turned to her young charge. "Why don't you show me your favorite toy? Is it a doll?" She paused, searching the room for toys.

Any animation that had lightened Violet's face vanished. "I have nothing." Tears pooled in her eyes and spilled onto her cheeks. The girl sank to the floor, her soft sobs filling the silence of the room.

Rhiannon didn't know what to do, how to comfort the girl. She sank down beside her and gently stroked her back with halting strokes. "It will be all right, Violet. You'll see."

Yet even as she said the words, Rhiannon had no idea how anything would ever be all right again. For it was in that moment that she realized the magnitude of what Violet had lost. Her family. Her home. Her clothing. Her toys. Everything she had ever possessed was gone.

Rhiannon's throat tightened with unshed tears. It wasn't right that one little girl should suffer so much loss. Agony tore through her. A part of her heart that she thought had turned numb from her own sorrow cracked wide, exposing wounds both old and new.

She forced back tears. She could never reclaim any of her losses. But for now she could savor her companionship with a girl who desperately needed someone who cared.

"It will be all right, Violet," she said, this time with more conviction. Because she intended to do whatever it took to see her young charge smile once more.

Chapter Five

"Where's Cory?" Dougall Ruthven asked himself. He frowned at the empty roads leading to the town of Lee, then shifted on his horse, searching in all directions. His brother had sent word to meet him there shortly before dusk. Dusk would slide into night soon, and Cory and their men were nowhere in sight.

Dougall tamped down a shiver of dread. Cory was just late. Perhaps he'd had trouble getting past the muck in the roads left by the late afternoon rainfall. Dougall dismounted, giving his tired horse a rest from the breakneck pace he'd traveled from Glasgow. The horse nickered, then moved to the side of the muddy expanse to munch on a tuft of soft green grass.

The wind picked up, and Dougall shivered, this time not holding the sensation back. He pulled the edges of the tartan cloth tossed over his shoulder closer around his body and listened for the soft sound of hoofbeats approaching.

Nothing.

Dougall fixed his attention on the north road. As soon as Cory arrived they would head in that direction, traveling all night if they must to reach Taturn Abbey.

It was beyond time for them to retrieve their sister, Rhiannon. She would bring a pretty price—enough funds to continue the battle against the Lockharts their father had started decades ago when James and Camden's father had stolen the woman their father wanted. And even though their father was dead, killed by the English, his sons had made a promise to avenge him until the day they died.

They had tried to kill the Lockharts for years, but until James had split the clan in two, dividing its members and staff between both Lee and Lockhart Castles, the Lockharts had been too powerful an enemy. Yet with James's relocation came their opportunity. They'd waited and watched until the time was right.

Killing James had been a start to their long-awaited revenge. But until all the Lockharts were dead, they would not rest.

Rhiannon knew nothing of their vendetta. They'd kept her isolated most of her life from what it took to be a Ruthven. But now it was time for their sister to pay her debt to her family name.

The soft sound of hoofbeats broke into Dougall's thoughts. "Cory? Is that ye?" Dougall strained to see the dark figure approaching in the silver light.

"Why in God's name did ye summon me out here?" Cory complained as he continued forward. "I know we canna show ourselves tae many o' our countrymen, but this place is out o' the way fer even ye." Cory brought his horse to a stop alongside Dougall's and dismounted.

Cory's mocking tone brought a frown to Dougall's face. "Ye summoned me."

Dougall tensed. "Nay, ye left word wi' the innkeeper tae meet ye here."

An expression of unease crossed Cory's face. He twisted back toward the horses. "It's a trap," he cried.

An arrow flew through the night air with faultless precision, finding its mark in Cory's chest. Before Dougall could move, a searing pain in his chest robbed him of breath.

A whisper of sound came to his ears and a shadow detached itself from the night, heading toward them from atop a horse. "What do ye want?" he asked even though he knew the answer.

The man said nothing, only continued his progression forward. Dougall's heart was pounding, hurting. He could see Cory's body outlined against the silver moonlight. He saw his brother twist, then fall to the ground as a second arrow protruded from his chest.

Oh, God, they could not die. Camden Lockhart still had to pay for his father's misdeeds.

The large muscular man brought his horse to a stop and dismounted. He headed for Dougall, his bow extended before him.

"Don't!" Dougall tried to run. Pain exploded inside him. Once. Twice. He dropped to his knees as something warm and salty filled his mouth.

He was dying. And he was afraid. The big man dropped his bow and reached for the sword at his side. In an instant the sword whipped against his neck. The weapon swung, sliced, and was free.

At first light, Camden rode out of the castle alone, retracing his steps from a few days ago. He had to find the assassin he had hired. He had to cancel the attacks on Rhiannon. For another bag of coins, he was certain the blacksmith would guide him to the assassin.

Back at the castle, he'd left Orrin in charge of Violet and Rhiannon's protection, never explaining exactly why he needed such a service of his friend. Orrin was wise enough not to ask.

Camden had even demanded that the occupants of Lockhart Castle, his brother's castle, be made to wait outside the gates of Lee Castle until his return. He wanted to screen every new resident as they entered the protection of his home. He could not afford to allow an assassin to slip into his castle.

Pushing his horse as hard as he dared on the half-frozen roads, Camden entered Glasgow at midday. He headed

straight to the river green, where he'd found the blacksmith the other day. He dismounted outside the smithy's
yard and strode toward the forge. Two men, both fair in
coloring, leaned over the open flame. From iron clamps
they rotated red-hot metal over the glowing coals. One
man looked up at his approach.

"Good day, milord."

Camden bowed his head in greeting. "The blacksmith,
the one with dark hair, where is he?"

The two men exchanged a look of surprise. "Nolan?"

"Aye," Camden said. "That was the man's name. Where
might I find him?"

"He's dead," the older of the two men replied.

Dead? Cold rose in Camden's throat and danced down
his neck. "That's impossible. I just spoke with him two
days past."

The younger man set his piece of metal back into the
fire. "He was robbed then murdered last night."

A sinking sensation filled him. Had the assassin come
after Nolan for the other half of the money Camden had
promised? "How did he die?"

"Strangled," the younger man said. "The odd thing was
when we found Nolan, we also found the heads of two
other dark-haired men."

Camden didn't need to hear anymore. He turned back
to his horse and with a renewed sense of urgency spurred
the animal toward the shadier part of town. A heavy fog
crept across the streets near the river, making the twining
stone corridors eerie and confusing despite the daylight.

The air hung heavy and stagnant, filled with the odor of
rot and slime. Camden stopped at a nearby inn, then a pub
farther down the way, asking after the man he had em-
ployed. A long litany of negative responses greeted him at
each stop. No one seemed to remember the man.

Determined to press on until he found what he searched

for, Camden eventually reached the long, dark alley he had visited a few nights past. In the daylight, the river waifs lingered in the alley, leaning against the crude stone walls, watching with curious eyes as he rode by.

At the turn in the alley, right before the stairs that led down to the riverbank below, Camden dismounted. He surveyed the area with a frown. Where was the darkened doorway his assassin had appeared from the other night? Or had there been a doorway at all?

"Ye lookin' fer somethin'?" One of the waifs pushed away from the wall and headed toward him, slowly, appraising with each step.

"I hired a man here two days ago. I need to speak with him."

The young boy continued toward him. "What ye want with him?"

"That is between me and the man."

"Well, since he ain't here and I am, ye might want tae take it up with me."

"I have no time to waste. The man, where is he?"

"Ye might not have time but ye have funds me and the boys would like to relieve ye of," the waif said with a bark of laughter that brought a round of chuckles from the other boys behind him. He pulled a dagger.

Camden's muscles clenched, and his hand drifted to the hilt of his curved Saracen sword, ready to strike. The river waif's weapon would be out of his hands in the blink of an eye if Camden chose to attack.

On the river below, a ship's whistle sounded. Camden startled at the flash of memory it evoked. *Over the high-pitched squeal of a whistle, he heard the shouts of the clans riding into the seaport town of Dunbar, the wailing of the pipes, the echo of a day long past.*

The English had invaded, but the clans refused to be tamed. As Scots born and bred, 'twas in them to fight, to the death if needed, to save their country, their heritage, each other. Men in tartan plaids weighted down with weaponry fell upon the English. Camden and Orrin were really too young to fight, yet their hearts were big and they refused to be left out of the action.

But fate had been cruel. Instead of being in the midst of battle, they found themselves on a low slope near the shore, bound, gagged, with backs burning from the whip that had tried to tame them. As the fight raged, he and Orrin had been ambushed by Malcolm Ruthven and his men. With revenge on their minds, the Ruthvens had sold them as slaves. Camden and Orrin were tossed aboard a ship bound for who knew where.

"He's daft, he is." Harsh laughter preceded the swipe of a blade.

Camden jumped back out of harm's way as he shed his disorientation and years of pain. The streets of Glasgow, not the shores of Dunbar. Camden grasped his sword and fell immediately into a loose defensive stance. "You do not want to rob me."

The boy startled at the oddness of Camden's sword. The Saracen weapon had surprised many of his enemies. "Not alone I don't," the boy said. He glanced behind him, and with a nod of his head, the other waifs started forward. The boy dived at Camden, slashing. The others stood behind him, weapons raised to strike.

Camden's heart pounded, yet his brain remained calm. He was a better fighter than any of them. But they could overtake him with their numbers alone. Camden allowed the anger that had been stirred up by the memory of that black, hard place he'd been in his youth. Fury propelled him forward. He would never be a victim again. Neither would anyone he loved. There must have been something in Camden's face that frightened the boys, because their faces paled, their eyes widened. They ceased their advance. With an inhuman shout, he flung himself at them.

They turned and ran. Camden's anger dissipated as he strode back to his horse. Orrin had been right when he'd said, "Revenge had a way of coming back at you."

Truer words had never been spoken. Because of his need for revenge, he would be forced to defend a woman he hated from an assassin he had hired.

Rhiannon managed to coax Violet to sleep after fitful hours of tossing and turning. She'd even cried out a few times in fear, startling herself and Rhiannon as she tried to sleep. Only when Rhiannon had settled in the bed beside her had Violet fallen into a deeper sleep, into a place free from the terrors that haunted her.

Rhiannon sighed, stroking Violet's now clean and tangle-free yellow-gold hair. Even though she'd managed to coax the girl into sleep, restlessness built inside Rhiannon. Sleep would not come anytime soon for her, not unless she walked off some of her own anxiety. She needed something to occupy her mind.

Her gaze wandered about the neat and tidy nursery until it came to rest on the small soiled and tattered dress at the base of the bed. In that moment she knew what she needed to do.

She tucked the thick woolen blankets tight against Violet's sides and slipped off the little bed. In her own room she picked up a candleholder above the hearth and lit the candle with the flames.

She had never been in a castle before. Her family's holdings were nothing elaborate when compared to the grandeur of Lee Castle. But castles, because of their size, were drafty and cold, she'd discovered. She grabbed a woolen shawl she'd found in the room and winding it about her shoulders, she entered the corridor. The long hallway was quiet and eerie, bathed in a glow of golden light, as she headed for the stairs. Moving slowly down the corridor, she paused at each of the portraits displayed there. Male Lockharts, in the traditional dress of their countrymen, stared down at her. The candlelight illuminated their faces, most notably their eyes—eyes that seemed to mirror the same anger and revulsion she'd seen on Camden Lockhart's face.

With a frown, Rhiannon quickened her pace, her eyes no longer on the portraits, but on the floorboards beneath her feet. She did not seek their approval.

Belowstairs, she stepped into the great hall that despite the late hour was filled with the castle's residents. A group of women huddled before the overly large hearth. They each held two large wooden combs that they used to card raw wool from one side to the other, preparing the material for spinning.

Men gathered around the long tables, drinking from wooden mugs as they played a game she recognized as Merrills. Orrin, and several other men who had escorted her and Violet to the castle earlier, looked up when she entered the room.

Orrin broke away from the others. "Is there something you need, milady?" Orrin asked.

"Lady Violet needs a new gown," Rhiannon said, noting that the women's gazes had shifted to her, gazes that were none too friendly. "Is there somewhere I might find a length of fabric in this castle to make her one?"

He nodded toward the women at the hearth. "Mistress Faulkner or the other women can help you with that." He returned to the other men, leaving her to stand alone.

The muscles in Rhiannon's shoulders stiffened before she forced herself to relax. Violet needed the fabric, not herself. That fact might bring their cooperation. Rhiannon pressed forward, coming to a stop before the older woman she'd met earlier. The woman raised her gaze to meet Rhiannon's. She read inquiry there, but nothing else. No welcome, no warmth. Rhiannon cleared her throat, suddenly nervous. "Mistress Faulkner, might you have a length of fabric I can use to make Lady Violet a new dress?"

Before the woman could respond, one of the other older women stood and tossed her carding combs to the floor. Her face contorted in disgust. "Your family killed my dear Harold."

Another of the younger women to her left murmured "Scot killer," just loud enough for Rhiannon to hear.

A young redheaded maid next to her giggled. "More like Mistress Plague."

Other women joined in the laughter. "Mistress Plague," they repeated, and continued their laughter until a sharp gaze from Mistress Faulkner cut the merriment.

"That is enough," Mistress Faulker reprimanded. "Sophia, you will show Mistress Ruthven to the storeroom."

"Me?" the maid whined. "I'd rather—"

Another lethal gaze from Mistress Faulkner halted her reply. With a grunt of disgust, she stood. "Follow me." Without waiting for Rhiannon to catch up, she hurried down the hallway on the opposite side of the great hall. The corridor twisted to the right several times before they came to stairs leading down. "Watch your step, Mistress Plague," Sophia giggled over her shoulder as she disappeared into the dimness ahead.

Rhiannon stumbled in her haste to keep Sophia in sight. Catching herself before she tumbled down the stairway, Rhiannon slowed her pace. And Sophia vanished.

A blast of cold, mold-laden air washed over Rhiannon at the bottom of the stairs, where a short hallway led to two doors. She peered in the first doorway, extending the candle ahead of her. The weak flame pierced the darkness for only a few yards before her.

Rhiannon stepped farther into the room. The scent she had first thought was mold shifted to that of pungent wood mixed with something she couldn't identify. She took another step into the darkness only to reveal stacks of wooden barrels in neat rows across the room.

Suddenly, the door slammed behind her. An instant later, she heard the screech of metal as a bolt slid into place, barring the door. A soft laugh followed, then nothing.

A shiver went through Rhiannon, and she braced herself against the impulse to pound on the door. Who would let her out? None of those women would help her. She frowned into the darkness. She'd experienced this kind of torment before from her brothers. The trick, she'd learned, was not to play the game. They wanted a reaction, some response that would confirm their suspicions of who they thought she was.

The candle flickered as she stared into the darkness. She had to find a way out without help and without fuss. But how?

She clutched the candleholder tightly, watching the flame sputter. Again, she held her arm fully extended before her, searching her surroundings. She was in some kind of cellar room filled with wooden barrels. Now that she'd become accustomed to the overwhelming scent, the air in the room smelled pungent with just a hint of spice.

Rhiannon ignored the barrels and blocked out the scent, concentrating on the darkness. No, not complete darkness. She could see a dim glimmer of light in the distance. Another door on the opposite side of the room?

Only one way to find out. She strode forward, her eyes straining to pierce the darkness outside of the ring of light cast by the candle. As she wound her way between the rows of barrels, the small line of light grew bigger, brighter, until she could see light coming from beneath the bottom of a door.

A few steps more, and her fingers closed around the door latch. One pull and the heavy door opened easily into yet another corridor. The temperature on this side of the castle was colder, most likely closer to the outside wall of the keep. The door at the end of the hallway proved her assumption as she stepped out into the night air. The door to the courtyard had enabled her to escape that trap. No sooner had the thought formed than a dark shape appeared before her.

"What were you doing in that storeroom?" Camden Lockhart stared down from atop his horse with his usual look of displeasure.

Rhiannon couldn't tell him the truth. For he would never believe his people capable of such deviousness. She also couldn't lie because that's what everyone expected her to do. Lie, cheat, steal, murder. She was capable of none of those things, yet damned by them all. "I couldn't sleep," she said, truthfully enough.

He dismounted and as he did, something in his gaze shifted, softened. Candlelight flickered over his dark hair and his light blue eyes, making the startling contrast even more pronounced. "You should not be out of the keep at night. Alone," he said, emphasizing the last word.

She was always alone. But what did that matter to him? "Thank you, milord, for your concern." She ducked her head, shielding herself from his appraisal, and set out for the castle's entrance.

She heard him dismount, but kept walking until a hand on her arm stalled her. "Why were you out here?" he asked, his gaze intently on her face.

"You might say I was given no choice." She gave him a cool smile and continued toward the door.

He fell in step beside her. She suddenly wished she did

not feel so dwarfed by his presence. The man exuded confidence and power with his every step, a fact that made her knees unsteady. She grasped the door latch that would take her back inside his lair for support.

What did he want from her now?

Chapter Six

Rhiannon Ruthven's face paled in the golden light cast by her candle, and guilt radiated from her. And yet Camden sensed all was not as it seemed. What wasn't she telling him?

"Why did Mother Agnes send you here?" He fell into step beside her as she scurried for the keep. "I sent a messenger to her at the abbey to verify your claims."

She gazed at him in surprise. "Are you always so suspicious?"

"I will know the truth—from you or her." He gazed at her thoughtfully. "Why are you here?"

She grasped the door latch of the keep, her fingers remaining there without opening the door. A raw vulnerability appeared on her face where there had been none before. He hardened himself against her attempt to manipulate his emotions.

"Do you want to know why I'm here? Because I'm desperate. I have nowhere to go. I gave myself to the abbey, but the abbess refused me, saying my calling was elsewhere."

He frowned at her unexpected confession. "You shouldn't tell me you're desperate," he said softly. At this moment, she was completely in his power. As he took in her lush body, his blood stirred at the thought of what that could mean.

"You wanted me to be direct." She studied him. "Besides, I have nothing else to lose."

"Oh, I can think of at least one thing." His gaze rested at the point where her shawl covered her breasts.

She lifted her chin, eyes blazing. "And will you take that from me, milord?"

He pictured it—stripping her bare and plunging into her hot wetness. His shaft started to harden. It would be his ultimate revenge. As suddenly as the thought came, it left him cold. She was a Ruthven, but she was also under his protection. "You have nothing to offer that I would want."

Yet he wasn't quite convinced of the truth in his own words as his hand met hers on the latch. He moved past her, their bodies connecting in a flash of shared heat, as he opened the door and strode into the keep.

Rhiannon took a deep breath to collect herself after Lord Lockhart went inside. At the sight of his broad, muscled back, she couldn't help thinking of his suggestive comments. She was completely at the man's mercy. Yet what on earth had possessed her to admit it? After another calming breath, she went back into the castle. Although she carefully avoided looking at Lord Lockhart, she could feel the heat of his gaze tracking her across the room and up the stairs. Oh, he was a dangerous man.

Inside her bedchamber, Rhiannon wilted against the wooden panels of the door. Her knees were unsteady and her heart raced. She had seen the lustful thoughts behind his eyes. She might be young and inexperienced, but that was one look she had not imagined.

She'd seen similar looks on the faces of her father's friends when they had come to visit and she'd played the role of hostess in her mother's absence. One of the few times she'd been allowed around other men. But these men did not want friendly conversation. Nay, their leering looks and not-so-discreet pinches had said it all.

Rhiannon shuddered at the memory. Thankfully, her father had never allowed any of them to pursue anything more.

But Camden Lockhart . . . she pressed her hand to her stomach, trying to stall the fluttering that had started there. He was no aged, leering philanderer. He was a handsome, virile man.

With a groan of disgust, Rhiannon pushed away from the door. She wasn't experienced enough to handle a man like Camden Lockhart. He would chew her up and spit her out before she even knew what had happened.

With a sigh, she went to the door connecting Violet's room to her own. Violet tossed and turned on the bed, writhing as if in some sort of pain. Rhiannon hurried to her side when the little girl bolted upright in bed. A scream pierced the stillness of the night.

"Don't let him get me. Mummy, don't let him take me away," she sobbed with her eyes still tightly shut.

A nightmare.

Rhiannon immediately went to the little girl's side. She sat on the bed, and her hands hovered above Violet's head. What should she do? How should she comfort her?

Violet's sobs continued. "Mummy, make him go away."

Rhiannon slowly brought her hand down to stroke the little girl's hair. "It's all right, Violet. No one will harm you while I'm here," she said softly.

The little girl pressed her body against Rhiannon's. Her sobs subsided, but waves of trembling wracked her body.

"Shh," Rhiannon cooed, continuing to stroke Violet's head until the girl's shaking stopped and soft breathing came from her lips. She'd fallen back asleep.

Rhiannon slowly lowered the girl to the bed and once again tucked the coverlet tightly about her small body. A sense of satisfaction mixed with joy came over her at her ability to help. Perhaps the abbess had been right to send her here with Violet.

As the girl slept, Rhiannon slipped off the bed, still restless. She *would* care for Violet, and she'd find some way to make the child a new gown that would not remind her of the horrors she'd faced. Violet needed a fresh beginning, and a new gown was a simple way to start her healing process.

From her adventure earlier in the dark storeroom, she knew she'd get no assistance from anyone else in the castle. One locked doorway and a few harsh names could never sway her resolve. She'd have to be more creative. She scanned the room. She'd find a way to make a gown out of something.

Rhiannon thought of her own sparse belongings. The only dress she had was the one she wore. She could use her cape for fabric, but that would leave her without a source of warmth when they took their lessons outside.

Still not defeated, she paced about the room as her mind inventoried the essentials she'd tossed into her one small bag. At one of the small beds, she paused to finger the fine dark blue silk of the bed drapes. And a length of ribbon came to mind—a lavender and blue tapestry ribbon her mother had given to her before her death. That ribbon would be the perfect accessory to a gown made from dark blue silk.

A lightheartedness she hadn't experienced in ages crept over Rhiannon. She pulled the drapes from the frame of the bed. If she worked all night, she just might do it. And with any luck, sewing into the wee hours might help take her mind off a decidedly handsome lord with a curious light in his eyes.

"Raise the portcullis and open the gates," guards at the gatehouse called out. The grinding of the metal chains filled the morning air as the fortified entrance opened, allowing those who had lived at Lockhart Castle entrance to their new home.

Camden felt he'd had no choice but to leave his brother's

castle empty while his efforts were divided between protecting his kin and the Crown. Lee Castle was closer to his enemy's border. To keep English forces from taking Glasgow or Edinburgh, it was best he be there to defend it. With its gateway cities strong, the rest of the country would be safe and he could make certain his brother's people would be safe.

"We need to speak to each of them," Camden told the men who had gathered at the gate to help him greet the staff of his brother's castle. "We must be certain only those known to us enter here."

Orrin's gaze narrowed on him. "I can appreciate that you'd want to care for your brother's people, but why such caution?"

Camden had not told any of them about the assassin he'd hired. Not even Orrin. He did not fully regret what he'd done. The image of James's disemboweled body would stay with him for all eternity. His revenge had been justified.

"No questions. Just do it," he growled.

"You heard the man." Orrin strode away.

Camden scowled. Damn the Ruthvens for forcing this upon him. He'd had his hands full just trying to keep the English at bay. And where he might have had a flair in matters of war, he had no skill for domestic concerns. He and Orrin had been back in Scotland for only three short years.

As the new residents crossed the drawbridge into the bailey, his men went to work, sending his way anyone of a questionable nature.

By midday they had welcomed over seventy-two of his dead brother's household, thirty-five of them warriors, trained and ready. They would be a welcome addition to his defenses. The remaining residents had skills of all sorts, ranging from cooks, weavers, scullery maids, a troubadour, a mason, ten huntsmen, two blacksmiths, a falconer, and two men, Hugh and Rhys, who had joined the castle's staff only the week before James's death. None of the other staff knew them well, but reported they were both hard workers, doing more than their fair share of the work.

"What should we do with them, milord?" Orrin asked, coolly.

"Let them pass. But we must be watchful."

Orrin nodded, then turned away, his movements rigid. "Orrin," Camden called, falling in step beside his friend as he headed toward the keep. "You were right."

"About what?" he asked, his expression puzzled.

"About taking revenge against the Ruthvens. I hired an assassin to kill them all."

Understanding settled into Orrin's dark eyes. "That explains your disappearance yester eve. I had wondered."

"I tried to find him, to stop him. He killed the two remaining male Ruthvens," Camden said quietly.

"You tried to stop him?"

"Aye."

"Because one of those Ruthvens is a female?"

Camden nodded. "I inadvertently placed Violet in terrible danger by hiring that assassin. No matter how many guards I surround her with, there is always a chance that she could be hurt if he comes after Rhiannon."

"You could always send the Ruthven girl away."

"I can't do that," Camden said, stung.

"Because?"

"Two wrongs won't make this right," Camden said, bitterly.

"Then what will?"

Camden sighed. "I wish I knew."

Orrin shrugged. "You've managed to bring Lady Violet here. The guards and I will be watchful. She is safe in this castle."

Camden clapped Orrin on the shoulder. "Thank you, my friend. I am in your debt."

Orrin smiled, his earlier stiffness gone. "That is true, and I am keeping tally of just how much."

The tension in Camden's neck eased as they fell into an easy banter that had seen them through their youth. Camden opened the door and stepped into the foyer outside the great hall.

"With me watching our two suspicious residents, whatever will you do to keep yourself occupied?" Orrin smiled.

Camden's thoughts immediately darkened. "I best go see what our uninvited guest is up to."

Orrin's teasing smile widened. "Truly? Is it that unpleasant?"

Camden frowned, his mood only darkened further at Orrin's taunts. "I'll let you know."

"Where are your ambitions, boy?" Mistress Berwick chided her son from her sickbed. She struggled to sit up, but a spasm of coughing sent her back down to the pillow.

Bishop Berwick brought her a sip of water from the pitcher at her bedside. "Drink this, Mother. It will help." Only because he'd laced it with juice of the poppy.

She drank from the cup, and with frail hands, handed it back to him. "We need to plan. We need to come up with a way to get the Charm Stone away from whoever has it now. It must be with Camden Lockhart. Where else would that woman have sent her precious Stone?"

The bishop set the cup on the bedside table with a smooth grace, despite the anger that seethed inside him. "You are sick, Mother. No planning today."

She scowled at him. "I am not sick. God would never punish me that way. I am the mother of a great bishop, a holy man."

The muscles of his neck clenched at her continued ranting. When would the tisane kick in? "Even holy men get sick, Mother."

"Nay," she said in a less forceful tone as her eyelids flicked closed once, then twice. "God would never strike me down," she mumbled.

Soon she would slip into a blessed sleep and he wouldn't have to hear her lectures any longer. Did she not think he wanted to be the next Archbishop of Glasgow? Did she not see what he had done, the horrible things he had been forced to do, to show to her that, aye, he did have ambition after all?

He wanted to make her proud. But even more, he wanted the power the office of the archbishop would give to him. He deserved it.

Finally, the woman sighed. A moment later her soft snores filled the room. He frowned down at her sleeping body. When had that flush of pink spots appeared upon the flesh of her neck and chest? His frown deepened. He should never have allowed her to journey to the Isle of Iona to see her sister with only a maid to support her. The maid had stayed behind when she'd suddenly fallen ill. Did his mother suffer the same illness now? Unlike his mother, he did believe God was capable of sending illness their way. A purification of sorts to keep them humble.

They were vulnerable. Except if they had the Stone. The bishop felt a flush of warmth move through him. The Charm Stone could cure his mother as well as secure for him the very ambitions he sought.

His excitement faded. He had used the Ruthvens to crush James, but still one obstacle stood in his way. Camden Lockhart. Somehow he had to find a way to remove the man. Then he would take the mystical Stone for himself and become a man of miracles. A holy man unlike any other the Church council had ever seen.

He could have everything he'd always wanted—power and status. He twisted back to the bed. His mother's soft snores filled the silence. And his mother would finally have the son she had always wanted.

If only he could get his hands on the Charm Stone.

Camden searched the entire castle and grounds for Violet and Rhiannon. At first, he had been annoyed that they had managed to elude him. Now, nearly two hours later, the muscles of his stomach knotted with panic. Where were they? The only place he had not checked was the orchard, and beyond that the fields outside the castle walls.

He nearly ran through the outer bailey to the orchard, drawing more than a few curious stares as he went. He threw the gate open, ready to call out Violet's name, when he saw the blanket on the ground. At the edge of the blanket lay two embroidery frames, one with stitching, the other blank. But still Violet and Rhiannon were nowhere in sight. Camden searched through the rows of dormant trees. The branches were showing signs of burgeoning into their spring growth. When he spotted two familiar shapes in the distance, Camden expelled a sigh of relief. They were safe after all his worry.

Rhiannon wore the same gray dress she had arrived in yesterday. His niece, however, looked like a springtime nymph dressed in a gown that in the sunlight appeared more purple than blue. He frowned. The color of the fabric made him pause. He'd seen that color somewhere before. And he was almost certain Violet had not arrived with anything more than the clothes on her back.

And what in heaven's name were they doing? With their backs to him he could not see them clearly. He hastened across the orchard.

Rhiannon pulled her arm back. An instant later, an arrow arched through the air. The tip imbedded in a wooden post not far enough from Violet to suit him. Camden made a sound low in his throat and raced forward. Had he been wrong about allowing Rhiannon to stay? Would she harm his niece just as her family had done to James and Clara?

Each step he took seemed to take forever. Horror chilled his blood when Rhiannon drew another arrow from her quiver. She aligned her bow, pulled it back. He rammed into her. She gasped. The bow veered off into the distance, away from Violet.

The force of his blow knocked Rhiannon off her feet. He carried her with him as he hit the ground, rolling her to the side.

"I trusted you," he said when he could draw breath.

They lay there together. Her soft body pressed against his war-seasoned chest. She smelled of lavender and lemons, as soft as a light summer breeze.

"What have I done to anger you?" Her breathing was sharp. Her gaze upon him sharper.

"You were about to murder my niece," he growled, disgusted at his body's reaction to her nearness. How could he still find her appealing despite this heinous deed?

Her face clouded with confusion. "I what?"

He thrust her away from him. "You aimed your bow—"

"At a target, you ninny." She sat up and scooted away, dragging her skirts in the dirt as she moved.

Violet stood to the side of them, her eyes wide, her face pale, a miniature bow and a quiver of arrows in her little hands.

Camden frowned. He hadn't noticed his niece also held a weapon.

Rhiannon stood and dusted herself off with angry swipes. "If you had stopped before barreling me down, you would have noticed that I am trying to teach her how to protect herself."

His frown deepened. "As her nursemaid, you should be

teaching her the things a lady needs to know." She stared at him without speaking, and Camden suddenly found himself uneasy.

Fury turned her tawny eyes to a deep, unreadable brown. "Lady Violet has more need for protection right now." Rhiannon bent down to retrieve the bow he had knocked out of her hands. "With all she has been through, she needs to feel as if she can defend herself against an assailant."

Regret knifed through him. "Why use a bow and arrow?"

She picked up one of the arrows that had fallen from her quiver. "That is the skill I know." With a quick, fluid motion, she nocked the arrow, turned toward the post and fired. Before he had time to register what had happened, her arrow hit its mark, not an inch from its twin. Her gaze returned to his, unflinching. "I can defend myself. I can teach Lady Violet the same skill."

He glanced away from her to Violet. The girl trembled violently, her shoulders quaking, her gaze cast to the packed earth beneath her tiny feet. So small, so innocent.

He scooped up Violet with one arm and cradled her to his side. "Uncle Camden will see that you are safe. Women do not need to know how to shoot." The little girl buried her face in his neck, and a pang of tenderness stirred within him. "You are both under my protection."

Violet nodded against his neck, but Rhiannon turned away and gathered the rest of her fallen arrows. At the target post, she plucked her arrows from the wood. Anger reddened her cheeks.

She had no idea of the danger she was in. But she could never know the truth.

She marched past him without saying a word. Her dusty gray skirts swayed as she bent to retrieve the blanket and embroidery frames that had gone unused.

Then she turned to Violet. "Lady Violet, would you

enjoy spending some time with your Uncle Camden for the rest of the day?

The young girl nodded eagerly.

A moment later, Rhiannon was gone.

Shock ran through him. Whatever reaction he had expected from Rhiannon, it wasn't this. What woman didn't want to be cared for? He frowned down at Violet's golden curls. And what was he supposed to do with a child?

Chapter Seven

"What is that woman trying to do to me?" Camden grumbled to himself several hours later. He'd accepted Rhiannon's unspoken challenge of watching over Violet, mostly because Rhiannon hadn't given him a choice.

Officiously he had escorted Violet to the lists where he and his men sparred with swords. He placed her on the fence to watch, but she didn't stay there. He'd pulled her away from two of his best warriors as they battled, swords swinging, unaware of their unschooled observer.

"Is that how you'll keep me safe, Uncle Camden, with your sword?"

Camden scooped her into his arms, realizing the lists were no place for a child.

Inside the castle, he took her with him down the back stair and into the storeroom where he kept his ale.

"What are you doing?" Violet asked as she watched him rotate the wooden barrels on the rack closest to the door.

"I'm making sure the fermentation spreads evenly through all the liquid."

"What's fermentation mean? Can I do it, too?" she asked, placing her small hands against the wooden barrel closest to him. She pushed, her cheeks turning pink at her effort. But the barrel remained where it stood. "It won't move." She skipped ahead to the next one, then the next one, until she was out of sight.

"Violet?" he called when he could no longer see nor hear the child. He found her a moment later when a thunderous crash filled the air. He ran down the long row to find her at the end, her pretty blue gown drenched with ale.

"I'm sorry, Uncle Camden." She stood in a puddle of ale left behind by the barrel that lay on its side, spewing liquid through the small opening that had once been closed by a cork.

He righted the barrel, suppressing the groan he desperately wished to vent. "Are you hungry?" he asked, praying it was somewhere close to their midday meal. Together they went upstairs, and after drying her skirts by the hearth, the meal was set.

Weary from chasing the young girl about, Camden gratefully seated her at the high table beside him, then filled her trencher with honeyed mackerel, braised turnips, and a slice of cheese.

He searched the room for Rhiannon with a self-satisfied grin. The afternoon had been difficult. He would be the first to admit it. Even so, he needed her to see that he and Violet had survived without her. It seemed essential that he prove to her he had lived up to her challenge.

His gaze moved from one table to the next, seeking a familiar head of golden hair. He frowned. The woman was nowhere in sight.

A tug on his sleeve brought his attention back to the little girl beside him. "I don't like mackerel. Mummy never made me eat turnips like this." Violet frowned down at her plate and rocked back in her chair. "Uncle Camden, why do I have to eat with you?"

The questions flowed after that, fast and apparently without needing a reply.

"Why doesn't that man use his knife to cut his food?"

"Can we play outside after we eat?"

"Can I have cakes with honey instead?"

"Uncle Camden, that man burped. Do you hear him? Mummy says it's impolite to burp."

Any triumph he might have experienced a moment before faded as the truth curled his ragged nerves into knots. Violet's high-pitched voice continued with one question after another until he wished he were temporarily deaf.

Camden scooted his chair away from the table. "Come, Violet. Let's go find Rhiannon. She'll know what you want for dinner. And she might be able to answer a question or two for you."

He assisted Violet with her chair. No sense suffering alone. A quick apology for insulting Rhiannon's skills earlier, and blessed silence would once again be his.

Rhiannon had just fastened the clasp on her cloak when a knock sounded on the wooden door of her chamber. In strode Lord Lockhart carrying a pink-cheeked Violet. By the joy that radiated from the young girl's face, Rhiannon would have to admit, he had done perfectly fine without her. Then she looked at Violet's dress.

"Oh heavens, what have you done to her gown?" she asked before she caught herself. She pressed her lips together. Who was she to question him?

He set the young girl on the floor in front of him. "She's a child in need of a nursemaid. Teach her how to protect herself with a bow and arrow." He offered her a partial smile. "Teach her anything you want."

"Anything?" Rhiannon folded her arms over her chest to hide the trembling reaction to his nearness that had set into her limbs.

His smile vanished. "Within reason."

"Thank you for your trust, milord. But you gave me much to consider in the last few hours." She hesitated. "Perhaps another nursemaid would be more appropriate."

Violet crossed the room to stand before her. "No."

She bent down to look into Violet's eyes. "This is between your uncle and me, I'm afraid. He has every right to decide what is right for you." She smoothed one of Violet's errant curls from beside her cheek. "Aren't you going for your ride this afternoon with Thomas?"

"Why don't you hurry along, Violet," Camden said. "You are keeping Thomas waiting. Then Rhiannon and I must talk."

Violet moved reluctantly toward the door. "Thomas said we could ride in the orchard this afternoon if it was all right with you, Uncle Camden."

"It's fine. But it's cold outside so remember your cape."

Violet nodded, her gaze still on Rhiannon as the girl let the door close softly behind her.

Rhiannon turned away. "Do the Ruthvens surrender so easily?" His voice was rough.

"I'm merely being practical. It's obvious you don't want me here. I should leave before Lady Violet becomes too attached to me. She doesn't understand that this was a mistake. Mother Agnes was wrong."

"It's no mistake." He gazed at her flushed cheeks and full lips. Something flickered in the depths of his eyes. He took a step toward her. She froze, unable to move away from his presence. Slowly he reached for her, gently tracing his finger along the sensitive flesh of her jaw to her chin.

She braced herself against the power of his touch as her resolution faltered. "Why the change of heart?" Her voice shook.

"I do not despise you." For a moment a shadow darkened his eyes. "Quite the contrary." His fingers slipped up then down the sensitive flesh beneath her chin. The caress felt far more arousing than it should have. "Lady Violet needs a woman she can depend on in her life." The heat of his body enveloped her.

She swallowed roughly, wanting desperately to step out of the web he'd woven around her, yet she couldn't seem to find the strength.

"You'll stay here with"—he paused again—"with Violet." The air between them was charged with tension—a different kind of tension than had been there before. Something dark and mysterious in his gaze reached out to her, beckoned her to risk staying.

At a loss for words, she nodded.

She remained still, unable to do anything other than force herself to breathe, slowly, evenly.

He withdrew his finger from her flesh. "You and Lady Violet can do what you wish within the walls of the castle as long as Travis and Hamish are present."

"Who?" she asked, suddenly confused.

"Your guards."

She could only blink. "My what?"

"You may proceed with the archery lessons. You have proved you are skilled. And, because I also know you to be a fine rider," he continued despite the angry color she knew he could see in her cheeks, "I will inform Thomas that you are to take over her riding lessons."

Camden ignored her growing anger, which only upset her more. He started for the door. "Hamish and Travis will assist you with anything you need."

The door closed with a firm click behind him, but not before she caught sight of the two hulking warriors who stood just outside her door.

He'd asked her to stay, as long as *her* two nursemaids stayed right by her side.

The realization that he still judged her by her last name stung.

Rhiannon moved to the bed and collapsed upon it. She lay there, nestled in a sea of crimson and wondered what her life would have been like had she been born as anyone else.

"Your Grace." His chamberlain's well-tailored form filled the doorway of the bishop's library in the small country home they'd been forced to rent on the outskirts of the town below Lee Castle. "You have a visitor."

Bishop Berwick studied his long, graceful fingers with a scowl. "Show him in," the bishop said, unable to keep boredom from showing in his voice.

"As you command." The chamberlain bowed, leaving the room.

Bishop Berwick's fingers wrapped around the ivory-handled mirror that lay facedown on his desk. He picked up the mirror and smiled at his reflection. A narrow, triangular face stared back at him. He could claim no attributes of beauty, except for his wide-set gray eyes. They sparkled with an exceptional brilliance that his mother had claimed proved he possessed the holiest of spirits.

He stared at the reflection of his eyes. They gleamed with pleasure, then impatience, then boredom. He set the mirror facedown once more. He hated the country. Hated that the youngest Lockhart had unknowingly forced him to take up residence in an area where people did not love him as he should be loved. This Lockhart might be green in age, but he was twice as wary, and thrice as well-guarded by his armed warriors as his brother had been. Getting him to fall would take some skill.

The bishop's lips pulled up into a sardonic smile. Fortunately, he had all the skill necessary to take the mighty Lockhart down. Then the Charm Stone and the little girl who knew its magic would be his to command. He needed that Stone. His position in the Church depended on it.

The bishop thrummed his fingers on the surface of the desk. Performing miraculous healings with the aid of the Charm Stone would guarantee that the Council would select him as the new archbishop over the other five contenders.

He needed a miracle. The Stone would give him that and more.

A shuffling at the door interrupted his thoughts. The chamberlain reappeared. He turned to the peasant beside him. "You may take three steps into the room, then bow. Wait there for His Grace to recognize you by offering his hand and ring for you to bow over. Only then may you speak."

The peasant did as directed. The bishop flinched as the peasant nearly touched his hand with his filthy body. "Report," the bishop commanded, stepping a safe distance away from his earthly subject.

The man's face was alive with eagerness. "The wee one is at Lee Castle. I saw her head of yellow-gold curls myself." A brownish-yellow smile followed the divulged information.

The bishop took another step away, wishing he had his perfume bottle nearby to freshen the air with anything other than the man's foul breath. But desperate times called for desperate measures.

"Is that all you have for me? Any sign of the Charm Stone?" The bishop waved his hand before his nose instead.

"Nay, no Stone. But Lord Lockhart has taken in a chit whom no one seems tae like. Someone named Ruthven."

A jolt of pure satisfaction rode through the bishop. He dug into his robe and pulled forth a silver coin that he tossed at the peasant. "You did well. Keep watching. I want to know the moment the Stone surfaces."

The man caught the coin in midflight and slid it hastily into the pocket of his tattered wool coat. "Aye, Your Grace." He bowed once, then again before heading out the door.

A Ruthven? Surely it was divine intervention. Her family had been loyal to him since he'd been appointed bishop.

He need not deal with pesky undisciplined peasants any longer. Nay, he had a new spy, one who would be more pleasant to his eyes and his nose. The Ruthven girl would tell him whatever he wanted her to.

She would betray her country and her new protector. She would have no choice in the matter.

A smile of satisfaction crossed his lips. And he allowed it to form, knowing that his cheeks looked less angular and more in the popular vogue when he did. "Perhaps it is time I pay my new neighbor a visit."

Chapter Eight

He had hurt her. Camden had seen the angry expression on Rhiannon's face at the sight of the two burly warriors he'd posted outside her bedchamber door. He would make it up to her.

Striding down the long corridor, he chastised himself for the thought. He had nothing to feel guilty about. He was doing the only thing he could do given the circumstances.

Or was he?

Could he trust her? Trust. One nebulous and dangerous word that could either bring him the peace he so desperately sought, or send him spiraling to his end. Had James trusted the Ruthvens? Is that how they had managed to get close enough to him to circumvent his guards?

Camden continued down the stairs and outside to where his niece rode through the orchard on his most docile horse with Thomas and a full contingent of guards.

Orrin broke away from the others and came toward Camden. "The men do not seem to mind 'protection' detail. Although they are curious as to why they need to guard the littlest Lockhart with their lives."

Camden gazed out at the young girl as she rode her horse down one long line of trees then up yet another, pushing the animal faster and faster. Thomas chased after her, his face grim with disapproval.

A smile came to Camden's lips. A bit of Clara's adventurous spirit existed in her daughter. "I cannot tell them why," Camden said, his smile fading.

"No one would question your actions. They saw what happened to James."

"I cannot risk it." Camden allowed an edge of steel to enter his voice.

"You can't risk Rhiannon learning the truth," Orrin corrected.

Camden paused before saying slowly. "It's too dangerous for any of them to know the truth. I will not allow the bishop to use any of my people as his puppets. Knowing nothing makes them innocent." Camden frowned. "If our last meeting with the bishop was any indication of events to come, the man will scrutinize every detail of our lives until he finds what he wants."

"What does he want?" Orrin asked.

"The Charm Stone."

"And Lady Violet? Why did he want her almost as badly as the Stone?" Orrin asked.

"Did I hear someone mention Lady Violet's name?"

Both men turned, drawing their swords more out of habit than necessity. Camden's sword pointed at the Bishop Berwick's heart. Orrin's aimed for his gut. One sword poised to kill, the other to cause suffering. Which outcome did the man deserve more?

"Lord Lockhart. You've certainly outdone yourself," the bishop said as he frowned down at the weapons pressed against his pristine robes. "You found your niece in record time. Anger and grief usually spur men to accomplish great deeds."

"What do you want, Berwick?" Camden asked, his sword steady.

"You wound me, Lockhart." The bishop's frown increased. "I've come to make certain that little girl has come to no harm." With a gloved hand, he pushed the tip of Camden's blade away from his heart. He scowled at

Orrin. "Would both of you cease this attack? I am no threat to you."

Camden sheathed his curved weapon. Orrin followed his example. But he remained close, and Camden could see the twitch in his hand as it hovered over the hilt of his sword. "I repeat. What do you want?"

"I've come to make you an offer. My dear mother would be most happy to take charge of your niece. She will instruct her properly in the ways of a noble lady."

The bishop's gaze moved to the orchard where Violet and Thomas had just finished their lesson for the day. They headed directly for them. For a moment, Camden wished he'd never encouraged Thomas to take his niece out for a ride. Even with a full contingent of warriors nearby the outdoors seemed suddenly too vast, and his niece too vulnerable with this man nearby.

"She stays with me," Camden said with icy precision.

"Then perhaps I may send my mother to you? She can train both your niece and your other young charge."

"We have no need of your help."

The bishop frowned. "Oh? But I know all about Rhiannon Ruthven. What I don't understand is why you would trust her, the spawn of a family of traitors, rather than me, a holy man?"

Camden's surprise vanished. His own experience with holy men might color his perspective, but at this moment he did prefer Rhiannon's help to that of the bishop's. And this bishop obviously had connections inside *his* castle. Only someone who lived inside these walls would have access to information about his niece and Rhiannon. "Rhiannon will teach Lady Violet all she needs to know."

Thomas led Violet up the slope to where he and the bishop stood. With each step, Camden's worry increased. He had to keep Violet away from this man.

The bishop's eyes brightened as the young girl approached. "Think of Lady Violet, not yourself."

"She is my first priority." Camden moved to stand beside his niece's horse. He caught the reins, holding them with a firm hand. Caution flared. His men filled in the space around them. They stood with their bodies tense, as though sensing Camden's tension.

"And what about the Ruthven woman?" The bishop's gaze strayed from Violet to the keep. "Perhaps a little repentance might do her good if she is to take charge of something so precious."

Unease passed through Camden. The bishop wasn't after Violet. Not this afternoon, anyway. Nay, he wanted to speak to Rhiannon. That was the true reason for his visit.

"Does she know you are here? Did she ask you to come?" Camden felt his body tighten as he once again questioned Rhiannon's motives for coming to his home.

"Nay," the bishop replied. "It is the shepherd who must find a sheep who has left the flock."

"There are no lost sheep here. The woman is ill. I wouldn't advise seeing her." He lied. But something inside him warned him not to give the bishop access to Rhiannon.

"You cannot dismiss me, Lockhart. I serve the people, all people. She might want me to stay."

"I asked you to leave." He didn't think, merely reacted—a survival skill that had seen him through his days in the Holy Land. He drew his sword. The rasp of steel filled the air as his men drew their weapons. "Or shall I force you?"

The bishop cast a furious glance at him before turning to hustle through the outer bailey. "You are treading on dangerous ground, milord."

"Danger has been my life," Camden replied, striding toward the gate with his men. Once the bishop left, Camden ordered the portcullis lowered and the gate closed, and to remain that way unless he himself granted entrance.

Only when the two heavy planks of wood slid into place did Camden feel the winds of dusk that blew crisp and cold on his face.

He needed that cold to focus his thoughts. He was the new laird of the Lockhart clan whether he liked it or not. With that position came certain responsibilities. The first and foremost, keeping his clan safe from anyone and anything that could harm them.

Could the bishop truly be the threat he seemed? A holy man? Camden frowned at his own thoughts. Shaykh Haashim had been a threat for seven years. Never would he allow any member of his clan to suffer as he and Orrin had at the hands of a holy man.

Camden slammed the door on his memories. He clutched the curved sword that was ever-present at his side. He was no longer a slave. He could protect his people from the invading English, from the bishop, or anyone else. Grasping the comfort the thought brought, he shifted his gaze to the sky now turning from a hazy pink to a pearlescent gray mixed with heavy dark clouds. There would be snow tonight.

He watched as Thomas escorted Violet inside and Orrin dismissed the men. When that task was complete, Orrin joined Camden near the gate.

"The man is a lunatic."

"That may be true, but he's one lunatic we will likely see again. He might claim to want to help with Lady Violet's training, but I am certain he has an ulterior motive," Camden said. "Whatever we do, we must keep my niece safe."

"The two of us along with your army will be all the protection she needs." Orrin's face took on a look Camden had seen so many times before—the look that dared anyone to prove him wrong. It was that look, and his fighting skills, that had kept him alive during their captivity.

Camden's thoughts moved away from the bishop and turned to Rhiannon. Was she the insider who had delivered information about Violet to the bishop? "I'm not so certain my army is all that is needed here."

"You think the bishop has that much power?"

Camden nodded. "Aye. We both know the power that lies behind a holy man."

Orrin's brow darkened as he, too, battled memories of their past together. "Then what are we to do?"

"We need to lure the bishop into exposing his true plans before anyone else is harmed," Camden said as darkly as the clouds billowing overhead.

Orrin met his gaze. "What will you do?"

"I need to speak with our new nursemaid. There is a connection between her and the bishop. I need to find out what it is and decide once and for all if she can be trusted."

Camden strode into the castle and up the stairs. At the door of Rhiannon's bedchamber, he dismissed Hamish and Travis, then entered the room after a brief warning knock. "Rhiannon, we must talk."

She lay upon the bed above the coverlet, asleep. He moved silently to her side and gazed down at her, seething with frustration. He should wake her up. He had every right to do so. And yet he hesitated.

Candlelight flickered over her pale blonde hair and stroked the silken smoothness of her cheeks and neck. She lay curled on her side, her cheek buried in the pillow, her pink lips slightly parted. All thoughts of finding the truth about her connection to Bishop Berwick faded as a different emotion took its place.

Desire.

Wanting hardened every muscle of his body as he gazed

at the soft shadows that the long lashes cast upon the curve of her cheeks. The long exposed column of her neck led down to the fullness of her breasts as they rose and fell against the bodice of her gray gown with each breath.

Just beneath the fabric of her gown he could make out her hardened nipples. The thought of stroking the sensitive buds sent his heart thudding against his ribs.

He bent closer, until the soft scent of lavender filled his senses. His blood pounded in his veins and the quickening in his loins hardened to an almost unbearable force. Why not wake her and take from her what he could? He had every right to take anything he wanted from his enemy. His own father had taught him that rape and pillaging were the rewards of overcoming one's enemy in times of war. He had pillaged many wealthy enemies in the Holy Land, but had never resorted to rape . . . yet.

He frowned at the direction of his thoughts. This was no war—only a battle between himself and Rhiannon Ruthven. And despite the fact he wanted to be the victor, he did not want her to yield to him because he forced her to.

Nay, he would prefer a slow surrender, one willingly given. With an effort, he straightened and backed away from the bed. He would wait to speak with her until the morning, just as he would wait to take from her everything she unwittingly offered.

He blew out the candle. Aye, he would wait until the time was right.

Death was all around him. Blood turned Jerusalem's rocky sand into a slick bog. Men who continued to fight found it difficult to find purchase, yet feared falling among those who were slain by the sword or trampled by horses.

Camden spilled his own share of blood. He fought back to

back with Orrin in the way of their countrymen, startling the Moors who had attacked them. And that brief hesitation was all it took to find their advantage.

They would not die. They would know injury and pain, but neither of them would leave this world surrounded by strangers. He did not think about that during battle. All thoughts centered on a cold, calculating way to kill the men before him, hold on to his fierce determination, and cripple his enemy's offense.

He would return home in just three years.

Home. Scotland. Freedom.

Camden startled awake. Another dream. He'd had them more regularly as of late. Ever since the Stone had come back into his life. He knew it wasn't the Stone itself that caused his memories to return. It was what it represented— a link to his past—to the Holy Land, and his captor, Shaykh Haashim.

Forcing the memories back into the recesses of his mind, he tossed his bedcovers back and got out of bed. He dressed quickly, watching the golden glow of light seeping beneath the door of Rhiannon's room across the hall. Thoughts of her stirred his blood once more, tempting him. Until he remembered his decision to make her come to him, to drive her to a need so fierce she would capitulate of her own will. That day would come. Sooner rather than later, if he had anything to say about it.

As the first rays of dawn streaked across the sky, Camden left his bedchamber to pace the battlements and try to assuage his growing lust. The crisp morning air would do him good and clear his senses before he accused Rhiannon of any treachery.

Fresh snowflakes settled on his head and his shoulders as he stepped outside. Snow continued to fall, as it had all night. Camden gazed out across his land. Snow blanketed everything for as far as his eye could see.

Pink streaks of dawn mixed with yellow and red, filling

the sky with color. A sense of peacefulness settled over him.

Until he saw the tracks.

Marring the newly fallen snow were two sets of footprints, one leading away from the castle, the other returning. The bishop's spy? Camden moved down the battlements, closer to the tracks, wondering where they had originated. He needed to know that information before he followed where they went.

On the north wall of the castle, the wind picked up and the flurries of snow forced him to slow his steps. He proceeded with as much haste as he dared.

Then he saw the rope. A thick jute rope encircled one of the crenellations and dangled down the entire length of the castle's outer wall. He picked it up, the coarse texture prickly against the flat of his palm. The rope, while sturdy, was not strong enough to support the weight of many of his warriors.

His thoughts drifted to Rhiannon once more. Had she left the castle during the night to meet with the bishop somewhere? Was the light behind her door a decoy to make him think she was within the room while she'd been engaged elsewhere?

He drew his sword and slashed easily through the coarse fibers, sending the rope plummeting down into the snow. He would not make it easy for whoever had used the rope to do so again.

He sheathed his weapon, then headed for his keep. This constant doubt about Rhiannon had to end. An inner turmoil had consumed him since the moment she'd stepped inside his home. He'd never felt anything like this before, alternating between revulsion and desire.

Camden scowled at the scenery he had moments before found breathtaking. He had to find a way to resolve his feelings and put an end to his doubts.

One way or another, he would have his answers this very day.

Rhiannon led Violet belowstairs and into the great hall for their morning meal. Her two hulking *companions* would not deter her from her plans. She had nothing to hide from Lord Lockhart.

This morning she wanted Violet to familiarize herself with the castle and its people. She hoped they would be more accepting of the little girl than they had been of Rhiannon.

She seated the girl at the head table, thankful the lord and master of the castle was nowhere in sight, then went to dish them each a bowl of boiled oats and cream. She sweetened Violet's with honey before returning to the table.

"Mistress Rhiannon, why is everyone staring at me?" Violet asked as she hunched down in her chair, conscious of the gazes upon her.

Those gazes were most likely directed at Rhiannon herself and filled with the same repugnance she had received yesterday. Rhiannon straightened her shoulders. Violet need not suffer because of her. "Because you are the lady of a great castle, these people look to you for guidance and support." She sat beside Violet.

Violet's brow furrowed in consideration. "But I'm only a little girl."

"You won't always be, and they realize that. Now sit up straight and show them how a *lady* breaks her morning fast."

Rhiannon smiled when Violet did as instructed. She looked every bit the young mistress in her new blue gown. It hadn't been easy, but Rhiannon had managed to clean the ale stains from Violet's dress during the night, drying it before the fire in her room. This morning the young girl seemed more at ease than she had been in days. Violet had slept through the night, her nightmares gone for the moment.

As she ate, Rhiannon peered at the others in the hall from beneath her lashes. The women glared at her, as she had expected. Well, no matter. Lord Lockhart had given her the freedom to teach Violet what she thought necessary whether they approved or not. Today's lessons would be about the responsibility Violet had to the people around her.

That they would receive Violet's assistance without further trouble did not look promising, as long as Rhiannon was near, but she needed to guide the little girl. For how else would Violet learn?

Rhiannon had just taken another spoonful of oats when the door to the great hall swung open, and a blast of cold air heralded Lord Lockhart's arrival.

His gaze shot directly to her. The cacophony of voices and laughter in the hall suddenly silenced. A warning not unlike the keen of a pipe went off in her head.

Rhiannon smoothed the creases from her dress with trembling fingers as he stalked toward her, his mouth pressed into a firm line. Her pulse gave a nervous leap when he stopped before her.

"Good morrow," he said with cool civility. "You will come with me."

"But Lady Violet—"

"Mistress Faulkner will attend her today." As if on cue, the chatelaine appeared at his side.

The two burly warriors he'd assigned to watch her every move stepped forward. "Shall we prepare to escort you?"

Lord Lockhart shook his head. "Stay and protect Lady

Violet. I'll take care of Rhiannon." He thrust a long, fur cloak at her. "Put this on. We'll be going outside."

"Why outside?" Rhiannon stood and accepted the cloak.

"To follow the trail of a traitor."

The coolness of his gaze suggested he meant her. Her stomach felt as if she'd been punched.

When she did nothing, he tugged the cloak from her grasp, tossed it about her shoulders, then with a tight grasp on her arm, nearly dragged her out the door and into the snow. At the bottom of the stairs outside, he had one horse waiting.

He mounted. "Give me your hand," he demanded. Of its own accord, her hand lifted, his fingers closed around it, and suddenly she was hauled up to sit in front of him atop the beast. Arms like bands of steel encircled her, and his warmth cradled her back.

"Where are we going?"

"You'll find out soon enough," he replied, turning the horse toward the gate. With a signal of his hand, the mighty wooden gates parted and the portcullis rose. Without explanation, he headed across the drawbridge, then turned the beast north.

Snow covered the world around them, silencing everything except the sound of their breathing. Tendrils of steam generated by their warm breath rose into the air to vanish a moment later.

They followed the outer wall of the castle for a distance until Lord Lockhart brought the horse to a stop in front of a rope partially buried in the snow. "Do you know anything about this rope?" His voice filled with suspicion.

"You sound as if you expect me to," she replied, tucking her hands more deeply inside of her cloak in an effort to ward off the chill from outside as well as within.

"A straight answer, please." He leaned forward to stare into her face, his blue eyes as frosty as the world around them. "Did you use this rope to escape the castle last night to meet up with Bishop Berwick?"

"Nay." She drew a sharp breath. What heinous things did he think her capable of? "Why would I do such a thing?"

"The bishop paid us a call yesterday," he said, watching her closely. "Someone inside the castle disclosed Violet's presence." He hesitated again before adding, "He asked after you."

She startled. "I've never met the man, but the abbess did caution me about him."

"What was her caution?"

"She warned me to be cautious around him. To never let Lady Violet near him."

Lord Lockhart frowned. "Why would she warn you of such a thing?"

"I don't know." Rhiannon lowered her gaze to the snowflakes gathering on the red velvet of her cloak. "She seemed very distraught that day."

A finger beneath Rhiannon's chin brought her gaze back to his. "The abbess trusted you."

"I am trustworthy." She held his gaze, refusing to buckle beneath his punishing appraisal.

"Time will reveal that truth or falsehood." He straightened and signaled the horse to walk through the heavy drifts of snow leading away from the castle.

The snow came halfway up their horse's legs, but their mount seemed undeterred by the lightweight powder. Rhiannon allowed her gaze to travel across the pristine blanket of white. It was then that she noticed the two sets of footprints partially filled by the newly fallen snow.

"Where are we going?" she asked.

"We're following a villain's trail."

"A villain? Anyone could have made those tracks. Maybe someone at the castle took an early morning walk."

"Someone who needed a rope to climb the castle walls? Nay, it has been made clear to me we have a spy."

"You assume I am that spy."

"Aye."

"Then for Lady Violet's sake I won't hold your assumptions against you."

He leaned close to her ear, his lips brushing her temple. The warmth of his breath sent a shiver right to her core. "That's kind of you."

"I'll prove my innocence."

"I look forward to that," he said in a low, inviting tone that brought a catch to her breath. She shifted away, trying to escape the intimacy the moment had wrapped them in.

They rode well over six miles as the snow continued to fall around them, fast and furious. "I can hardly see the tracks." Rhiannon ducked her head to keep the flakes from gathering on her face.

"The storm is picking up." His frustration was evident in the tone of his voice. He reined the horse to a halt and scanned the sky. "I was so certain the snowstorm had ended. But the weather has only grown worse."

As though in response to his words, the wind kicked up. Where it had been sighing through the trees, it now whipped the branches about.

"We should head back," Rhiannon called over the rising howl of the wind.

Camden frowned. "I've left it too late. It will take us more than an hour to return. We need shelter. I remember from my youth an abandoned cottage around here somewhere that was once used by my father's gamekeeper." He tightened his arms around her and dug his heels into the horse's side, sending them all forward into the storm. "We can find shelter there."

Snow covered them entirely, and they could barely see in front of them. Rhiannon no longer knew which way to take back to the castle. She shivered, wondering which would lead to her demise—the man behind her or the storm overhead.

Chapter Nine

Camden steadfastly spurred their horse forward. "I see something ahead," Rhiannon called out between chatters of her teeth.

A short time later, she realized it was a small cottage set deep in the woods. Rhiannon strained her eyes through the falling snow for signs of habitation. She smelled before she saw the smoke curling from the chimney. Warmth. She nestled deeper into her cloak. She could almost feel the heat now.

They came up to the cottage and Lord Lockhart slid from the horse before he reached up and plucked her off as though she weighed nothing at all.

"I thought you said the cottage was abandoned?" Rhiannon said, pulling the edges of her cloak more tightly around her as the cold seeped inside her, chilling her to the bone.

"It was." He gathered the horse's reins, moving toward the lean-to that would provide shelter for the animal. "Let's find out who might be here, shall we?"

Rhiannon hurried after him. She didn't care who might be inside as long as there was space near the fire. Her thoughts focused only on the warmth that awaited. She darted ahead of Camden to knock on the door. When no one answered, she tried the latch. The door opened easily and she stepped inside.

One open room made up the entirety of the cottage. She peered inside, finding no one there. When her gaze lit on the cheery little fire that crackled in the hearth, she smiled. Warmth wrapped itself around Rhiannon, drawing her into the room.

Camden entered the small cottage a moment later, carrying an arm full of wood. "I never would have taken you away from the castle had I known a storm was coming."

She turned away, toward the flames, rubbing her cold hands together. Pinpricks of sensation danced along her chilled flesh. "Not much deters you. Why would a storm be any different?"

He set the wood near the fire, then stood beside her. "It must seem that way to you," he said almost as an aside. He sighed as he bent his dark head to peer into the flames. "I am only trying to keep my people safe."

"Which is why you risked following those tracks despite the threat of a storm," she responded more to herself than to him.

"Aye."

"Do you still believe I made those footsteps?"

"I am finding it harder to believe. By the look of the fire, whoever inhabited this cottage left only a short time ago." He gaze lifted to hers. "It appears as though we will be here for a while." He put out his hand. "Give me your cloak."

"Nay." She took a step away from him as all the dark warnings she'd heard from her father about being alone with a man filled her head. She *was* alone. And stranded in the snow. Oh why had she been such a fool to get on that horse with him?

"Rhiannon." He spoke her name softly, gently, with reassuring calm. "You are quite safe here with me."

She narrowed her gaze on him. "I will trust you, if you will trust me for once."

He smiled, and she saw the tension in his shoulders relax. "Agreed." He signaled with his hand. "Your cloak. It's wet. There are pegs by the fire to dry it."

She unfastened the heavy cloak and handed it to him. He placed it on one of the pegs, then removed his own cloak, hanging it beside hers. The soft linen of his shirt molded to him, revealing wide shoulders, a lean torso that led to a narrow waist and muscular thighs. "Do you think this is where your spies have been meeting?"

"Since no one else is around, I'd say it's a safe assumption." He turned back toward her and she hurriedly dropped her gaze, although she could not hide the heat that rose to her cheeks. "Want to help me find some clue as to who might have been here?"

She nodded, grateful to do anything that would distract her from the sheer maleness of his body. The cottage was small, with a rickety wooden table and two chairs tucked in the corner near the hearth, a wooden bench placed near the fire. A straw-filled mattress with a dark woolen coverlet took up the far side of the cottage. A small iron stove made up the kitchen.

"There isn't much here to identify anyone," she said, exploring the area near the hearth. Aside from a few candle stubs on the floor near the hearth, she found nothing.

He explored the table, and the three shelves above the iron stove. "The stove is cool, and the shelves look as though they haven't been stocked in ages." He moved a pottery jar aside, as if to prove his point, and a tiny mouse scurried from behind the crock, down the shelf, onto the stove. It leaped for the floor, before scurrying into a small hole at the base of the wallboards.

"Whoever our spy is, he's careful." Camden tossed another log onto the embers of the fire, then reaching for the saddle bag he'd brought in with him from the horse, he sat on the bench.

Rhiannon moved to the shutters at the front of the cottage. Ice clung to the bottom of the casement. She moved to the door and peered outside. Heavy snow continued to fall. Restless, she watched as the delicate flakes hit the accumulating mass on the ground. The storm showed no signs of letting up anytime soon.

She closed the door and glanced toward Camden. Something in his expression made her look away. Yet she could still feel the warmth of his gaze as though it were something physical, almost possessive. She began to quake inside at the intimacy of the moment, once again realizing how truly alone they were.

"Come," he said, his tone as inviting as his gaze had been. "It's much warmer over here by the fire."

She hesitated.

"Can I interest you in a bite to eat?" He held up a small plank of wood that contained a wedge of yellow-gold cheese and a loaf of dark bread.

"Where did you find food? Not here, I hope," she commented as the image of that tiny mouse came to mind.

He smiled, a warm, friendly smile. "I made it a rule never to ride out without at least minimal provisions. The grooms are very conscientious about executing those orders. Sit." He patted the seat beside him. "You must be hungry."

"A little." She sat down as far from him as the wooden bench allowed and curled her feet up under her skirt.

His eyes glinted with amusement. He withdrew two mugs and a bladder from his saddlebag, unfastened the closure, then poured each of them an amber-colored beverage from within. He handed her a mug. "This should help to warm you."

She took a sip, then sputtered at the richness of the liquid as it flowed over her tongue. "What is this?" she asked in a raw voice.

"Ale. Using my own special blend of grains." He raised his mug to his lips and took a long, slow sip. "Last year's batch is the best yet."

Rhiannon frowned down into her cup. The bitter liquid would take some getting used to. But in the absence of
anything else to drink, and so as not seem rude, she took
another sip. "Interesting."

He offered her a smile that lit up his eyes. Their depths
became suddenly mysterious and inviting. She swallowed
roughly. When had he stopped treating her as yesterday's
pottage?

"Bread?" he asked offering her the tray of bread and
cheese.

She accepted the tray and sliced a wedge of bread, then
cheese, taking the opportunity to look away from him, to
gather her composure. She hadn't spent much time around
men other than her father and his friends. Over the years,
she'd convinced herself that all men were rough and
brutish. But in this moment, Camden seemed very distant
from her earlier assumptions.

Brutish men did not demand their men leave the stable
with some sort of provisions in case something went
wrong. They did not care about anyone's comfort but
their own. And they certainly didn't risk their own lives
for the sake of their people's safety. Suddenly nervous,
Rhiannon drank liberally from her mug. The flavor of the
brew seemed less bitter now. It was smoother, with hints of
spice. "What is the spice in this? Cinnamon?"

"Nutmeg." His gaze became warm, sensual. "You are
the first to ever observe that note."

"I've never heard of that spice," she confessed. "Where
did you learn of such a thing?"

"A long time ago." Some of the warmth in his voice
faded. He took a bite of his bread and cheese. "My father
taught me what he knew about ale-making. He's the one
who started growing the mixture of grains in our fields at
Lee Castle. I think my love of the land and the castle itself
is what prompted my brother James to build Lockhart

Castle farther north. He didn't want to take the memories of our family from me."

She nibbled on her bread. "It sounds as though James loved you very much."

"He did."

She grew silent as she thought about her own youth. Memories of her mother filled her mind, and she smiled.

"What are you thinking about?"

"You reminded me of a pleasant time from my childhood."

He nestled back against the settee. "Tell me."

"Well," she hesitated.

"Your best memory."

She tucked her feet more firmly beneath her. "There was this time when my father and brothers were away hunting." She frowned at the sudden realization that they hadn't been hunting at all. That's when the raiding had begun, when they'd come home not with game, but with coins, salted pork, and gems—the spoils of their raid.

"Are you unwell?" he asked, his face filled with concern.

"Just remembering." She shook off the horror the memory brought. "I was Violet's age, maybe a little younger. There was snow on the ground, much like there is today. My mother and I were baking oatcakes, but I was bored. I kept asking her if we could do something special, like Father and the boys were doing. I kept after her until she finally relented and tossed her apron aside. She told me to go to my bedchamber and not to come out before she called me."

Rhiannon smiled at the memory of hiding under the bedcovers, shivering with anticipation. "It seemed like forever until she came for me. But I'll never forget the glint in her eyes when she did. She tied a sash over my eyes, put my cloak and my pattens on me, then led me outside."

She drew a shaky breath as tears came to her eyes. "She

took the sash off my eyes and all I could see were a hundred candles, casting a rich golden glow over the snowbanks that lined the ice on our pond. She pulled me onto the ice, and we both skated in circles for hours and hours, laughing until our sides hurt. She looked down at me that day with such love in her eyes and I knew true joy."

Rhiannon swiped at one of the tears that trailed down her cheek. "Three days later she died."

"How?" His voice was soft, lulling.

A counterraid, she realized now. Her mother had paid for their raiding with her life. New tears joined the others on her cheeks. She turned her head away, embarrassed by the emotions that she could not control. "She died. That's all I know."

"I'm sorry," he said, sounding sincere. "You really do know how Violet feels, don't you?"

"My apologies." She wiped at her tears with the back of her hands. "You asked for a memory and I give you waterworks instead. You must think me terribly ill-bred."

"Quite the contrary. I find you fascinating." The husky sincerity in his deep voice brought a hitch to her breathing. "I want to know more." He settled back against the settee. "What is your worst memory?"

She shook her head. "Nay, I can't go there."

A shadow darkened his face. "I'll tell you mine in exchange for yours."

Tempting. She pressed her lips together. She wanted to learn more about this man, but was what he asked too high a debt to pay? She'd tried to keep her past a secret for fear of him hating her family even more. Or worse yet, feeling sorry for her. But she truly wanted to understand him. Even as confusion wracked her, she nodded her head.

"My worst memory." He squinted his eyes and mouth as though searching his thoughts. A moment later, his face cleared, and resignation reflected in his gaze. "I will have to backtrack a bit and tell you how this situation came to be first."

She nodded, listening eagerly.

"When Orrin and I were twelve, we were kidnapped by your father from the shores of Scotland and taken as slaves to the Holy Land."

Rhiannon gasped. She couldn't hold it back. Her fingers pressed against her chest. "My father?" His hatred suddenly made sense.

He drew a slow, deep breath. "Our Saracen master bound us in service to him for seven years. We had to do whatever he asked, or we would be severely punished."

Rhiannon couldn't speak, just listened as he continued.

"The worst day for me was when Orrin, who had been ordered to kill a woman and her children, refused. He absolutely refused to pick up the sword and cut them down. So one of the other men did, right in front of us. Then he and another man took Orrin's arms, and held tight while a third man took a whip to Orrin's back. I could not stand by and let them abuse him. But when I ran to help, two other men stopped me and forced me to witness Orrin's pain."

Camden's voice sounded distanced, raw. She could imagine how horrifying that would have been for him to helplessly stand by and watch when he could do nothing to help.

Rhiannon nodded to herself. It explained a bit about why he always seemed to obsess about protecting his clan.

He shook his head, as though forcing away the memory. "That was mine. Now what of yours?"

He would hate her and her family all the more if she told him a particular time where her family had abused her, so she generalized instead. "I have no particular memory I can cite as the worst," she confessed. "My entire youth was filled with moments like that."

His light eyes flared. "The watching or the lashing?"

"The lashing, I'm afraid." She flinched. "Even remembering brings back the pain."

"Who did this to you?" His voice sounded anguished. Because of her?

She shrugged. "My father until after my mother died. Then my brothers also took out their aggressions upon me."

"Why?" His eyes grew dark, restless.

"Mostly because I was not born a son. My father had no need for a daughter."

"Daughters have their place."

She shook her head. "Not in his world."

He continued to stare at her with dark, angry eyes. She looked down at the hands she clenched in her lap. "I did not mean to upset you. I felt you wanted honesty. . . ." She trailed off, suddenly wishing she'd concocted a lie instead.

"Rhiannon." He said her name with a note of familiarity. "Look at me."

"Please, don't ask me to," she implored helplessly, knowing that if she saw the compassion she heard in his voice, she would dissolve in a puddle of tears.

He took her chin between his thumb and forefinger and lifted it, forcing her to meet his steady gaze.

Compassion registered in the depths of his eyes, and something more. Tears did not come as she'd expected. Instead, her entire body tensed as his lips descended toward hers.

His lips covered hers, tender, almost hesitant at first, then bolder, as he wrapped his arms about her.

Sad memories faded as shivering waves of pleasure took their place. He left her lips to trail a hot path over her cheeks, brushing away the tears with his lips, to her ear. Slowly, he feathered his lips back and forth across her lobe, before he dipped lower, tracing each curve of her neck, her jawline.

The tension drained from her as his arms tightened around her, supporting her while his tongue explored her ear. His hand curled around her nape, sensually stroking it, and he began trailing scorching kisses down her neck, to her shoulder.

"I'll never hurt you like that." His warm breath stirred her hair and his whisper was achingly gentle as his mouth began retracing its stirring path to her ear again.

Imprisoned by his protective embrace and seduced by his mouth, Rhiannon clung to him, sliding slowly into a dark abyss of desire.

His tongue traced a hot line between her lips, coaxing them to part, and then insisting. The moment she yielded, his tongue plunged inside, stroking and caressing. Rhiannon surrendered mindlessly to the stormy splendor of his kiss.

Her hands shifted restlessly over his heavily muscled shoulders and forearms, her lips moving against his with increasing abandon as she unwittingly fed his hunger. Each time she stroked her lips over his, she felt him shudder, felt the thunder of his heartbeat against her own breast. The knowledge empowered her, encouraged her to go on, to explore him more deeply.

The shadow of time shifted within the small cottage. Neither noticed. And when he finally pulled his mouth from hers an eternity later, their breathing came in mingled gasps. His face was dark with passion, his eyes a smoldering blue.

"We have to stop," he whispered on a long tortured breath. He lifted a lock of her hair, tenderly brushing it off her shoulder. "I promised you'd be safe here from me, but if we continue . . ." His voice sounded strangled, as though it took everything he had to pull away from her.

Rhiannon mourned the loss of his lips upon her flesh, but then her swirling senses returned to reality, slowly at first, then with a sickening plummet. Passion gave way to anguished shame. "I didn't expect . . . I never should have . . ." Where had the wild attraction for his man come from? Was this just one more family "attribute" she had inherited?

Mother Agnes was right to call her a black seed. The passion he had unleashed in her went far beyond what was considered civilized and proper. What they'd shared had been wild and uncontrollable.

She issued a sound that was part sob, part groan. "What have I done?"

"You are not the only one at fault here, Rhiannon," he said softly, as though understanding her anguish.

"We must leave." She jerked out of his grasp and with wooden movements made her way to the door. She pulled it slightly open and nearly sobbed with relief to see that the snow had stopped. "We must leave now." She hurried to the hearth to snatch her cloak, but a loud crack startled her before she reached it. The door shattered, wood splinters flying everywhere. Camden surged for her, taking her with him to the ground.

She shrieked as her shoulder hit the ground. But before she could feel any pain, Camden rolled her on her side, his big body covering her own.

"What's happening?" she cried. "I thought you said this cottage was abandoned."

"It was."

"Maybe whoever started that fire has returned," Rhiannon whispered as silence settled around them.

"Whoever started that fire is no friend of ours." Camden shifted her to his side. "Stay down," he ordered. His muscles tensed and he strained to listen. Other than their own harsh breathing, silence surrounded them. Time seemed to stand still as they lay there on the floor of the cottage. Then a soft squeak of a floorboard sounded from near the door.

Before she had time to draw a breath, Camden sprang up, sword in hand. The clang of steel sounded.

Rhiannon sat up, scooting back toward the hearth. She could see that Camden had charged another man dressed all in black, his face partially concealed by a dark swatch of fabric over the lower half of his face.

The man slashed his sword toward Camden, who spun away, leaving the other man swinging at the air.

Camden whirled, then lunged. The attacker parried, then counterthrust with deadly precision. Each thrust intensified in a lethal game where only one man would walk away.

Camden said something, but above the clang of their swords, she could only make out a few words. "Mistake . . . changed . . . do not . . ." Their blades came together, sliding to the hilts. The stranger spun away, feinting to the left while he cut with an agile backhand high across Camden's upper arm, leaving a streak of red on the exposed flesh.

Rhiannon gasped. Camden bared his teeth and with a savage roar went on full attack, forcing his opponent out the door into the snow. In the background, a horse shrieked, and Rhiannon knew what she had to do.

She gained her feet and hurried to the open doorway. Her heart thundering in her chest, she slipped outside to where they had tied their horse. With fingers that suddenly felt as though they were weighted with lead, she untied the stranger's horse, and gave it a whack on the rear to send it racing off into the distance.

A moment later, she'd freed their horse and hoisted herself onto the animal's back. With a prayer for luck, Rhiannon kicked her heels into the horse's flank, thrusting herself and the horse into the battle. "Give me your hand," she yelled a moment before she reached Camden and the stranger as they fought in the snow that came up to their knees.

Both men startled at the sight of her. Taking advantage of the moment and drawing on strength she did not know she possessed, she hauled Camden onto the horse behind her. Tucking her head against the wind, she spurred the horse into a sprint, putting distance between them and the swordsman in black.

A roar of outrage filled the air. No doubt the man had discovered that his horse was missing. Rhiannon smiled to herself.

Camden sheathed his weapon and grasped her waist, balancing himself on the back of the horse. "What are you doing?"

"Saving your life."

"Risking your own."

"It worked," she said, spurring their horse into as fast a gait as possible in the deep snow. She cast a quick glance at the wound in his arm. "Who was that man?"

"God's blood," he swore beneath his breath. "He's no friend of ours. Keep this horse moving. I'll not rest easy until we are safe behind the castle walls."

At the pain in his voice, Rhiannon glanced back again, to the thick gash in his arm and the rivulets of blood that trailed down his arm and leg, then onto the horse's flanks.

"Your wound is worse than I thought. We have to stop." She slowed the horse.

"Don't stop this beast," he said between his teeth. "Keep going, with as much speed as possible. No matter what happens to me, promise me you'll keep going until you reach the castle."

She wanted to tell him he was wrong, that they'd left the stranger far behind. But a sick feeling in her stomach told her otherwise. It would be foolhardy to stop until they were certain of their safety. She'd watched the dark stranger fight. She'd seen the lethal look in his eyes that said he'd come to kill.

"I promise," she whispered, and some of the tension in his body eased as it pressed intimately against her own. She kept the horse moving. Her soft shoes dug into the horse's side, urging the beast to continued speed. They had to reach the castle soon.

The chill air of the early evening fairly crackled with tension. How had anyone found them in such an isolated place? No one had known where they were headed. Or did they? And who exactly was the man after? Violet was not with them as she had been when the man had attacked before. Even though the man had concealed part of his face, Rhiannon had recognized him as the same assassin who had attacked her and Violet in the horse cart only a few days past.

Rhiannon gripped the reins, her fingers frozen in the bitter cold. In her haste to escape, she'd left both of their cloaks behind. The cold seemed to soak through the layers of her clothing until prickles of ice wrapped around her spine, and seemed to be all that kept her atop the horse. She could almost believe she floated just above her chilled body; there was room for action only, and her feelings were remote to that need.

The moon was a crescent-shaped sliver rising over the top of the mountains. Stars hung suspended by the millions. The last traces of pink touched the evening sky when Lee Castle came into view.

She kept the horse moving, as pace by pace they approached their goal. Her mind, her body, her senses were numb from cold. The great iron portcullis rose and the gate opened wide. She felt as though she hung suspended, watching but not participating as someone stopped the horse, then pulled Camden and herself from the animal's back.

"We need boiling water," a voice from outside herself called. Mistress Faulkner? Orrin? She could not be certain as gentle hands guided her into the keep, up the stairs, and into the master's bedchamber.

Chapter Ten

Pinpricks of sensation coursed over Rhiannon's flesh, wringing a gasp from her lips. She was too cold and too hot all in the same moment. She writhed in the bathwater, seeking freedom from the torture she now endured, only to be pressed back down into the copper tub. More buckets of steaming water joined the others. Slowly Rhiannon felt the chill that had permeated her bones melt away.

Relaxed now, she closed her eyes and leaned back into the side of the tub, allowing the hot water to flow all around her, turning her flesh a reddish-pink. Had she ever been that cold in her life? She shivered just thinking about it.

The soft voices that had filled the room vanished. The door to the bedchamber closed. Silence settled over the room. And suddenly she became aware of another presence beside her.

She snapped her eyes open. Camden sat in a tub next to hers. His torso was bare and had turned the same reddish-pink as her own flesh. Her eyes widened, and she stared at him. She'd never seen a naked male before. She swallowed and drew a shaky breath as her gaze met his. Wild heat flooded her cheeks at her unusually bold appraisal.

But hers was not the only exploration. His gaze lingered on the rise of her breasts just above the surface of the water. A stirring low in her belly brought a new wave of heat to her cheeks. "Why did they bring me here instead of the chamber across the hall?"

"I told them to." His gaze rose to her face, and he offered her a reckless smile. "You are an excellent horsewoman."

"Thank you," she replied, dipping deeper beneath the water.

"It takes great skill to handle a horse the way you did back in the forest." He feigned a sigh. " 'Tis a blow to my manliness to admit I was rescued by a female."

"How is your arm?" she asked, suddenly aware of a subtle difference in their banter. He played with her. And his underlying sense of suspicion had vanished.

"Bertie wasted no time in sewing the wound." He shifted in the water, hanging his bandaged arm over the side of the tub, closing the distance between them. "I shall live for other adventures." The words were spoken with silken sensuality. His gaze moved slowly across her shoulders, her breasts, and further below the surface of the water.

"As will your pride, I am sure." She found herself staring at him, unable to look away from those light blue eyes. She could feel her heart beating harder, her skin warming as the blood ran faster in her veins.

"In time perhaps."

She could see the pulse drumming in his temple and watched as the feathery curve of his lashes came down to hide the blue of his eyes. She caught his scent—musk and mint—and inhaled deeply, committing the fragrance to memory. Rhiannon wished she could think of something to say that would bring an end to the tension building between them.

His gaze moved to her neck, tracing the curve of her flesh from her shoulder to her ear. She willed herself to breathe slowly. How did he do it? All he had to do was look at her and she went weak in the knees. Thank goodness she was sitting down.

"Lord Lockhart," she breathed, her voice barely above a whisper.

"Camden."

She drew a deep breath and tried again, knowing the question she had to ask. "Camden, who was that man?"

The warmth in his eyes faded. "An assassin."

"Why was he after us?"

"I suppose it had something to do with us being at the cottage."

The explanation seemed reasonable, yet she could hear the tension in his words. She knew he was the same assassin as before. But who exactly was he after, her or Violet?

"I'm getting out of the bath," he warned. "Close your eyes or look your fill." The water rippled.

Rhiannon squeezed her eyes shut, though her cheeks heated once more at the image of his naked body that appeared in her mind. She listened as he stepped out of the bath. The sound of shuffling cloth followed before he said, "You can open your eyes."

As if on command, her eyes drifted open, immediately seeking him out. He stood before her, his upper body bare, his lower body concealed by a soft linen towel. Warmth spread through her at the sight.

He held a towel out to her. "You want some help?"

The heat turned to a slow flame at the suggestion. "That would leave me unfairly exposed," she said boldly, with a hint of huskiness in her voice.

Just then, a knock sounded on the door. "Enter," Camden called.

Mistress Faulkner hustled in.

"Would you allow Magdeline to assist you?" He held the towel out to Mistress Faulkner. The woman accepted the cloth with a frown.

"I would be grateful," Rhiannon said.

Camden turned to Mistress Faulkner, sparing Rhiannon any further censure. "Magdeline, please find Mistress Rhiannon something suitable to wear down to supper. The whole castle will be wanting to gaze upon the woman who saved their lord."

When he was gone, Rhiannon stood. Cool evening air caressed her skin, dispelling what remained of the heat between herself and Camden. She turned to face the chatelaine. "Mistress Faulkner, if you'd rather not assist me, I'd understand. I've grown used to caring for myself over the years."

"Nonsense," the woman said, wrapping the towel around Rhiannon's body. "I am capable of performing my duty regardless of my feelings for you. What the master does is his own business. He is the one who has to live with his choices at the end of the day."

The chatelaine turned away, toward the tall wardrobe on the wall opposite the door and swung the doors open wide. "I cannot pass judgment on what goes on around here. If the master wants to dally with the woman who's responsible for killin' his kin, what do I have to say about it?"

It seemed as though the woman had *a lot* to say on the subject. Rhiannon moved toward the fire and stared into the flames as they licked the logs, devouring them, as surely as her family's reputation did devour her. No matter what she did, nothing would ever change the fact that she was a Ruthven.

The usual emptiness that she carried inside her returned. For a short while today at the cottage, she and Camden had talked like friends. He had not judged her then.

But they had done more than talk. Heat crept into her cheeks at the memory of his lips upon hers. She touched her lips with the back of her hand. This evening he had continued to treat her in a friendly manner. The heat in his eyes did not reflect hatred, only desire.

And in those moments she had felt different, satisfied, almost as if she mattered to someone else on this earth.

Almost.

Rhiannon shifted her gaze back to the chatelaine.

With her back turned, Mistress Faulkner hummed a lilting tune that Rhiannon recognized as a Celtic prayer. "Lady Lockhart must have left something behind here that would fit you."

While Mistress Faulkner sorted through garments, Rhiannon toweled her body dry, then set to work on her hair.

"This will do just fine." The chatelaine stepped back from the wardrobe, a triumphant gleam on her aged face. She gathered a few other things before coming to stand beside Rhiannon at the hearth. "While you don't deserve to wear her things, this dress will look lovely on you."

Rhiannon's throat burned with unshed tears, but she held her emotions in check. The woman continued her belittling rambling as she slipped a sheer linen chemise over Rhiannon's head, followed by a sapphire blue velvet gown.

Rhiannon remained silent, trying to force her mind on to other things until the woman finally stood back, satisfied with what she saw. "The evening meal is being served. If you want to eat, you will have to join the others." With those last words, she left as quickly as she had come.

Feeling unwanted and suddenly alone, Rhiannon nervously smoothed her fingers over the luxurious fabric of the dress Mistress Faulkner had chosen. The color reminded her of Camden's eyes as they'd filled with passion earlier this afternoon.

Heat came to her cheeks again at the memory. Would he have kissed her like that if he still hated her? It was hard to imagine so. Rhiannon forced a smile to her lips. Perhaps she wasn't as alone as she imagined. With Camden and Violet on her side, she could handle the rest of the household.

Gathering her tattered pride, Rhiannon moved to the door only to be greeted by the two hulking warriors Camden had placed at her door the night before. "Good evening, gentlemen," she said as she strode past them down the hall. They followed.

A cacophony of sound greeted her as she stepped into the great hall, followed by the savory scent of roast mutton and onions. She paused for a moment, fortifying herself for the night ahead, when the sound in the room suddenly died and all eyes fastened on her.

More people than she had ever seen together in one room before sat at long tables in neat rows across the entire hall. Lord Lockhart and Violet sat at the table in the front of the room, and on legs that trembled ever so slightly, Rhiannon made her way into the room.

She had no idea where to sit. No doubt not with Camden at the high table, but where else? Open spaces on the benches seemed to close as she drew near. Weaving her way between the tables, Rhiannon did not miss the scowls directed at her. One woman spit on her as she passed, and several people hissed. The man she knew as Camden's steward, Bertie, stared at her with hatred in his eyes.

She held her head high as she continued forward, looking for a quiet, perhaps isolated place to sit. Her legs wobbled beneath her now.

"Mistress Plague," cursed a scullery maid as she passed.

"The devil's daughter," another woman hissed.

Rhiannon kept moving forward. A moment later, her foot snagged something and she catapulted forward, hitting her elbow and her thigh against the wooden bench on her right before she slammed against the hard stone floor. She hitched in a breath. Tears threatened from the pain as well as the humiliation that burned in her chest. Someone had tripped her intentionally.

"Fill your heart with forgiveness." Mother Agnes's parting words to her played through her mind.

Mustering everything she had inside, Rhiannon let go

of her anger, her pain, as she forced her thoughts to that of forgiveness.

"Are you all right, milady?" Hamish asked as he and Travis gently lifted her from the floor.

Travis drew his sword and turned, aiming his weapon at a dark-haired warrior's heart. "You dare to harm a guest in this castle, Garrett?"

The warrior's face reddened. "She should sleep with the dogs, not eat with us."

Travis pressed his sword more firmly against the man's chest, drawing a gasp. "That is for the master to decide and not you. If you value your position here in this castle, I suggest you remember that."

The warrior's face paled and his gaze dropped to the floor. "Aye."

Travis sheathed his weapon. A low murmur rippled through the room. "Come, milady," he said, taking her by the arm. "You have us to support you."

Rhiannon gazed at the two big men, and offered them a soft smile. "My thanks," she said, grateful for her new champions. Together, the three of them made their way past the remaining tables, until there was no doubt in Rhiannon's mind that they headed to the high table. Once there, Travis released her arm. Rhiannon breathed a sigh. The worst was over.

She stopped and consciously braced herself before she brought her gaze to Camden's. He looked so different tonight, dressed in a dark shirt and dark breeches with his hair tied back at his nape. He looked tough, sleek, elegant.

"You look well," he said, his gaze lingering on the rise of her breasts as they pressed against the low-cut bodice.

She tried to control her response to him as she remembered the countless lectures about staying away from him that she'd given herself since their time in the cottage. Her mind might want one thing, but her body responded otherwise. Her breasts swelled beneath his gaze and heat moved through her body in mindless, melting waves.

She forced a calm smile as she approached the empty seat between Camden and Violet. "Good evening, Lord Lockhart, Lady Violet."

"No!" Violet cried, her distress echoing throughout the room. The room plunged into silence. Her chair crashed to the floor. She threw herself at Rhiannon. Tears rolled unchecked down her reddened cheeks.

Rhiannon froze, startled by the little girl's attack.

"Take it off," Violet sobbed, raking her small fingers across the fabric of Rhiannon's dress. "Take it off!"

"Violet, what is the matter?" Camden thrust back his chair, coming to kneel beside his niece. He grasped her hands gently with his own, protecting Rhiannon from Violet's violent attack.

"Violet, what have I done to distress you so?" Rhiannon asked, as she also knelt beside the hysterical child.

"Make her take it off." Violet writhed in Camden's grasp. He pulled her tight against his chest. "That's my mum's dress."

Rhiannon felt the blood drain from her face. "What have I done?" she whispered, realizing the grief she caused Violet. To her knowledge, the little girl had never truly grieved her mother and father's loss. No doubt she'd been so traumatized by the events to truly do so.

Grief poured from the little girl now. The sound of her wails knifed through Rhiannon's chest.

Camden stared at Rhiannon. She could read the uncertainty in his face. How could she explain the trick Mistress Faulkner had played on her? Would he believe her if she did?

"Excuse me." Rhiannon raced for the stairs. The faces of the people and the names they called her became a blur as her sight fastened on one woman's face. Mistress Faulkner stood near the staircase, a satisfied smile on her face.

A cold sickness settled in the pit of Rhiannon's stomach. Rhiannon stopped before Mistress Faulkner. "How could you do something so hurtful to Lady Violet?"

The woman's gaze flew to the front of the room. "I hadn't thought . . . I never considered . . ."

"Next time you want to hurt me, hurt *me*. But leave Lady Violet out of it. That girl has been wounded enough."

Mistress Faulkner's mouth gaped open, trying to form words, though none would come.

Feeling slightly redeemed, Rhiannon raced up the stairs to her chamber and after fumbling with the lacings at her back, she ripped the dress from her body. She hurriedly put on her old gray dress. She opened the chamber door to find Hamish and Travis heading for her chamber. "We are going back downstairs," she said as she passed them. She needed to reassure Violet that she would never wear her mother's clothes again.

Rhiannon braced herself for the barrage of hateful words that would no doubt come her way. The others might think that Ruthvens were good for nothing. But *this* Ruthven knew her duty, and would let nothing or no one stand in her way.

Camden stared at the sleeping form of his niece. Her eyes were closed, free from the horror he had witnessed in them earlier this eve. "Are you sure she's asleep?" he asked Rhiannon.

From her position on the opposite side of Violet's bed, she nodded. "Absolutely."

"Will she be all right?"

Rhiannon nodded. "Give her time. She's lost much. Grief comes out in odd ways sometimes."

"You sound as if you know something about grieving."

She dropped her gaze to her hands. "I still miss my mother after all these years."

He could hear the pain in her voice and he felt an answering echo in his own chest. "Aye."

Camden shifted his gaze to Violet. He stroked a yellow-gold curl that lay against the girl's rosy cheek. Out of necessity, he'd been forced to see to Violet's grief, to reassure the girl that she was safe here with him. Yet Rhiannon needed his reassurance almost as much. Not with her grief, but about her position within his home.

He hadn't missed the hateful glances and vicious words Rhiannon had had to endure on her journey through his hall. He had watched her progress from the moment she'd stepped into the room. He'd witnessed her fall, and had started to rise to assist her when Hamish and Travis had intervened.

He was to blame for the way his people had treated her. He had set the precedent the moment he'd learned who she truly was. He'd made his feelings for her abundantly clear, and his staff now rallied behind him.

When had his feelings about her changed? What exactly did he want from her? She'd come here to care for Violet. Did he want something more? This afternoon he'd experienced lust, pure and simple. His body quickened at the memory of her warm and willing flesh pressed so intimately against his own.

Camden frowned at the woman across the bed. Candlelight flickered over the rich gold of her hair and stroked the creamy rise of her breasts as they pressed against the square bodice of her gown with each breath she took.

She gazed at him, a question in her soft, tawny brown eyes, her lips parted. If Violet were not between them, he would take her in his arms and . . .

And what? Satisfy his need for her? Because that's where

his desires would take him if he allowed himself to forget who she was and what her family had done.

Was he ready to move beyond that? This evening, his household's response to her and the anger it had invoked within him had proved one thing: Something had to change.

"Rhiannon." His voice was thick, and he clamped his fingers together before him. Saints above, he wanted to touch her. "I saw the way you were treated tonight by the other members of my household."

Her body stilled, she stared at him, not speaking.

"They had no right to treat you that way. I shall speak with them."

She appeared momentarily disconcerted. "You don't have to do anything for me," she said, shifting off the bed, moving away from him.

"I don't have to," he said gently. "I want to."

"Why?" She shut her eyes tightly. "It makes no sense."

"It's the right thing to do."

Her eyes opened to reveal glittering tears. "And duty means everything to you."

He stood. "Aye."

"Well, I am not your duty," she said, her voice suddenly fierce. "I can take care of myself." She turned away, and with jerky movements headed for the door.

Chapter Eleven

Before Rhiannon could clear the doorway of the bedchamber, a young woman, her face pale and her hands stained with blood, nearly knocked her down.

"Forgive me for intrudin', milord, milady," she panted. "I need your help. Well, not me, exactly. Charlotte and her baby." The young woman's eyes were wild as she shifted her gaze between the door and the bed.

Rhiannon tensed when she sensed Camden behind her. "Explain," Camden demanded.

"Somethin' is wrong. The baby is not comin' as it should," she said. "I sent one of the men for the midwife in Glasgow, but I fear she will arrive too late. Charlotte needs assistance now."

"I'll go to her. I might be of some help." Rhiannon started down the hallway.

"I shall accompany you." Camden strode beside her down the stairs through the hall and into the western rooms of the castle. They followed the young woman into a chamber. There were only a few candles scattered about the room, making it difficult to see anything. "We need more candles," Rhiannon commanded as she made her way to the bed. She took charge of the situation, and Camden let her.

In the middle of a straw pallet on the floor lay a young woman in a pool of blood. She clutched her distended belly with white-knuckled force.

Four women crowded the space around her feet; Mistress

Faulkner and three other women Rhiannon did not recognize. "Can you see any part of the baby?"

Mistress Faulkner nodded, her face pale. "One foot."

"Breech," Rhiannon said, her voice low, barely above a whisper. She'd seen two other breech presentations before—unfortunately, they were both with horses, not humans. But were the dynamics of birth much different between the species? For Charlotte's sake, she hoped not.

"Any chance we can change her pallet and get rid of all this blood?"

Mistress Faulkner signaled to one of the other women in the room. She hurried away to return a moment later with two young men carrying a straw mattress. They set it on the floor near the hearth, then returned to Charlotte's side. "We are going to move you, miss." The two men easily transported her to the clean bedding.

"Many thanks," Rhiannon said.

Both men made a bow before slipping from the room.

The light of the fire made it easier to see. Rhiannon took in Charlotte's flushed face and glittering eyes. "Are you thirsty?"

The woman nodded. Rhiannon stood, then turned to Mistress Faulkner. "If you want her to live, you'll help me without interfering. Understood?" Her firm tone left no room for argument.

Mistress Faulkner nodded, her eyes misting with tears. "This is my granddaughter. I'll do anything."

Rhiannon nodded with relief that she would not be challenged. "I'll need someone to mix a tisane of valerian and germander to numb her pain while I try to turn the child."

"Turn the child?"

"What kind of witchcraft is that?" two of the women questioned in unison.

Camden came to stand beside Rhiannon. "Do you know what you are doing?" he asked.

"Aye," she said with more confidence than she felt. Now was not the time to tell him all her experience had been in observing her mother with deliveries of the village babies and helping with the animals in her father's stable. Charlotte would no doubt lose her baby and possibly her own life, if someone didn't at least try to help her immediately.

"Then proceed." He left the room briefly only to return with two large candelabra that he set on the hearth near the bed. He sat in a chair across the room from her. He clutched the small linen package that Mother Agnes had asked her to deliver to him. He stared at the bundle in his hands with a dark expression on his face, as though he were trying to make a difficult decision.

"I won't die," the young woman whispered, bringing Rhiannon's attention back to the pallet. "You'll see. My baby and I will live."

"Of course you will." Rhiannon smiled shakily. "You are a fighter. I can see it in your eyes."

Mistress Faulkner returned with the steaming tisane. Rhiannon accepted the mug from her, then held it to Charlotte's lips. "I need you to drink as much of this as you can."

"Wait," Camden said. "It looks too hot. Allow me cool it by the window for a moment."

"That isn't necessary," Rhiannon said, unsettled by his interference. Her nerves stretched taut with the responsibility of what she was about to do.

"I insist." He took the cup from her hands and made his way to the window on the far side of the room. There, he threw the shutters open and with his back to all, cooled the liquid contents in the midnight air. He fumbled with something in his hands, then turned back toward the room's occupants. "That should do it. I appreciate your indulgence."

He returned the cup to Rhiannon's hands, his fingers lingering upon hers a moment longer than was necessary. Warmth that had nothing to do with the fire roared through her blood. Even now, in the direst of situations, her body responded to his. Rhiannon accepted the mug with careful precision and brought the liquid to Charlotte's lips. "Drink."

Charlotte closed her eyes and took a small sip, then another before pulling away. "It tastes terrible."

"Aye," Rhiannon agreed. She knew how bitter the concoction must taste. "But it will help save your baby."

Charlotte brought her lips to the mug again and drank deeply. When she was through, she collapsed back against the linen on the mattress, clutching her belly once more. "It hurts," she cried.

"Stay focused on your baby, Charlotte. Picture in your mind what the child will look like. It will help."

A calm settled over Charlotte's features. She released her grip on her belly. Her eyes drifted shut, and she lay quietly beside the flickering flames of the fire.

"The medicine has taken effect," Rhiannon said, grateful that her mother had allowed her to assist when she'd been called to help the villagers' wives deliver their babies.

"I need two of you to help me. Position yourselves so that one of you can kneel on either side of her." Mistress Faulkner and one of the other women followed her instructions. When the two women were in place, Rhiannon said, "I need to put the foot back inside her. Then once I do, as I move the baby, place your hands on her belly to keep the child in place."

With a prayer for guidance, Rhiannon dug her hands into Charlotte's flesh, locating the baby's head. Slowly, carefully, with the help of the others, she guided the child downward.

Despite her induced sleep, Charlotte cried out, her distress obvious.

Tears rolled down Mistress Faulkner's cheeks in response to Charlotte's distress, but she remained silent.

"Lord Lockhart," the other woman cried. "Please, milord, can you not use the Charm Stone to ease Charlotte's pain? Lady Lockhart must have passed it to Lady Violet before she died. 'Tis said that the Stone has been in your family for years."

Camden appeared uneasy at the woman's request. "Lady Violet has no knowledge of the Stone's location."

Perhaps Violet did not, but did he? Rhiannon paused in her manipulation of the baby's head. *The Charm Stone.* She'd heard tales of the legendary Stone since she was a child. It had come back to Scotland from the Crusades. When had the Lockharts become its keeper?

Rhiannon returned her attention to Charlotte, but her thoughts remained on the small bundle of linen she'd seen Camden with earlier. He no longer held the package in his hands.

Charlotte groaned again and her eyes flickered open.

"We are almost there, Charlotte," Rhiannon soothed, while applying a final thrust of pressure. The baby's head slid down, and dropped into place.

The rest of the birth proceeded quickly. Just as dawn's first light appeared in the sky, a lusty cry heralded the baby's safe arrival.

Mistress Faulkner burst into tears. After a slight hesitation, she threw herself into Rhiannon's arms, burrowing her face in the fabric of her gray gown. "Thank you," she cried, the sound muffled. "I gave you more than enough reasons not to help my dear Charlotte. Yet you did. I am so ashamed of myself and this entire household for judging you so harshly."

Rhiannon stiffened, not knowing what to do, how to respond. She'd done what was needed. And she'd do what she could to help anyone else, despite how they had treated her. Was the woman asking for her forgiveness? A Ruthven?

"Please say you forgive me," Mistress Faulkner said.

"All is forgiven," Rhiannon said, awed by the change in the woman. She gently stroked the back of the woman's head, remembering yet again Mother Agnes's words of forgiveness.

Joy bubbled up inside Rhiannon. The world seemed suddenly enveloped in a soft golden haze. Life was newly born and brimming with possibilities for Charlotte, for her baby, for herself.

Camden had never understood why his sister-in-law risked so much to use the Charm Stone.

He did now.

At first he'd wrestled with the decision to use the Stone or not. Now he was glad he'd gone to the chapel to retrieve the Stone when he'd left the birthing chamber in search of candles.

The thrill of doing something that helped to save lives rippled through him. He saved the lives of his people each time he went to war, but not like this. This time the enemy had been death itself. And in his experience, death usually won. Carefully, he slipped the healing Stone back into its hiding place in the chapel and stepped back.

An odd sensation prickled the back of Camden's neck—as though he could feel someone's eyes upon him. He turned toward the door and searched the shadows of the room. No one was there. 'Twas only his own excitement at the miracle the Stone had brought forth this night.

The Stone had only been one part of tonight's miracle. Rhiannon's contribution had been every bit as important. He never would have thought to turn the baby. He'd never seen or heard of such a technique before.

She continued to amaze him with her unselfishness. His people had treated her poorly, but she always seemed to overlook that fact to do what was right.

He stared up at the crucifix that hung above the altar.

Her family had placed James's body on a cross similar to that. Camden tried to bring forth hatred for the woman, but intrigue rippled through him instead. Why? She was beautiful, he would not deny. But her appeal was something more, something intangible. A familiar frustration welled inside him. He moved restlessly toward the three stained-glass windows behind the altar, staring up into their multicolored brilliance. If only he could lose himself in thoughts of something other than Rhiannon Ruthven.

He had thought he could stay remote. To have Rhiannon near to tutor Violet and provide her with motherly support, yet remain unaffected by her presence. Each day she stayed, he found his feeling shifted to—what? Guilt at what he'd done?

He had no reason to feel guilty. Not really. He'd been desperate to protect his family. And angry, he reminded himself.

Restless, was more his current state of mind. He flexed his fingers as he remembered Rhiannon's silky flesh beneath his touch, her tawny eyes staring up at him in wonder. As he'd explored her body with his mouth, the faint tremor that shook her had only encouraged him more. Rhiannon might be inexperienced, but her passionate response to him had been purely elemental.

He was hardening just remembering those brief moments in the cottage, and felt a renewed burst of frustration. Why did he have to feel this way about *her?* Lust had never been this obsessive for him before. His feeling for her interfered with everything he did—in his work with his men, in his duty to the people of this castle, to his country. He had to put an end to his distraction.

Perhaps, he should deal with the situation more directly—to satisfy his need for her? Once he tasted what she had to offer, his obsession would no doubt vanish, and he'd be himself again.

Excitement quickened the tempo of his heart as he strode out of the chapel. He would put an end to this torture. And he knew just how to accomplish the deed.

Chapter Twelve

The door to Bishop Berwick's study opened and a black-clad footman stepped inside. Irritation broke the bishop's concentration, for he had been lost in thought.

"Forgive me, Your Grace," the footman apologized with a bow, no doubt assuming that Bishop Berwick had been deep in prayer.

"What is it?" he growled. He picked up his quill, dipped it in ink, then signed the missive he'd penned to the Church council.

The footman flinched at his tone. "A man to see you, Your Grace."

"It is not yet fully morning." He scowled at the interruption.

The footman backed away until he stood framed by the door. "He said you'd know who he was, Your Grace."

"Send him in," the bishop ordered, knowing exactly who had called at such an inappropriate hour.

Impatiently he threw his nib aside. After folding the sheet of linen, he took out his wax and warmed a small chunk until it turned a liquid red. He quickly poured it on the loose edge of the paper, then stamped it with his insignia ring. The mark of his station, and his mother's pride and joy.

He frowned at the thought of his mother. Her health showed no signs of improvement. The spots on her chest had spread to her entire body. Her temper had turned sharp, and she spent most of the day rambling at him about how he needed to do something special to catch the Church council's attention.

He'd written to the council and asked them to come to their humble home to witness a miracle. His mother's miraculous healing would be a great enough triumph for them. But to perform any sort of miracle, he would need the Charm Stone.

He pushed the missive toward the corner of his desk. His clerk would see to its delivery. If the council members accepted his invitation, they would arrive in little under a week. That left little time to secure the Stone. He'd have to hasten his plans.

The bishop rose and moved across the room to stare out the window through the haze of dawn at the snowcapped mountains of the Highlands in the distance. A leaden gray sky hovered over the mountains while blacker clouds rolled in from the north. A storm was coming—several storms, in fact, if he were truly honest with himself. The weather would unleash itself with a vengeance, as would his mother if he wasn't selected to fill the vacant position of arch-bishop within the month.

Which brought him to the storm brewing between himself and Camden Lockhart. The man was doing everything in his power to protect his family. No matter. Lady Violet and the Charm Stone would be the bishop's to command, giving him everything he had ever wanted.

A sound came from the doorway, and the bishop turned. The man he'd expected slipped inside the chamber, this time without offering a bow over the bishop's ring. He merely sat uninvited in the chair across from the large mahogany desk.

"I've news, Your Grace," the man announced, placing his wet, muddy boots atop the spotless wood.

"Do tell." The bishop narrowed his gaze on the filthy boots defiling his property.

The man brought his feet to the floor. "Last night a woman and her babe survived an impossible birth."

The bishop sighed deeply. "That's your news?"

The man smiled as he met the bishop's dark gaze. "Lord Lockhart and the Ruthven woman were both there. The baby came first by the feet, but the woman turned it around. The mum and babe survived and are thriving. 'Twas a miracle to be sure."

The bishop gazed coolly at the man, disgusted. "They must have used the Charm Stone. I need that relic, you idiot. Someone must have witnessed something. When you have something more, you may return. Until then, be like the shadows."

The man's face darkened with a frown. "I've done everything ye asked me tae do, Your Grace."

Bishop Berwick moved to his desk. "Your son's life is at stake if you do not cooperate."

"Please, don't hurt him," the man pleaded.

"Then do exactly as I ask."

The man nodded. "I'll not let ye down."

"See that you don't."

The man departed, closing the door softly behind him. No sooner had the door stilled than another knock sounded.

"Enter," the bishop growled.

His footman nearly quaked in his shoes as he stepped once again into the chamber. "Another caller, Your Grace. This one says he's—"

"I'll give me own introductions." The hulking man swatted the footman aside and surged into the chamber. The man was dressed in leather. Strapped to his body were several lethal blades.

And the bishop knew just who the man was. "That will be all," the bishop said to his chamberlain, striding to the doorway and pulling the portal shut. This discussion needed no audience.

Once the chamber was secure, the bishop turned back to the assassin. He had recently learned from his sources in Glasgow that Lord Lockhart had hired this man to wipe the Ruthvens from the land. "What do you want? Are Lockhart and the woman dead yet? Did you kill them this morning then?" the bishop asked, moving back behind his desk. While he did not fear the man, somehow placing the desk between them gave him peace of mind that the openness of the room did not.

The man growled as he gripped the far edge of the mahogany wood with clenched hands. "Nay," he cursed, revealing a brown, rotten-toothed grin.

The bishop frowned. "Don't tell me you missed."

The man's gaze darkened. "I was interrupted."

"By whom?"

"The Ruthven girl saved 'em both."

The bishop stiffened in shock. "The girl saved them?"

The man rocked the desk with his hands. "She's a bruisin' rider and took me by surprise. 'Twas more than that, though. All the while I was battlin' Lockhart, he kept beggin' me tae stop tryin' to kill her. He'd changed his mind, he said."

"That matters not."

The big man straightened. "How can I be sure tae get an intercession from the Lord above if the man no longer wants her dead? The sin of her death wouldna be on Lockhart's head but mine."

"You stupid man." The bishop slapped his hand upon the desk, the sound echoing throughout the chamber. "An intercession is just that. It allows me to intercede for you in all manner of sins and gain for you a place in the afterlife that you might not achieve on your own."

"Lockhart changed his mind."

The bishop could almost taste the man's fear, and for an instant it brought him a smug sense of satisfaction. He was the master to all his lost sheep. "The world would be better off without her. No one in this life cares for her."

"I dinna know," the assassin said. "The way he fought tae protect her would prove otherwise."

The man's doubt suddenly filled the bishop with fury. He threw back the lid of the golden box on the corner of his desk. "How much will it take?" He ran his fingers through the silver and gold coins inside. The clink of the coins wiped the doubt from the assassin's face. That was better. Let the man remember who was in charge here.

"He paid me twenty gold pieces."

"Then I'll pay you forty."

The man nodded eagerly. "That'll do."

A smile of satisfaction came to the bishop's lips. His sheep were always so attracted to the sound and feel of gold. Gold could wring anything he needed out of his flock. "Now, get back out there and do what you were hired to do."

With an eager smile, the man left the room.

Such enthusiasm. The bishop turned a cold gaze on the door. Too bad that once he'd wrung all he needed from the man, he would have to die. The trail of death would never lead back to the bishop's own doorway.

Never.

"I don't want to learn to sew today. I want to go outside and ride the horses." Violet's voice drifted out into the hallway outside the castle's solar.

"After you learn to sew," Rhiannon said, her tone patient.

Camden edged closer to the door, listening. He'd tried to find something to occupy his mind, yet all he could think about was Rhiannon. Before he'd known where he was headed, he found himself at the door of the solar. The anticipation of touching her once again sent a thrill to his core.

"All great ladies must learn to use a needle, Violet. Without clothes to wear or blankets to keep warm with, or even tapestries to inspire, where would your people be?" Rhiannon's voice cut into his thoughts, pulling him back to the moment.

Camden peered inside the room. Rhiannon sat on a bench near the hearth. Violet sat at her feet. An embroidery frame with several untidy stitches lay in Violet's lap. She tossed her needle aside.

"I am no great lady. So why should I?" Violet pouted.

"You are a daughter of a great man, and you will become a great lady in this castle for your uncle. Your people already look up to you as an example. In time, you will lead them."

The young girl's eyes went wide. "Me? A leader of my people?"

Rhiannon smiled, her face radiant. "Many women have become leaders and examples over the centuries."

Violet scooted closer, staring up at Rhiannon with adoration in her eyes. "Tell me of these women."

Rhiannon's brow arched in question. "Did your mother ever tell you stories?"

Violet shook her head. "My mummy was very busy healing people in the local villages. She didn't have much time for other things."

A twinge of sorrow moved through Camden at the young girl's confession. James and Clara had had many responsibilities. He wished he'd taken more time to help them with those obligations after his return from the Holy Land.

Violet stared down at her embroidery frame, then smiled. "Tell me a story, and then I promise to pay more attention to my sewing."

Rhiannon dropped onto the floor beside Violet, absently stroking the little girl's fair hair as she pressed her lips together in concentration. "A story . . . that might have meaning for you." She hesitated, then smiled, her face radiant as she drew Violet closer to her with her arm. "There is the story of Esther from the Bible. She was a woman of deep faith, courage, and patriotism, and ultimately risked her life in order to save her people."

Violet stilled, her attention caught as she waited for Rhiannon to continue.

Camden found himself edging into the room, just as eager to hear what Rhiannon would say.

"Esther was an orphan and a descendant of those taken from Judah in the Babylonian captivity. She lived with her cousin, who held an important office in the household of the Persian king. This cousin of hers, Mordecai, was responsible for thwarting a plot by two palace guards to assassinate the king.

"King Ahasuerus was a wealthy man. He held a feast for one hundred and eighty days in order to display his vast wealth and the splendor of his kingdom.

"To further show his prosperity, he ordered his wife, Queen Vashti, to join him and his guests. When she refused, the King asked his wise men, the seven princes of Persia and Media, what he should do. They advised him to make an example of her for other disobedient wives, and he had her banished from the kingdom."

Camden edged closer to the pair. They were so engrossed in the storytelling they did not hear him approach.

"The king then began a search for a new wife. Beautiful young women were taken from their homes within the province and brought to the palace. Esther was one of the chosen women.

"Before she was taken, her cousin Mordecai advised her that if she were chosen, she should hide her true heritage from the king. There was much unrest in the land, and one of the princes, a man named Haman, wanted nothing more than to put all the Jewish people to death because of crimes committed against his family. Mordecai, afraid for his cousin's life, advised her to change her name from Hadassah to Esther. He also begged her to stop worshipping in the ways of her faith so that she might not be identified as a Jew and killed."

Violet frowned. "Why did they want to kill the Jews?"

"That is an excellent question that has a very involved answer. For now, let's just say that the Babylonians disliked the Jews. And because of that intense dislike, they wanted to see them dead."

Camden froze as the impact of her story hit him squarely in the gut. His own dislike for the Ruthvens had caused him to make a similar decision to put them to death. At the time he'd made the decision, it did not seem as heartless as it did in this moment.

"What happened to Esther?" Violet asked, breaking into Camden's thoughts.

"She and the other women entered the king's harem and over the course of twelve months were cleansed and groomed to meet the king. Each woman appeared before the king. And it was from that meeting that the king chose Esther to be his new queen."

"What's a harem?" Violet interrupted.

Rhiannon sat back as though considering her answer. "A harem is a special place in some cultures where women live."

"Do you and I live in a harem?"

"Do you want to hear the rest of the story?"

Violet nodded.

Camden held back a chuckle. She would answer Violet's question by not answering it at all.

"King Ahasuerus was distracted by warring factions

surrounding his territory. In order to protect his people while he was away fighting, the king gave Haman all the power and authority of his kingdom."

Violet's eyes went wide. "But Haman was a bad man. He wanted to kill the Jewish people."

"King Ahasuerus did not know that at the time. Haman planned his assault against the Jews carefully, waiting patiently for the time that the king would leave for war.

"Esther learned of Haman's plans to put all Jewish people in the Persian Empire to death after the king left for war. Putting her own safety aside and defying warnings to remain silent, she approached the king uninvited on the eve of his leaving for war. To appear before the king without permission was punishable by death."

"Esther had to have permission to see her husband?" Violet interrupted again.

"In some cultures, women have very few privileges. You are fortunate to have an uncle who will allow you many freedoms."

Violet straightened. "What happened when she approached her husband?"

"Esther risked everything in order to stop the killing of her people. As she approached, the king held out his scepter to her, showing her that he accepted her visit. She told the king of Haman's plan to massacre the Jews, and with much trepidation, revealed her own identity."

Violet frowned once more. "That is like what happened to you, when Uncle Camden learned of your last name. He was angry at first, but he's not so angry now."

Camden stilled. Had he hidden his anger at Rhiannon from no one?

"Aye," Rhiannon replied. "But just like the king, your uncle had his reasons."

Her understanding knifed at his guilt. Would she be so forgiving if she knew he had sentenced her to death? He knew the rest of the Bible story. The king had accepted Esther for who she was. Had he truly accepted Rhiannon? He no longer wanted her dead, but did that mean he had forgiven her for her family's sins against his family?

"Tell me how the story ends," Violet asked.

Rhiannon continued, "The king, enraged with Haman for using the privilege of his station to further his own goals, ordered him to be hanged. Then the king appointed Mordecai as his prime minister and gave the Jews the right to defend themselves against any enemy."

Violet's lips flattened with uncertainty. "What does that story have to do with me being a leader of my people?"

"Just like Esther, you have been orphaned, but that does not mean you do not have everything inside of you to become a great woman someday. Your Uncle Camden will need your help to keep our people free from English persecution. Some of the English feel the same way about the Scots as Haman did about the Jews."

Violet released a heavy sigh as she picked up her embroidery frame and needle and started sewing once more. "I will be a great lady, and I will learn to lead my people." She paused in her work. "Mother Agnes was right. She told me before we left the abbey that you would be the one to guide me in everything I needed to know."

Rhiannon dipped her head, hiding her reaction.

Even so, Camden could imagine the flush that rose to her cheeks and the soft sentiment that would fill her eyes. He strode the short distance from where he stood to the two women he'd been spying on. "The abbess was correct to send you to care for Violet."

Rhiannon startled. Her wide-eyed gaze flew to his face. "How long have you been listening?"

"Long enough to hear a rather insightful story." He held his hand out to her, offering her assistance up from her seat on the floor.

She hesitated a moment before she slipped her fingers into his hand. "Thank you, milord."

"Camden." Awareness rippled across his flesh. He tightened his fingers around hers, unwilling for the moment to let her go.

"Camden," she repeated, her tone breathless.

The sensation had flowed through her as it did him. He released her fingers to brush her cheekbone with a motion that was almost but not quite a caress.

Instead of his fingers, he allowed his gaze to caress her skin. Warmth brought a touch of pink to her cheeks. She leaned toward him, as though drawn by the same irresistible force that flowed through him.

Camden held himself back because of Violet's presence, despite the overwhelming desire to kiss Rhiannon. His emotions veered crazily, crackling around him until he realized it was not his emotions but a loud boom that shook the room.

Violet shrieked, and catapulted into Rhiannon's legs, almost knocking her down had Camden not pulled both into his arms to steady them.

"Violet, what's wrong?" Camden asked, stroking the top of her head.

"It's the same noise that came just before the men took my daddy away," she cried.

A cannon? Before Camden could respond, the door to the chamber burst open. Five warriors dressed in full battle gear erupted into the solar—Orrin, Hamish, Travis, Garrett, and Hugh. "Milord," Orrin said. "We are under attack."

"From whom?" Camden spun toward the door, leaving the women behind.

"We watched them approach, a small army of fifty men. They were flying the colors of the Lockhart clan, so we assumed they were more of the men from Lockhart Castle come to join us here. That was, until we saw the cannon."

"They fired on us?" Camden asked, his thoughts now fully on the coming war.

"Aye, milord."

"Call the men to arms," Camden ordered. "Hamish, take Rhiannon and Lady Violet to the storeroom. No one will think to look for them there."

"You think this attack is targeted at them?" Hamish asked with a puzzled frown.

"I am certain of it."

Chapter Thirteen

An explosion rocked the castle. Rhiannon clutched Violet's arm as the ground shook beneath their feet. She could hear the shouts of the men as they raced through the passageway, preparing for battle. Shrill screams pierced the afternoon air in the great hall below.

Rhiannon's gaze flew to Camden, but he'd turned away, toward the door.

A violent shiver wracked Violet's small body. "I'm scared." The young girl buried her face in the folds of Rhiannon's dress.

Pushing her own fear aside, Rhiannon gently stroked Violet's back. "I'll keep you safe," she soothed, hoping that she could do just that.

Orrin burst through the door of the solar. "They are firing cannon balls at the outer wall. We will be breached before we can stop them."

"Who is attacking?" Camden asked, his voice tight.

"We don't know exactly." Orrin's features became strained. "Although we know it's not the English."

Rhiannon fervently prayed that the attackers were not members of her own family.

"Meet me in the courtyard," Camden said to Orrin, then turned back to her. "Go with Hamish to the cellar. You'll be safe there."

Fierce intensity entered his bright blue eyes. Did he know who attacked? He seemed almost as protective of her as he was of Violet. Did he fear her family had come to take her away? Or was it something more? He had accused her of partnership with the bishop. Did he suspect the bishop was behind the attack?

Rhiannon frowned. How would she ever know the truth unless she saw the situation herself?

Camden made his way to the door, but paused before Hamish. "Do not let either of them out of your sight," he said, his voice suddenly fierce.

At Hamish's nod, Camden was gone.

Rhiannon moved to the window. Great curling clouds of black smoke rose to the sky just outside the outer bailey. She could not see who attacked. Yet the brief glimpse left her with the feeling it was not the members of her family come to raid. The Ruthvens would not have had enough resources to afford a cannon and shells. The threat came from someone else, she was certain.

She caught sight of a familiar figure striding through the wisps of black smoke in the courtyard. He still wore a tartan of the Lockhart colors, but his chest was now covered with a leather doublet. His hair was unbound, the thick ebony length curling above his shoulders.

He approached his horse and checked the tension of the cinches while the animal's long and graceful head turned, nudging him with affection. Camden stroked the beast's neck before he mounted.

The animal swung about, and Camden looked toward the window. Rhiannon flinched back, embarrassed to be caught spying on him. She backed away, her throat tight as she realized the danger that lay ahead for him at the gates of his own castle.

"Come, ladies," Hamish called. "We must hurry."

Rhiannon scooped Violet into her arms and followed Hamish from the chamber. She paused, remembering the sound of men running through the hallway and the clang of metal that sounded as they did. "Hamish, is the armory near here?"

"Just down the hallway, milady."

"Then that is where we will go first." Rhiannon didn't wait for Hamish to agree. If they were at war, she wanted to be prepared. She could not protect Violet without some way to even the odds should they be discovered in the storeroom.

With a renewed sense of urgency, Rhiannon continued down the hall until she came to an open doorway. Inside she found armor in neat rows against the walls and weapons of every kind hanging on the walls, ready to be plucked down from their pegs and put into service.

Her heart racing in her chest, she scanned the room, looking for a familiar weapon. She breathed a sigh of relief when her gaze lit upon a bow hung alongside a quiver of arrows. She snatched them both down. Slinging the quiver over her shoulder, she turned to Hamish. "Now I'll go wherever you lead."

"Hurry," Hamish urged as he motioned for them to go back the way they had come.

Clinging to Violet and the bow with equal force, Rhiannon followed the big warrior through the great hall and into the hallway on the other side, down the long corridor she'd visited the other day on her quest for fabric, and down the stairs leading to the storeroom.

The pungent scent of fermenting grain assaulted her senses as they plunged into the semidarkness. It took only a moment for Rhiannon's eyes to adjust to the dimness. She recognized the chamber from her previous visit. The room was filled with barrels all stacked in neat rows.

She held on to Violet's hand as she searched for a place to hide the girl in case they were discovered. Another explosion shook the walls, and the barrels groaned from their perches slightly above the floor. "More cannon fire?" she asked.

"Aye," Hamish replied. "I'll stay here and cover the doorway."

"There are two doorways."

"Two?" Hamish asked, clearly startled. "How do you know?"

"Experience," she replied.

Hamish shrugged. "Find a place to hide, and I'll do what I can to cover both entrances."

"May luck be with you," she said, picking up Violet and holding her against her chest.

"I'm scared," Violet whispered against her shoulder.

"Fear isn't always a bad thing, Violet. It keeps us alert," Rhiannon said as she turned into the darkness of the storeroom. It would be wise to hide Violet somewhere close to the hidden doorway in case it became necessary for the little girl to escape.

Rhiannon quickly moved through the hazy darkness until she came to the end of a row of barrels. She tried to tip each one, searching for one that was lighter than all the rest. "If only I can find an empty barrel."

"I know where one is," Violet said, lifting her head from Rhiannon's shoulder.

"You do?"

"I accidentally spilled the ale the other day when Uncle Camden and I were playing."

Rhiannon stifled a smile at the memory of Violet's stained dress. "Show me."

Violet wiggled out of Rhiannon's grip and headed down the row of barrels on the far side of the room. "This way," she called, no longer afraid.

The container stood empty at the end of the last row at the back of the cellar's wall. Rhiannon had hoped for something closer to the door, but this would have to do.

"How do we get it open enough for you to slip inside?" Rhiannon pondered to herself.

"Allow me."

Rhiannon startled at the sound of Hamish's voice behind them.

"I will need to know where to lead the intruders away from." He moved around them and with a grunt, lifted the barrel from its shelf before positioning it against the wall. He took several steps back, then hurled himself forward, landing with both feet firmly planted against the wood that formed the bottom of the barrel. A sharp crack filled the air as the wood collapsed beneath his assault. Hamish hit the floor with the force of his blow, but rolled once, and in a fluid motion came up on his feet.

The new opening in the barrel gaped wide enough for Violet to slip inside. Once she was hidden, Hamish brushed all the wood slivers beneath the racks that held the barrels, hiding any evidence of an open barrel, then lifted it back onto its shelf with the open side facing the wall.

"She'll have plenty of air to breathe, yet be fully concealed," Hamish said with a note of satisfaction. "Excellent idea."

"Thank you," Rhiannon said, deeply touched by the compliment.

"Now, where do we hide you?"

"There is no time," she said as a thunderous crash filled the air. The sound went on for what seemed like an eternity. Just as silence settled, the sounds of battle emerged as the roar of men's shouts mingled with the thunder of hoofbeats.

"The wall has been breached." Hamish put into words her greatest fear.

Rhiannon clutched the bow in one hand and drew an arrow from her quiver with the other. "You take one doorway, and I will cover the other."

"Only if you promise that if we are discovered, you will run and hide yourself among the barrels."

"Agreed."

At her consent, Hamish turned away to head for the doorway that led to the storeroom from inside the castle. Rhiannon positioned herself near the other door. She aimed her bow at the doorway and waited, her heart thundering in her chest.

She had to protect Violet. After several long minutes, the door on Hamish's side slammed open. Bright light and the shouts of men followed. Rhiannon spun toward the sounds. She kept her aim on the shapes moving within the hazy darkness until a single figure broke away from the others, heading her way. She waited. Prayed he would turn. But nay, he continued toward her. Halfway across the room, she loosed her arrow and hit her target in the thigh. He stumbled to the ground.

Without thought, she nocked another arrow, allowing it to sail into the same space where the man she'd just hit had stood. A cry of agony pierced the air. Her fingers trembling, she set another arrow. The door slammed open behind her. She twisted around and let the arrow fly, missing the man. He surged forward.

With a gasp of fear, Rhiannon plucked another arrow from her quiver and darted behind a long row of barrels.

"She's got tae be here somewhere," a voice called out of the darkness. Could this be the man who had betrayed Violet's presence to the bishop?

"I watched her go down here with the child and the warrior," an unfamiliar voice said.

A chill moved through her at the realization that these men were after her and not Violet. Rhiannon crouched behind a wooden barrel as the men ran past. Even if they were after her, she had to lead them away from Violet. She couldn't take a chance like that with Violet's life.

Rhiannon braced herself and bolted for the open door. A shout behind her told her she'd been spotted. She twisted around to see who followed. Two hulking men came at her, their features distorted by the shadows, but she knew their intent from the menacing grins on their faces.

She let another arrow fly. One man fell to the ground. She hurried up the stairs in the darkness, her heart pounding and her hands shaking. Rhiannon broke through into the light only to hear footsteps coming swiftly up behind her. With a burst of desperation, she sped forward only to be hauled back against the solid wall of a man's chest. He wrenched the bow from her fingers and jerked her hands behind her.

"Goin' somewhere, my sweetlin'?" he breathed against her ear.

Rhiannon shuddered. He smelled of sweat and fish and rotten teeth. She twisted in his arms. She gasped at the sight of the man who'd fought Camden at the cottage. A scream tore from her throat, only to have his brutal hand clamp over her mouth.

"Yer comin' with me," he said with the look of hatred blazing from his cold, dark eyes.

Chapter Fourteen

Rhiannon struggled against the hands gripping her. Despite her efforts, the man held tight. She twisted and writhed in his arms, only to have a large burlap sack tossed over her head, engulfing her in darkness and the stench of dead fish. Her stomach roiled.

She kicked and squirmed, her nails tearing the flesh of his forearm. The man grunted at the assault, and pain exploded in her cheek and temple as his forearm connected with her head. He dragged her across the ground, then threw her atop a horse. Her skirts bunched up about her legs. The man mounted behind her a heartbeat later, his rough hands pinning her to the saddle.

They were moving very quickly. The shiver of apprehension that coursed through her body did not go unnoticed by her captor. He laughed, the sound grating.

The sounds of battle echoed all around as they rode for what felt like forever. The air seemed warmer than it had a few days before when she and Camden had been forced to take shelter in the cottage. And by the fast gait of the horse, Rhiannon could only assume much of the snow had melted. As they continued and the sounds of battle faded she became increasingly uneasy.

"Where are you taking me? Why are you doing this? Who are you?" The bag was lifted from her head as the man slowed his pace. Rhiannon pulled a breath of clean air into her lungs. Her eyes adjusted to the brightness, though she was uncertain of where they were.

"Where we're takin' ye is of nae concern of yers. If ye

behave well enough, ye might live tae see it." His grin was a dark, evil slash across his face.

"Lord Lockhart will come after me. You'll see."

The man's face brightened. "I'm prayin' that he does." He narrowed his eyes and let them slide down to the thrust of her breasts. "And if he takes his time, mayhap I can sample what ye have tae offer."

She gasped.

He laughed coarsely. Grabbing a fistful of her hair, he jerked her head to one side. Her cry of pain opened her lips to the revolting feel of his mouth sucking wetly upon hers. She brought up her fist to beat him away.

He caught her wrist and twisted it behind the small of her back. He released a husky laugh. "God's teeth, yer goin' tae be a fun one tae tame."

Two riders edged closer to them. "Stop playin' with yer catch, Axel. We have tae get her out of here and hand her over before we'll be paid."

The man called Axel grunted and replaced the burlap sack over her head, kicking the horse into a faster gait once more.

"We've captured the cannon!" one of his men shouted. Camden couldn't see exactly who it was inside the blue-black cloud that had fallen over the crumbling mass of stones once comprising the outer wall of Lee Castle.

"Then the victory is ours," Camden called to his men. They hadn't been able to stop the breach, but they'd ended the conflict shortly after. Now that the cannon was no longer in their attackers' control, many of the enemy had turned and fled. Yet Camden had seen a group break through to the castle grounds before anyone could stop them.

"Orrin, do we have any idea where the men who breached the wall were headed?"

"They got into the keep before we could secure the gates."

"Bloody hell," Camden swore under his breath. "They're after Violet."

"Or did they come for Rhiannon?"

Stunned by the question, Camden froze. "Where are Violet and Rhiannon now?"

As if in answer, the sound of hoofbeats filled the air. A dozen well-armed men raced past the fallen rubble of the wall and out into the open land. As they passed, Camden did not miss the feminine outline of a leg that draped against one of the horse's flanks. The rest of Rhiannon's body was concealed beneath a dark woolen sack.

Camden fought the urge to kick his horse into a gallop and follow. "God's blood, how did they find her so quickly?" His voice vibrated off the fallen stones from the wall. "Did they take Violet as well?"

Camden turned his horse back toward the keep. In the courtyard he dismounted, then raced for the door that led from the courtyard to the storeroom. Orrin followed close behind. In the dim light Camden could make out several bodies lying on the floor with arrows protruding from their flesh.

"Violet," Camden shouted into the void. "Hamish, where are you?"

A scraping noise sounded off to his right a moment before Hamish appeared. "Milord, I failed you." He drew closer. "Mistress Rhiannon fought valiantly, but there were too many of them. Four men attacked me. I tried to help her. . . ."

"You did what you could, Hamish," Camden said, noting blood on his chin, his arms, his thighs, though nothing looked fatal. "Where's Lady Violet?"

Hamish nodded, his eyes wild in his white face. "She's safe. That I know." He turned toward the back wall and as

Camden hurried after him, Hamish grasped one of the huge wooden barrels. Orrin helped gently lower the barrel to the floor. Violet crept out from the back.

Camden threw his arms around his niece, hugging her tightly. She returned the embrace, her small body melting into his. His breath caught in his chest. "Praise the saints you are safe."

A shudder wracked her small body as she pulled away, her wide eyes searching his. "I heard men shouting. And Rhiannon screamed." Tears filled her eyes. "They took her away. Just like my mum and daddy."

Gratitude for her safety mixed with fury at his failure to keep Rhiannon safe. "I'll find her and bring her back," he said, his voice trembling with rage. Camden placed Violet in Orrin's arms, then moved to leave the storeroom.

With one hand, Orrin grasped Camden's arm, holding him back. "Are you certain you want to go after her?"

Camden turned to stare at the hand clutching his arm. "Are you suggesting we abandon her to those marauders?"

Orrin released his grip. "I'm suggesting that perhaps they are doing you a favor. They've taken her away, a Ruthven, your sworn enemy. Perhaps it is for the best."

Camden's blood ran cold in his veins. "They are murderers, Orrin. How can I desert her if I am the very cause of her abduction?"

"We have to think this through," Orrin reasoned. "Did they steal her to murder her, or did they do so because they knew you would follow? Who is the real target here? We need to have a plan before you charge into some sort of trap."

Camden knew he wasn't thinking. He was only feeling. *I promised to keep her safe.* "She's Lady Violet's nursemaid."

"Is that all?"

Guilt twisted Camden's gut. He had unleashed the demon that had captured her. And she needed his help.

Or did he need to help her to appease his own guilt?

Camden released an unearthly growl at the mix of emotions that tortured him—fury and guilt, and if he were truly honest, fear, welled up inside.

"I fear for her life because something changed, Orrin. I don't know when. I don't know how. But I stopped hating the sight of her and find I look forward to seeing her instead. She might be a Ruthven, but she is still a living being. And despite her name, I swore I'd protect her."

Camden clasped Orrin's arm, and the tension between them drained away. "If they had meant to kill her," Orrin said, "they would have done so here. They took her away instead. To me that means they're looking for information from her or plan to use her as a trap for you instead."

"I must take that chance," Camden said. "Now that the battle has ended, I will take a small contingent of men with me. You and the others should remain here and set things to rights." He headed out the door toward his waiting horse.

Orrin nodded and followed, carrying Violet with him.

Camden mounted, and signaled five of the men who were mounted and ready to join him.

"At least they left us a trail in the snow," one warrior said as he fell in behind Camden, waiting for the order to move out. The other men followed his example until all six were ready to continue the battle elsewhere.

Camden surged forward, leading the way. The wind blew cold and crisp against his face as he rode out of the gate of Lee Castle. An overwhelming sense of urgency spurred him to put his horse into a gallop.

He had to find Rhiannon and ensure her safety. But more important, he realized with a sudden start, he had to keep her from learning the truth about what he had done.

What would he see in the depths of her eyes if she learned that he'd hired an assassin to kill every member of her family? An assassin who had already killed both of her brothers?

He could picture the pain and the betrayal in her bright tawny eyes. "Nay," he swore into the wind. They would reach her before her trust in him came to a bitter end.

A dark figure followed Rhiannon's captors through the woods. He slowed his horse, keeping his distance. If they caught him now, they would not be kind in their punishment. They wouldn't believe he was merely a spy, reporting what he saw for a few silver coins.

He hung back behind the dormant heather shrubs and scrub trees. Their lanky branches did not conceal him fully, but enough to keep him from being detected by either horse or man when he stayed completely still.

He didn't want to be here, tramping through the snow. What had started out as justified revenge now seemed cruel. The girl hadn't hurt anyone, even though everyone at the castle had treated her poorly. She tried to help. And she was good to Lady Violet, gentle like the girl's own mum would have been.

In return they hurt her. But what could he do to stop the torment? He had to stay out of harm's way himself.

He had no choice but to follow, to observe, and report what he saw, no matter how much he might want to help the poor girl. He'd sealed his fate with that first silver coin he'd taken.

As the cold wind burned his cheeks while he waited, he wished he'd made a different choice.

Rhiannon shivered in the saddle as she sat in front of her captor on the horse. The trail they followed had deteriorated into hardly more than a sheep track as they descended into a gorge sparsely dotted with shrubs and trees. The light of day was beginning to fade. Dusk cast gloomy gray shadows across the land. The sparse pines created a ghoulish scene as their long, leering limbs hung down over the path.

She and her seven captors reached a small clearing and came to a stop. Rhiannon detected a sigh of relief from the man in the saddle behind her. "Now tae set the trap for Lockhart."

Rhiannon startled. "You are using me to lure him away from the castle?"

He jumped from the horse and leered up at her, keeping a firm grip on the reins. "Too true, but I expect ye'll be gone afore he arrives."

Rhiannon tried to keep her expression neutral. "You're going to kill me?"

A flicker of grudging admiration lit the man's face. "I'd hoped ye'd be more afraid."

She was afraid and sick to her stomach, but she wouldn't let him know that. She cast a furtive glance at the reins in his hands. If only she could yank the reins away, she might have a chance to save herself. "Wouldn't it be better to use me to bargain with?"

The man's smirk of satisfaction faded. "Why would he bargain for ye? Yer family helped tae murder his kin. I'm sure he'll be more than grateful tae be rid of ye."

Rhiannon flinched at the truth of his words. Why would Camden waste his time on her?

"Fear not, sweetlin'. I won't kill ye right away. The men and I are lookin' forward to a bit o' sport." He drew a dagger from his belt, running the blade of his long knife between his fingers. "Get down."

When she remained on the horse, he yanked her foot, hard. She landed in the snow with a thump. Cold, wet clumps of snow clung to her skin, chilling her even more.

With a sharp laugh, her captor left her there while he and the others tied the horses to the surrounding shrubs, then lit several torches to illuminate the area.

Rhiannon gained her feet and sprinted away from the men, only to be dragged backward a moment later. "Ye aren't goin' anywhere, sweetlin'," her captor growled. He forced her back toward the others, then tossed her on the ground once more before he joined the other men. Her body ached, and her temples throbbed. A crescent-shaped sliver of moon hung in the sky. Stars twinkled by the millions, but their light did little to alleviate the ghostly shadows that had fallen over the land.

Again, Rhiannon slowly rose to her feet. When the men started to argue with one another about what should be done with her, she took two steps back into the shadow of the trees. She hoped her captors were as disoriented by the falling darkness as she was. She cast a glance at the horses several feet away. Should she risk it? Could she slide over to the beasts unnoticed this time, untie the tethers, then slip away?

She took another step toward the animals. A branch, partially hidden in the snow, caught in her skirts. She tugged the fabric, praying for silence. The branch snapped. The sound seemed overly loud in the quiet of the trees, but the others seemed not to notice as they continued to argue.

"We should wait 'til he gets here," a large man growled.

"He won't want her. He's a holy man, ye idiot," a smaller captor said, jabbing the first man in the gut with his elbow.

The big man staggered back a step as he doubled over. His arm flew out to deliver a lashing blow to the right side of the man's face. While the two men brawled, the others surged forward, trying to stop them.

Rhiannon ran for the closest horse and untied the reins with trembling fingers. Her heart thundering in her chest, she threw herself onto the animal's back. She put her heels to the horse's flanks and rode out into the darkness.

A thunderous shout sounded, followed by hoofbeats.

Rhiannon leaned forward and pushed the horse into a faster gallop. Wind whipped at her cheeks, and the loose ends of her hair flew into her face. With the back of her hand, she forced the hair out of her eyes. All thought centered on the black path before her. She had to find a way to veer off into the trees and hide the horse's footprints before she could be safe.

She pressed her cheek against the horse's trembling neck. The animal was scared. Probably as terrified as she was. "Come on, boy. We have to go faster," Rhiannon urged.

"Ye little hellion. Ye've gone too far this time." A cold, hard edge had crept into the man's voice. He rode alongside her like a man possessed.

Rhiannon pressed her horse harder, plunging ahead one moment, only to be ripped from the back of her horse a moment later by his cruel grip on her hair. Flung sideways in the darkness with nothing to catch her, Rhiannon hit the ground, her head cracking against something unexpectedly solid beneath the snow. Pain exploded through her right temple moments before she was plunged into darkness.

When she awoke, the world was pitched in darkness, not from the night, but from the blindfold that pressed so tight against her eyes she could not force her lids to open. She realized that she stood upright, her hands bound behind her back. She seemed to be tied to a pole by the waist, arms, and feet. With a surge of panic, she struggled against the bindings but found no slack.

Robbed of sight, Rhiannon listened to the world around her. She could hear shuffling off to her left. She drew in a quick breath of the pungent odor of her captor's breath.

"It's about time ye woke up," the voice said, from close to her head. "I'd started tae worry I killed ye too early." He chuckled, then stepped back; she could tell by the less intense scent of his rotten teeth.

A shudder of fear rocked her. What did they intend to do to her? By the scent of pine and musty leaves, she knew they had not left the cover of the trees. An odd stack of timber rattled beneath her feet.

They would burn her alive.

"Please," she begged, thrashing her head back and forth.

"I'll make you an offer." This voice sounded a little more cultured, more sophisticated than the others. A newcomer?

"What offer?" she asked.

"Spy for me, and I'll let you go."

"What do you mean?" Rhiannon's heart leapt. A way out?

"Tell me where the Charm Stone is kept and bring me that little girl, and I'll see that you stay free from harm."

"Who are you?" she asked. *Betray Violet? Hurt Camden?* Rhiannon stilled as she realized that she could never do it. Tears welled in her eyes and slipped beneath the cloth that blinded her. Perhaps she did deserve such an end. After all, she was a Ruthven—a dark and evil seed.

"They would not hesitate to betray you." The man cruelly pressed his finger against the bruised flesh of her cheek. "What's it to be? Death or freedom?"

Rhiannon couldn't speak. Her throat locked up as she desperately twisted her hands, searching for a release. She didn't want to die, at least not this way.

A hand cracked across her cheek with violent force. Agony rocked through her. "What's your answer?" the man demanded.

Rhiannon shook her head, trying to clear it of fear and the ringing pain of the blow. She wouldn't bring further suffering upon Violet or Camden. "I'll never betray them."

He struck her other cheek.

Pain exploded inside her head. "I might be a Ruthven, but I will not hurt those who have helped me."

"Then you're a fool." He backed away, the wood snapping beneath his feet as he did. "Burn her. It is the only way for God to purify her soul." The sound of his voice grew more distant. "I cannot tolerate the scent of burning flesh, so I'll leave her disposal to you. Do not fail me this time."

The sound of hoofbeats came to her ears. For a moment hope burst inside, until she realized they moved away, not toward her.

She heard a soft hiss. She struggled against the bonds that held her firmly to the pole, frantic to escape. The ropes stayed tight as the acrid scent of smoke filled the air.

"Damn this smoke," a gravelly voice cursed. "The wood is wet from the snow. Help me fan the flames to get the wood to catch faster." A shuffling of footsteps told her the men drew near, no doubt doing as they'd been ordered.

Oh, God's Mercy, this is real. Horribly, hideously real. She wrenched her shoulders back and forth. She tried to kick her feet. But the ropes held. She would die, and Camden could do nothing to save her. Pain compressed her chest as a sob escaped her.

Swamped by hopelessness, she leaned her head back against the pole, toward the heavens. She tried to re-create the brilliance of the stars in her mind. She had to think of something, anything but the inevitable end that awaited her. But even her imagination abandoned her.

"Please help me," she pleaded, not really expecting any sort of divine intervention. When had God answered her prayers as of late?

Then she felt it, a featherlight dust of cold against her cheek. Then another. Snow. She smiled at the sky overhead. An answer to her prayer. Though the snow would never be enough to douse the flames once they licked at her feet.

At least she could picture in her mind's eye the flakes as they fell to the earth. A small comfort compared to the agony she would feel very soon. But for any distraction, short or long, she was grateful.

Chapter Fifteen

amden smelled the smoke before he saw it. "Hurry," he shouted to his men. He dug his heels into his horse's sides, praying for even more speed.

In a surge of motion, both man and beast burst into the clearing. Camden drew his sword and cleaved through the warriors before him without slowing his stride. He had to reach her.

Rhiannon was trapped, flames licking at the wood at the edge of the stack. Yet her face was serene, accepting of her fate.

Damn her for not believing she deserved more. Camden charged forward, sword flashing. He knew his men were near, but he only had eyes for Rhiannon.

He did not let fear enter his thoughts, for it would only slow him down. He had to reach Rhiannon before the flames consumed her. The world around him slowed. He lashed out, and the men who charged him fell.

He called her name, his throat raw with fury.

Her head snapped toward the sound of his voice. "Camden?"

Hope blossomed in that one simple word. She was still alive. For now.

Through a haze of smoke, he focused on his goal. He guided his horse behind her, away from the others, and dismounted. He quickly sliced through the bindings at her waist, wrists, and ankles. Free of her bonds, she sagged, her knees failing her. The bottom of her dress caught fire.

The stench of burning cloth filled the air as he yanked

her from the flames and smothered the fire. He scooped her up with one arm and held her against his chest. The pile of wood shifted, and the subsequent roar of the flames filled his ears. The scent of blood assaulted his senses. He forced the realities of battle aside and with a gentle hand loosened the binding over her eyes. The fabric slipped over her cheeks to settle at her neck.

"You came for me." Her faint voice held a touch of awe and gratitude. Her fingers wrapped around his bloodied sleeve. "Thank you."

"We are survivors, you and I." He reveled in the softness he saw in her eyes, grateful she did not know the truth.

All around them, the battle raged with the screech and clangor of steel, the grunts of men. Two warriors charged him, swords raised to strike. Camden quickly set Rhiannon on her feet and tucked her behind him. "Get behind the horse."

He drew his sword.

At the sight of his long curved blade, the men paused, frightened momentarily by the unknown.

Camden took advantage of their confusion and charged. He lunged left, right, using his curved scimitar like a saber. A sharp cry told him he'd hit his target. A body thumped to the ground. The other man, a big one, snarled and made for him. Camden thrust forward, upward, sideways, blocking every blow.

The man heaved his weapon over his head and charged like a giant, ready to cleave Camden in two. But Camden easily spun away as the force of the man's blade came down to plow through snow and earth instead.

Camden brought his boot down against the back of a leg, crumpling the man to the ground. Suffocating in the heavy smoke, the man hacked and coughed, then gained his feet.

Camden readied his sword. The hook of his blade sliced clean through the warrior's arm, followed by an upswing of his weapon that sliced the man's throat, ending his agony.

In the next heartbeat, Camden turned to block the thrust of yet another warrior's blade, coming face-to-face with the assassin he'd hired. The world seemed to freeze as they stared at each other, swords locked at the hilt.

"You killed the blacksmith," Camden said past the ache in his sword arm. He blocked out the pain, fixing on his enemy.

"I'll kill whoever I please tae get what I want," the assassin said through his brown and pungent teeth.

"I released you from your obligation." Camden pulled his blade away.

The man's gaze shot to Rhiannon. "I work fer another."

Rhiannon's face appeared pale in the glow of the red, flickering light. Growing flames climbed the pole where she'd been staked.

Camden turned back to his newest enemy and raised his sword. "For Rhiannon," he said as fury propelled him forward. *Kill him, kill him,* his blood commanded for all the innocents he'd been unable to save. He would save Rhiannon. He would save Violet. He would save himself.

His blade plunged deep, straight through the killer's chest, delivering a death blow. The assassin's sword fell from his hand and he dropped to the ground, clutching the gaping wound.

Camden sheathed his sword and bent down beside the man. "God be with you—"

A hand groped his arm, dug nails into Camden's flesh. "Beware . . ." He tried to breathe, only to choke on his own blood. "The bishop," the man warned before his body went limp and his eyes drifted back in his head.

The bishop? Camden brought his hand down over the man's eyelids, closing his eyes forever.

"Go in peace," he whispered.

Again time slowed as the battle died all around, until only his own men remained standing. Eager to make his way home, Camden stood and made his way to Rhiannon's side. He placed Rhiannon gently in the saddle, then signaled to his men to ride out.

Swinging up into his saddle behind Rhiannon, he charged ahead, leading the way back home. With the assassin's death, his secrets and his people were safe.

As a warrior, he understood death. As a man, he hated that he had caused it for his own selfish gains. He pulled Rhiannon closer against his chest. The warmth of her body comforted him somehow, working its way inside him, soothing his conscience.

Snow continued to fall lightly as he and his men made their way home. Camden frowned as they neared the rise to the castle. A dark pile of rubble and a gaping hole in the outer wall remained a reminder of the deception that had taken place here this day.

The group of men did not go to the gate, but entered the castle over the tumbled and obliterated stones of the wall.

Camden came to a stop, frowning at the damage. "How long?" he asked as Orrin came up beside him.

Orrin understood the question. "I can have the wall repaired within three days."

Camden shook his head. "Too long. We'll be too vulnerable to attack."

"The men will serve a constant guard."

"It is the spy within our own midst that has me most concerned. How easy for him to pretend to guard the breach at night or rebuild it during the day, then slip away unnoticed?"

"I'll not make it easy. I intend to guard the breach myself."

Camden cast a smile of appreciation at his friend. "Even you must sleep."

Orrin straightened. "No one will enter or leave this castle without my notice, I give you my vow."

"We'll both share the duty, as we always have."

Orrin nodded, and turned away to resume supervising work on the wall.

At the stairs to the keep, Camden dismounted and grasped Rhiannon's waist, assisting her from the horse. "We need to get you cleaned up. I will send for our healer."

"Please, I just need to rest."

He studied her for a long moment before he nodded. "If you will not see a healer, then you must promise me that you'll drink the tonic I send to your chamber."

"I promise," she said. A few moments later Rhiannon found herself ensconced in her bedchamber. Despite the chill that wracked her body, she hesitated to approach the crackling flames in the hearth.

She glanced down at the charred hem of her dress and what was left of her shoes. She slipped them off, leaving crumbles of ash and leather on the floor beside them. Several large blisters covered the skin where her slippers had been. Red burns streaked up her legs, discoloring her flesh. A stinging pain rippled across her legs. She was lucky. Burns and blisters she could heal from. Rhiannon shivered at the memory of the heat creeping up her legs. If Camden had not arrived when he did, she would have perished in a blaze of flames.

Before her thoughts could turn down darker roads, a parade of servants entered the room. Two placed a copper hip bath near the fire. Four more men entered behind them and dumped large buckets of steaming water into the waiting bath. Two women brought a linen towel and a plate of freshly baked bread with a chunk of golden cheese. Mistress Faulkner brought up the rear of the procession. She placed a mug of cool liquid in Rhiannon's hands. "The master asked that you drink this. All of it."

Rhiannon brought the mug to her lips and drank the bittersweet ale inside. When she finished, Mistress Faulkner took the mug from her fingers and handed it to a waiting maid. Then she proceeded to lead Rhiannon to the bed, where she carefully laid out a green damask dress along with a pair of soft leather slippers.

"Milady," she said when the others had left. "I made this dress for you, to thank you for your help with Charlotte and her child." Mistress Faulkner cast her gaze to the thick woolen carpet as she spoke. "I treated you poorly. I shall not do so again."

"The dress is beautiful," Rhiannon said, uncertain about what to think or do. "Thank you for your kindness." Could she trust the chatelaine? She seemed sincere enough. Or was this another attempt to humiliate her?

Mistress Faulkner helped Rhiannon take off the ruin that was her dress, then assisted her into the hip bath. Pain streaked across her feet and up her legs as she settled into the water. She lathered her body and hair quickly with the lavender soap, then rinsed, as eager to wash the smell of smoke from her skin and hair as she was to be freed from the heat of the water against her burns.

When she was done, the chatelaine assisted her from the bath, wrapping her body in a soft linen towel. Rhiannon settled in a chair near the fire, careful to keep her legs and feet from getting too close to the heat. At the sight of the flames, she flinched but forced herself to breathe slowly. This fire would warm her and help her dry her hair. This was not a fire of destruction.

As her hair dried, the pain in her feet and shins lessened. Rhiannon drew her legs up, placing her feet on the chair. She studied her legs. Where the red streaks used to be, only smooth flesh remained. She frowned, suddenly confused. "Mistress Faulkner, what was in the tonic that Lord Lockhart sent for me to drink?"

"I have no idea. Why?"

How could she explain what she didn't understand herself? " 'Tis nothing," she said as she lifted first one foot then the other, inspecting the soles that used to be covered in blisters. They were now only slightly red, and the pain had vanished. Utterly astonished at how rapidly she had healed, Rhiannon placed her feet on the floor and stood, moving to the bedside. There, she smoothed the elegant fabric of the dress Mistress Faulkner had made her. The luxurious softness planted the seeds of temptation in her chest. Could she wear the garment? Did she have a choice with no other clothing in her possession?

"Mistress Faulkner, do you promise me that this was not Violet's mother's gown?"

The older woman's face paled. "I know I've given you no reason to trust me." Her eyes filled with remorse. "But it's true I made the gown for you. I made one for Lady Violet as well."

Rhiannon believed her. In an uncharacteristic move, Rhiannon hugged the woman, bringing a startled gasp from the chatelaine's lips. "Thank you," Rhiannon said. "I have not had a new dress in ages."

"You're welcome, milady." An excited sparkle came back into the older woman's eyes. "Let's try it on." When the task was complete, Mistress Faulkner stepped back, admiring her work. "You look lovely. Just as mistress of the castle should look."

Rhiannon inhaled sharply. "I am not the mistress here. I am just Lady Violet's nursemaid," she rattled on, suddenly nervous.

Knowing reflected in the older woman's tired gray eyes. "You are here. Make the most of it." She gave Rhiannon a squeeze on the arm and left the chamber.

Unsettled by the woman's words, Rhiannon paced the

room. Dear heavens, is that how they saw her? An opportunist come to stake a claim?

Her legs became unsteady. She stumbled toward the bed and collapsed against its softness as a queer jolt of pain centered in her chest. Aye, the Ruthvens had been notorious for their unabashed attempts at advancement, through any means available. When proper and decent means slipped through their fingers, her family had become ruthless and unfeeling in the ways they chose to get ahead.

When she was young, her own father had abducted the king. Then later, he'd sold Camden and Orrin into slavery, no doubt along with countless others. Her brothers had murdered so many of their neighbors that she had lost track. They'd raided, pillaged, and done anything to foster their own gains.

Why did she expect anyone to believe she was any different from her family? Rhiannon shut her eyes and leaned back on the bed, suddenly exhausted. She'd almost been burned alive because of her family name.

A startled gasp escaped her. She sat up, her body tense. That wasn't true. She'd almost been killed because she'd *refused* to be like her family. The man had asked her to betray Violet and in turn Camden.

And she had refused.

"Wake up, ye bastard."

Bishop Berwick awoke with a start, his eyes wild and unfocused in the darkness of his little country bedroom. Where were his servants, the armed men he'd hired? He paid them handsomely to see that he remained safe.

He heard a rustle of movement from somewhere in the room.

His hand slid beneath his pillow. His fingers closed around the grip of a dagger.

"Yer Grace," the voice came again.

The bishop rolled off the bed, hitting the floor hard, his eyes straining to pierce the darkness. Then he saw it. The light of the moon revealed a solid silhouette near the window. The drapes billowed in the light breeze, creating undulating shadows in the now silent chamber.

The bishop got to his knees and crawled to the foot of the bed, his pristine nightshirt dragging on the floor. "Who's there?"

"Ye used me."

"Who the hell are you?"

"I hate bein' used."

The words came not from the window but the opposite corner of the room. The bishop spun toward the corner. How had the man moved so quickly and silently?

There was no one there.

"What do you want? Money? An intercession? Just name it, and it is yours."

"I want out. I won't tell on 'em anymore."

The voice came from near the window again, but there was nobody there.

The bishop's heart thundered in his chest. "Who?"

"Lady Violet and Mistress Rhiannon."

He had to keep the man talking to get a fix on his location. He strained to listen. "Rhiannon is dead."

"Nay, she isn't."

"Lockhart." The bishop frowned into the darkness. Damn the man.

A movement came from the opposite corner. "I'll not be a party to killin' them girls. For God's sake, ye tried to burn one alive."

The man stepped in front of the window. Moonlight illuminated the silhouette to reveal the warrior he'd hired a few weeks ago—a man who'd said he'd do anything to keep his son from harm. A surge of relief rushed through the bishop. He cautiously rose to a half crouch. The man posed no danger.

"If you want silver in addition to my promise not to harm your son, Rhys, I can be generous." The bishop stood, moving slowly toward the man.

The man's face was distorted in the half-shadow. "I'll take yer promise that my son will be safe, but I don't want yer silver. I want out, with my conscience intact. Ye've lost, and I won't go down with ye."

"Nonsense. Nothing has changed because the girl lives. Although I cannot say the same for you." The bishop lifted his dagger and with a snarl drove the weapon into the man's ribs.

Shock froze the man's expression. He staggered, then fell to his knees in a pool of his own blood.

The bishop tossed the dagger onto the floor beside him. With a slight tremble in his hands, he reached for the bell that would bring his manservant to his side.

A moment later the door opened, and his sleepy chamberlain appeared. "You rang, Your Grace?"

"We've had an intruder." The bishop scowled at the man on the floor. "I had no choice but to defend myself."

A flicker of fear crossed the man's features. "I shall take care of it, Your Grace." The servant bowed, then left the room only to return a moment later with two grooms.

"Put this around him, like a shroud." The bishop tossed an old sheet at the men, a sheet from his mother's sickbed. "We must do this properly," he said.

They did as they were told. Draping the body in the sheet, then silently, they rolled the man's body up in a woolen blanket.

"Dump his body in the loch," the bishop ordered, savoring the godlike power that surged through him.

A renewed surge of determination straightened his spine. Ridding himself of the man had been easy, as though it were God's will. If this exhilarating sensation came to him each time he condemned a man to death or saved his life, he wanted more of it. Surely that meant he was doing the right thing, trying to get the Stone away from the Lockharts. For who deserved it more than a man of God?

"Then get back here. Time grows short. The council could arrive at any time. We must find where Lockhart hid that Stone."

Dampness surrounded him. Rhys pushed against the darkness. Agony shot through his side, and the salty taste of blood came to his mouth. Where was he?

He tried to flail, but his limbs were caught against his body. A cold sweat swamped him just before he felt a sensation of flight followed by a hard thump and a rush of freezing water. He struggled even more, frantic now as the water rose and cut off his air.

Just when he began to despair, the barriers that confined him loosened. Cold sapped the breath from his lungs. Water crushed down over his head.

He stared up, or was it down, into the dark void that hungrily swallowed him. His lungs tightened at their lack of air. A hazy fog entered his brain. The dark waters seemed to stretch into eternity. A bittersweet smile came to his lips at the thought. Eternity was where he would be heading unless he could break through to the surface.

Please God, let me find air. If he lived, he vowed he'd confess to Lord Lockhart.

Even if Lockhart killed him after, at least his conscience would be cleansed.

He clawed at the blanket that trapped him, forcing it apart. Once free, his instinct told him to surge ahead. But was that up or down? He calmed his thoughts and drew the small iron ring from his finger. He knew that objects always fell down, whether on land or in the water.

The ring moved upward, so he twisted his body in the opposite direction. He gritted his teeth as hot, sickening pain seared his lungs. He thrust with his legs and slowly moved toward the surface.

Too slow. Much too slow. He had to live. He had to warn Lord Lockhart of the bishop's plans.

Chapter Sixteen

*D*ays. Mere days remained of battling yet another army with a Saracen sword. Camden and Orrin charged into the melee, at each other's sides. They were no longer the gawkish boys who had been foreigners in a foreign land. Now they were men, battle seasoned, ruthless, and desperate to remain alive. Freedom would be theirs in a few more days.

He and Orrin fought together in the midst of the carnage, bonded as brothers by all they had suffered. They stumbled over dead men, dying men, slipped on the blood-soaked ground, their voices raw from the Scottish war cries they had never left behind.

The holy man who held them prisoner for six years, three hundred sixty-one days, had sworn to release them. A part of Camden wondered if Shaykh Haashim would keep his word. And still he fought on. He would survive. He would protect Orrin.

This would be the last battle among the great enemy . . . the last battle.

Camden awoke with a start, staring into the darkness, willing his heart to steady its wild cadence. It was only a dream, he told himself. He no longer battled in the Holy Land. He was no longer a slave. He and Orrin had earned their freedom. Camden lay in his own bed, thousands of miles away from Shaykh Haashim's mad desires. It was only a dream.

The walls of his chamber seemed to be drawing closer. He drew a calming breath, then got up and quickly dressed. He had to leave the chamber, to go outside on the wall walk and look at the land, to breathe the fresh, heather-scented air he had come to associate with home. Aye, that was what he needed. Just the thought brought peace to his soul, banishing the tumult and blurring the memories he longed to forget.

In that instant, another scent came to mind—one of lavender and lemons. Rhiannon. Perhaps instead it was her scent he needed. Perhaps having her warmth in his arms would vanquish his dreams of the past with the joys of the present.

A knock sounded on the bedchamber door. Rhiannon sat up in the bed and tossed the woolen coverlet aside, wondering what emergency would bring someone to her room so late at night. She snatched up the coverlet and wrapped it about her shoulders, then tucked her newly healed feet into a pair of slippers Mistress Faulkner had provided, before she raced across the room and threw open the door.

Camden stood in the hall, dressed in fawn-colored breeches, tall boots, and an ivory linen shirt. His hair was combed back away from his face. The sight set her heart pounding.

He frowned. "You shouldn't open this door to just anyone."

Rhiannon narrowed her gaze. "With Hamish and Travis guarding my door, I doubt anyone with ill intent could make it into the bedchamber."

"You have a point," he replied, stepping inside.

She closed the door softly behind him.

"Were you asleep?" he asked, watching her closely, his gaze a soft caress.

Her breath caught at his expression. "I'm still too unsettled."

"How are your burns? Do they pain you much?"

She shook her head. "It's the most amazing thing." She almost pulled up the edge of her night rail to reveal her shins, then thought the better of it. "Whatever was in that tonic you sent to the room made the burns all but disappear."

"Good," he said striding toward her, and slowly encircling her hips with his hands. He pulled her closer, as he had in the cottage.

"If you hadn't arrived when you did . . ." Her words trailed off as a warm glow rippled through her. Her body wanted desperately to melt against his. Her mind warned her to keep her distance. "I never thought I'd meet my end that way."

"Hush." He pulled her against his chest. Her cheek pressed against the linen of his shirt. His fierce voice vibrated low beneath her ear. "It is in the past."

"I'll be haunted by the memory for the rest of my days," she said.

He pulled back to stare down at her. He simply stared, as though trying to find the right words to say. "Talk about it, then put it to rest."

She hesitated. "What good will that do?"

"Tell me," he persisted.

And so she did, haltingly at first and then in a rush. The words tumbled from her. Her fear. Her feelings of abandonment. Her pain.

He listened, his face impassive, his gaze fixed upon her.

Her words finally slowed, then ceased altogether. And she felt lighter somehow, less burdened. Sharing her terror with him had lessened it. "Thank you for listening."

He said nothing, simply pulled her back into his arms, crushing her to him. She could feel his heartbeat, as though he'd run for miles instead of standing perfectly still. He buried his fingers in her hair, gently stroking, soothing, until his heart slowed. "Things will be different now. I promise."

"Don't make promises you can't keep," she whispered against his chest.

"I can keep this promise. I will."

Warmth curled inside her stomach when he returned his heated gaze to her face. "I appreciate your efforts."

A curious half smile tugged at the corner of his mouth, making the cleft in his chin more pronounced. "Come with me."

"Where?" Her voice sounded as breathless as she felt. She pulled the coverlet tighter around her. All he had to do was look at her and the world seemed to stop.

"To a special place." His hand slipped from her hip to curl around her hand.

The heat of his touch melted whatever reserve she might have mustered. She nodded, her fingers twining with his. "Will we need an escort?" she asked as they headed for the door.

At his puzzled frown, she added, "Hamish and Travis."

Dark humor lit his eyes. "I bid them to find their beds for the rest of the night."

Her heart leapt with anticipation. She followed him down the hallway, away from the stairs, around several corners, then up a long spiral staircase that led to a bolted door.

"I used to come here as a child," he explained, dropping her hand to pry the thick metal bolt from its latch. He opened the door and motioned for her to proceed. "You can see all the way to the sea from here."

She stepped outside onto the wall walk. The area was deserted except for the two of them. A small watch fire burned in a metal grate nearby, keeping the chill of the night at bay. "Where are your guards?"

His smile turned reckless. "I gave them the rest of the night off as well."

"And the fire? Who set it?" she asked, not really needing an answer as much as she needed a moment to adjust to his nearness. *He wanted them to be alone.* Understanding softened his smile. "The fires are always set at night to keep the guards warm." He turned to the wall and picked up two small logs from the pile there, then added them to the grate. "Now the fire will keep us warm instead."

She moved to stand between two crenellations, gazing out at the silvery light of predawn. Her heart raced. She should return to her room where she'd be safe from her feelings for this man. How many times had her mother warned her that proper young ladies did not walk about unescorted, especially in the dark? Dangerous things happened if they did. God knew her father had ordered some of those dangerous things to happen.

She kept her gaze focused on the landscape, looking out at the sea. She felt him come up behind her and encircle her waist with his arms.

Instinctively, she leaned back against his chest. His embrace closed around her, his head resting near her ear. "What are you thinking about, Rhiannon?"

"That I shouldn't be here with you."

He smiled against her temple. "That was honest."

"I am an honest person."

He turned her around in his arms. "To be honest with you," he paused, "I want more of what we shared in the cottage." He slipped the coverlet from her shoulders as his hands skimmed the thin white linen that covered her arms.

The early morning air pressed her night rail against her body, caressed her limbs, heightening her awareness of her bare skin beneath the thin layer of cloth. His gaze traveled over her tousled hair, the curves of her breasts and hips, to her slippered feet. And again, warmth surged inside her, flowed through her veins, tuning all her responses to the warmth of his touch.

"You are dangerous to me," she replied, making no attempt to move away. "When you touch me I can't think." His lips brushed her temple. "I can't breathe."

She closed her eyes, trying to block the riotous sensations

his lips created. The darkness only intensified the effect. She opened her eyes as her power to resist him ebbed away.

"I'll never hurt you."

He *would* hurt her. He was hurting her now with his soft touch and honeyed words. He would hurt her over and over again, every time he touched her. The kind of magic they shared could never last. She was certain of it. Her heart would break, and she'd only have herself to blame.

Today's horrific events had taught her one thing: Life was unpredictable. Staring death in the face helped to clarify her desires. And she desired the man who held her in his arms. She would willingly risk her heart to be with him, even for a short while.

The night smelled crisp, fresh snow mixed with the soft scent of heather, bewitching her further as she relaxed against his chest.

His breath hitched at her surrender. "I will stop whenever you say the word," he whispered against her ear as he pulled her forward until the sheer linen of her night rail pressed against his shirt.

Her nipples hardened.

"We belong together like this, Rhiannon. Let's not fight whatever destiny brought us together. Let's enjoy what we can, without guilt or remorse."

"Resisting you is like resisting the tide." She could feel the heat of his body against hers building a maddening tension. The muscles of her limbs felt heavy, weak, unable to support her weight.

He pulled her closer and brought his lips down to explore the length of her exposed throat.

She inhaled sharply and a shiver ran through her.

He pulled away from her. Before she could mourn his loss, he hitched himself up on the stone ledge, then brought her forward to stand between his legs.

He lifted her gown to just below her breasts and brushed her flesh with his lips. She groaned at the exquisite feel of his hard cheek against the softness of her chest and her abdomen.

"This is no good," he said and pulled back. A moment later, he stripped off his shirt and tossed it to the ground. "I need to feel you against me."

With gentle hands, he guided her chemise over her head. Before her skin had a chance to cool, he pulled her to him again. His head lowered and his mouth closed over her right breast as if he were starving for her.

Rhiannon gasped as a streak of hot fire burned through her. The muscles of her stomach clenched. Boldly, she tangled her fingers in his hair, holding him against her, wanting more.

His tongue was so warm, each sensation he wrought robbed her of thought and breath. His lust for her was wildly exciting—primal, intense, fierce.

His left hand slid down her abdomen to the thatch of curls surrounding her womanhood and began to rub back and forth. "Your skin is so soft, like nothing I've ever touched before. It makes me want to—" He broke off, his voice hoarse. He looked at her with fire in his eyes, warming the blue to the color of the sky on a hot summer's day.

Rhiannon shuddered in response to his stroking. He created a strange ache between her thighs. "Open yourself to me," he commanded, his voice gentle.

She watched with fascination at the acceleration of the pulse at the base of his throat as she opened her stance.

"Wider," he said hoarsely.

She obeyed, and his hand slipped inside the warm, moist folds. He pressed his thumb and forefinger against the most intimate part of her. She bit her lip to keep from crying out as unbelievable ripples of sensation spread from his hand to every part of her body.

She arched toward him, into the pulsing manhood that pressed against the fabric of his breeches. She wanted more. She wanted him. Her hand moved down to the laces of his breeches. One tug on the ties set him free.

He jumped down from the ledge and pulled her close, his rigid manhood pulsing against her. "Are you sure this is what you want?"

"As sure as I've ever been about anything." She didn't want to stop. She couldn't. She closed her eyes, and swayed against him, blocking out all sensation but the feel of his hands on her heated flesh.

He lifted her. "Clasp me with your legs," he commanded, leaning back against the castle wall.

Her limbs encircled his hips. He settled her atop his flesh and he pulsed into her. When he met with resistance he stopped, before thrusting up in one swift stroke. He covered her lips with his to absorb her cry of pain. Rhiannon's entire body tensed. Then the sensation faded as his presence inside her sent waves of heat through every muscle in her body. His palms cupped her buttocks and held her to him.

"So tight." His eyes glazed with an expression of primitive pleasure, and his body trembled, shuddered as he moved her slowly up and down, his breathing coming in sharp gasps. The intensity of his need filled her with a heady excitement and increased her own hunger tenfold.

She clenched around him and heard Camden give a low groan. He lifted her, drawing all the way out, then plunged to the heart of her.

Rhiannon arched her neck back and gave a low cry. A hotness she had never known poured through her, merging with him, until they moved as one entity trying to reach . . . *what?*

Then she knew. The knowledge broke over her in a release of rapture that left her gasping and shivering in the aftermath.

He held her to him, breathing heavily, his flesh hot against her own. Even so, his hips still moved yearningly, as if he hadn't had enough of her even though he'd reached his satisfaction.

She'd known the moment she put her hand in his in the bedchamber below that something would happen between them this night. She'd wanted it. But she had never expected this—a joining that had been both primal and urgent.

Camden's breathing gradually steadied and slowed. "I was too rough." His voice was uneven. "I lost control."

"We both lost control. I had no idea it could be that way." She looked up at him, uncertain of what she would see. "I watched our horses mate once before, but this . . ."

Desire, hot and hard, reflected in the depths of eyes. He pulsed inside her, hardening, readying for her once more. "I want you again." His voice sounded pained. "I promise not to be so primitive this time."

She smiled, feeling fully alive for the first time in her life. "I liked primitive."

His eyes darkened. "Then allow me to indulge your primitive instincts again."

Her body barely registered the chill of the morning air as he pulled her to him and set her senses spiraling. By the time they collapsed against each other, the apricot fingers of dawn stretched across the sky, heralding a new day.

"We should go back belowstairs," he said, reluctantly moving away to collect their clothing. "The morning guards will be here soon."

Her cheeks flamed as she boldly explored the hardened contours of his body, remembering how his muscles had flexed, reacting to her touch.

With tender care, he pulled her night rail over her head, then wrapped the coverlet about her shoulders. "What are you thinking?" she asked, surprising herself at her boldness.

He smiled the same wicked smile he'd given her last night. "Honestly?"

"Absolutely." She tensed, awaiting his response.

He leaned toward her, his gaze caressing her face. His light blue eyes narrowed with intent. Strange how she first thought those eyes were icy. "You're beautiful."

Honesty. "Thank you," she whispered, touched by his words.

He kissed her forehead. He held out his hand, his fingers curling protectively around hers.

The blare of a clarion cut through the morning's silence.

Startled, Camden released her hand. He moved back between the crenellations. Rhiannon followed him, followed his gaze.

A group of armed men gathered around the castle's gate. "A call to arms. I must go."

He left her there, alone on the wall walk. A chill crept across her skin that had nothing to do with the light morning breeze.

A call to arms? Against whom?

Chapter Seventeen

"Why now?" Camden bit out the words. He clutched the missive in his hand. The bold wax seal of Robert II, King of Scotland, taunted him as he strode back and forth in front of the men at the gate. The king had sent riders with the orders to raise a force against the most recent army of English invaders.

Half the castle's warriors gathered in the courtyard at Orrin's command, armed and ready to ride. In the morning mist they appeared to be mythical creatures floating on a cloud, instead of men of flesh and blood. They would once again put their lives on the line for their king and country.

They were the best of men, honorable and true. Camden had no doubt that together they would drive the English back behind their own border. But at what cost to his own household? Would leaving half the warriors behind be enough to keep his people safe?

His men awaited orders. "Repairs to the wall will take at least two more days. I don't like it," Camden said with sudden violence.

"We don't have a choice," Orrin reminded him patiently. "You cannot ignore a summons from our king."

Camden's hand tightened on the missive. "What if this is a trick to draw us away from the castle?"

"The king's seal could not be forged without great difficulty," Orrin reasoned.

Camden frowned down at the bold mark of the king's authority. "It seems incredibly suspicious."

"Or it could be merely bad timing."

"The worst."

Orrin shrugged. "We could send everyone back to Lock-hart Castle. The walls there are solid."

Camden shook his head. "It's too dangerous for them to travel with only half the warriors as protection. They're safer here even with the wall breach than out in the open."

Camden crumpled the missive.

"We are not defenseless," Orrin reminded him. "Even with the wall down, even with half our men left behind, we would still be a strong force."

Camden knew that was true. Yet he hesitated. "That is why the king relies so heavily on us. But that doesn't change the fact that with us gone, Lady Violet and Rhiannon are vulnerable."

"We could take them with us," Orrin offered.

Camden frowned. "Battle is no place for women." He continued to pace. "There has to be a solution."

"I will stay behind with them," Orrin offered. "Will that give you peace of mind?"

Camden's gaze shot to his face. "You would do that yet again?"

"If it keeps you from committing treason and from the hangman's noose," Orrin said with a smile that quickly vanished at Camden's dark frown. "I did not mean to—"

"No offense taken. I accept your offer to stay behind. With you nearby, I know what happened to Clara will not be repeated." He strode to his horse.

"Mount up, men," Camden ordered. He would do what had to be done. Yet a sense of impending doom pressed down upon him like a heavy shadow. That shadow darkened the dawn as the gates opened and he and his men proceeded south.

The sooner he rid himself of the English who violated

Scottish lands and their way of life, the sooner he could return home, where he belonged.

The storms that had plagued the skies over Lee Castle finally moved on, and the sun made a weak appearance through the mist that refused to dissipate. The snow had started to melt, leaving patches of green and brown among the traces of white. Regardless, Rhiannon ventured out with Violet for archery lessons in the outer bailey. The silent shadows of Camden's warriors marked their every move.

Her body ached in unfamiliar places from last night's passion. Camden had been so passionate, yet so gentle when he'd touched her. How had he learned such tenderness when he had matured into manhood in the most hostile of situations?

Violet stood before the makeshift target, her small bow in her hands. She concentrated on the target, then let the arrow fly. The arrow hit the target this time.

"I did it." Violet's wide grin brought a smile to Rhiannon's lips.

"Excellent work. Try it again. This time aim just a bit more to the right."

Violet skipped to the target to retrieve her arrow. She raced back to Rhiannon's side, then nocked the arrow once more. A study in concentration, she pulled back the bowstring, squeezed one eye shut, and carefully lined up her shot before loosing the shaft. She squealed in delight as the arrow thudded solidly into the target. "This is fun!"

Rhiannon tried to be as enthusiastic as her young charge, but her mind was whirling with anxiety. Was Camden safe? Was he going off to battle her own family? She prayed the threat was English, though she knew her brothers were just as capable of treachery.

But as ruthless as they were, did she really want Cory

and Dougall to die? With them gone, she would be the sole remaining Ruthven. Even though she hadn't considered herself part of the family for years, she still felt a pang of grief at knowing she could be the last of the line.

Rhiannon cast a quick glance to the little girl who skipped back and forth at her side. Rhiannon had been alone until Violet and Camden had entered her life. But maybe now she had a new family of sorts. It was then that another chilling thought occurred to her. If her brothers found out she was living with their sworn enemy, would she be putting Camden and Violet at risk? Would her brothers inflict upon them the same painful end as Clara and James?

Fear twisted around her heart. When would her family's villainy stop?

"Rhiannon?" Violet ceased her archery lesson. She moved to Rhiannon's side and took her hand in her small fingers. "What's wrong?"

What could she say to make Violet understand her turmoil? Even if Camden could eventually learn to see past her Ruthven name and into her heart, could she accept his love knowing that doing so could place him and those he loved in danger?

"I'm merely overtired," she said, hoping Violet would not detect the lie. "Perhaps we should head back inside."

Violet nodded. The little girl gripped her bow in one hand and tightened her grasp on Rhiannon with her other as they headed back to the keep. They had barely entered the courtyard when Mistress Faulkner raced up to greet them.

"Mistress Rhiannon. Lady Violet." She skidded to a halt in a swirl of gray hair and brown skirts. "We need yer help."

Rhiannon's heart dropped to her knees at the woman's pale face and wild eyes. "Has something happened to Lord Lockhart?"

"Nay." She shook her head.

Relief washed over Rhiannon with such intensity that

she staggered. Violet's firm grasp on her hand stabilized her. "Then what is the matter?"

"One of the warriors is hurt. It's bad. Please, you must come help the man, or at least tell us what to do."

Rhiannon was no healer. Assisting in the birth of Charlotte's child did not qualify her for anything more. And yet words to the contrary came out of her mouth. "Take us to him."

Mistress Faulkner led them to the keep and into the great hall where the injured warrior had been moved.

"Why did you do it, Rhys?" Orrin asked the man, who stood with the help of two warriors holding on to his arms. His shirt and breeches were wet and soaked in blood, and his hair was a wild wet mass. The man's pale and drawn face made Rhiannon smother a gasp of alarm. She feared it was already too late to do anything for him.

"I . . . had . . . no choice," Rhys said, his breathing raspy and labored. "He . . . threatened to . . . kill my son."

"Who?" Orrin asked, his voice harsh. "Who threatened your child?"

"The bishop," the dying man whispered.

A dark frown settled over Orrin's face.

"Ye must . . . believe me."

"I do." Orrin shook his head. "Seems that man's influence has touched many of our lives."

Rhiannon strode toward the small gathering, curious to know how the injured man had become separated from the others. "Were you one of the warriors fighting with Lord Lockhart?"

"Nay. I was not with . . . Lord Lockhart."

The man brought his glassy gaze to Rhiannon's face. Contrition reflected there. "I'm . . . sorry. I dinna . . . help ye. They shouldna have . . . tried to burn ye."

Rhiannon's throat thickened at the mention of her own terror.

"What do you mean?"

Orrin spoke for the man. "Because of a threat to his child, this man was forced to help the bishop and his assassin capture you."

The implications of Orrin's words tumbled through Rhiannon's mind. The bishop had threatened this man's child? The bishop had tried to burn her alive? A riot of emotions threatened, but she forced them back, her gaze returning to the injured man.

"Lay him near the hearth," she commanded the men. "We must help him."

Orrin signaled the men to move the man to the floor near the warmth of the flames.

"Bring him blankets, strips of linen to bind his wound, and some warmed ale," Rhiannon said with authority, though fearing the residents would ignore her as they always had.

Much to her surprise, two women stepped forward. One brought a mug with her. The other, thick woolen blankets that she settled about the man's body. A third woman placed a pile of linen next to Rhiannon, who tied long strips tightly around the man's body, trying to stop the flow of blood. When that was done, she brought the rim the mug of ale to his lips. "Drink." Her gaze slid to the floor beside the man, then to Orrin's watchful gaze. "If we cannot heal him, is there anything we can do to make him more comfortable?"

"We could use the Charm Stone," Violet said.

A collective gasp echoed through the hall. All eyes turned to the little girl, who moved to stand beside the dying man.

Orrin knelt, staring into her face. "What do you know of the Stone?"

"Mummy told me about it. She said our family had a duty to heal our people. That when the time came, I should not fear my destiny."

Orrin's eyes turned hard, expressionless. "Using the Stone could be dangerous for anyone. More so for a child. No one wants you to bear the same burden as your mother."

"The Stone is good," Violet protested. "It's the bad men who want it who are dangerous." She tugged on Rhiannon's hand. "I know where Uncle Camden hid the Stone."

Rhiannon knelt beside Violet, studying her determined face. "How do you know where it is?"

She lifted her chin with pride. "I watched him hide it in the chapel after you helped Charlotte deliver her baby."

Rhiannon startled. The packet she had delivered from Mother Agnes had contained the Charm Stone? Had she known at the time, she would have been terrified. Rhiannon frowned. The bishop had demanded the Stone from her before she'd nearly been burned alive.

The Charm Stone.

Was that how Charlotte and her baby had survived the difficult birth? Rhiannon's gaze dropped to her feet. Was the Charm Stone also the reason her burns and blisters had healed so quickly?

Over the years she'd heard of magical healings performed throughout their country, but she never thought they were true.

Apparently the stories were real. As was the danger to Violet if she used to Stone to heal this man. "Nay, Violet. This isn't a good idea. Especially not while your uncle is away."

Violet pulled her hand away from Rhiannon's. She frowned down at Rhys. "I can help you. But you must promise to never harm anyone ever again."

"I . . . promise." Rhys's fingers trembled as he raised them from the floor, trying to touch Violet's hand. But he was too weak. His dirty and bloody hand collapsed against the stone of the hearth.

Rhiannon met Orrin's gaze, registered the uncertainty there. "Lord Lockhart will not like this," Rhiannon said.

"I will bear his displeasure if he does not," Orrin said. "Lady Violet, show me where the Stone is hidden."

Rhiannon followed Orrin and Violet up the stairs and down the hallway to the chapel. The chapel's three narrow windows sent streams of hazy light into the small chamber. Violet crossed the room, and the play of sunlight and shadow shifted on her form as she approached the wooden crucifix that hung against the far wall. She slipped her fingers between the wall and the wood, and pulled out a small parcel wrapped in linen.

Violet unwrapped the sacred Stone, allowing the linen protection to tumble to the floor. She held her prize from a short silver chain. At the end dangled a silver circle. A small bloodred Stone at the center winked in the filtered sunlight as if in greeting.

Was the Charm Stone a prize worth dying for? Rhiannon stared at the Stone, transfixed.

"It has always amazed me that something so small can hold so much power," Orrin said, reaching for the Stone.

Violet tugged the Stone out of his grasp. "We need to help the man."

"Do you know how to use it, Violet?" Rhiannon held out her hand to the girl, lending her more support than guidance.

"Mummy never showed me. But I have to try." Violet took her hand.

Anxiety filled Rhiannon as they made their way back to the great hall. A low rumble of sound greeted them when they reached the chamber. Rhiannon paused at the bottom of the stairs. The room had filled with people come from all corners of the castle. They conversed with each other excitedly.

Violet's grip tightened on her hand. She buried herself in the fabric of Rhiannon's skirt. "Why are they here?" she whispered.

"Curiosity, I would imagine." Rhiannon kept moving slowly forward. "It will be all right. Keep the Stone hidden."

From across the room, Mistress Faulkner hurried to greet them.

"Is there no way to put the man somewhere more private? If news of this gets out, Lady Violet could be in terrible danger," Rhiannon said, her anxiety growing.

"Since James and Clara's deaths and Lord Lockhart's return with her body, there has been talk among the staff about the Charm Stone and its connection to the Lockhart clan. Everyone wants to witness the magic that cost Lady Lockhart her life. Those who have seen the Charm Stone used before say there is no witchcraft involved. Those who haven't want to see it for themselves." Mistress Faulkner's gaze narrowed on Rhiannon. "If you know what's good for you, you'll not turn them away. They wish to be present during a miracle."

"This is not wise," Orrin said from right behind them.

"Do we have another choice?" Rhiannon asked, wanting his advice more than ever.

"With so many of our warriors gone, there are not enough of us left to enforce rule should they grow restless." He eyed the growing crowd. "But I'm not sure insisting on privacy is the better choice. The Stone was spoken of—and they want to see it in practice."

"Heaven help us, for Lady Violet doesn't know how to use the Stone."

"I know its secrets," Orrin said, escorting them through the crowd to the hearth. "The Stone should be dipped into a mug of liquid three times, then swirled to the right. Lady Lockhart always ended each use by making the sign of the cross over the body she'd just healed."

Rhiannon knelt beside Rhys, who lay so still before the hearth. Blood seeped from his newly bandaged wound.

She pressed a thick length of linen atop the bandages, hoping to further slow the bleeding. "There's no incantation? No ceremony?"

"None."

She frowned. "How is any of that considered witchcraft?"

"It's not." He scooted Violet toward the man. "Be done with this thing before they realize what you are doing."

Rhiannon nodded at Violet's questioning gaze. Rhiannon grabbed the mug of ale the women had brought to the man. "We must hurry, Violet. Do as Orrin instructed."

The little girl nodded. She bent over the mug of ale. Quickly, she withdrew the Stone from her gown. She dipped the Charm Stone in the amber-colored liquid three times, then swirled the talisman to the right. Once done, she made the sign of the cross over the man as her mother had done. She wiped the Stone on her hem, then handed it to Rhiannon who tucked the Stone safely into a small pocket inside her gown's skirt.

Someone in the room must have noticed the movements near the hearth. A shout went out across the room, "Prepare for a miracle."

A hush settled over the great hall. With fingers trembling at the audacity of what they dared, Rhiannon brought the mug of ale to the man's lips. "Drink, Rhys." She'd heard Orrin call him by that name. "You must drink."

Rhys tried to lift his head, but could not. Every eye in the chamber rested on her, Rhiannon slipped her hand beneath Rhys's head. She lifted both the cup and the man's head until the two connected and forced the "charmed" liquid past his lips. He swallowed roughly before a spasm of coughing overtook him. Several tense moments passed before he ceased coughing. Blood trickled out his nose and down his chin.

The room was cloaked in silence, as if no one dared to

make a sound for fear that the Charm Stone would some-how fail them.

"You must take more liquid," Rhiannon pleaded softly for his ears alone, forcing the liquid past his lips once more. This time he swallowed smoothly. He took another sip, then another until the liquid was gone. Rhiannon sat back.

"What happens now?" Violet asked from her perch near Rhiannon.

"We wait," she replied, forcing a reassuring smile.

"How long?

"As long as it takes." She patted the young girl's hand with confidence even as doubts plagued her. The man was so close to death. Could anything save him?

"Give it time," Orrin said, as though reading her thoughts.

Time was something this man did not have. Yet time it-self seemed to stretch out endlessly before them as they waited, watched, and prayed.

Chapter Eighteen

By late afternoon many of the castle's residents had given up witnessing a miracle. One by one, they wandered away to return to their daily routines until only Rhiannon, Violet, Orrin, Hamish, Travis, and Rhys remained near the hearth. Hamish and Travis sat at a table to the side of the hearth, keeping watch as they always did. Rhiannon had to admit that in Camden's absence, the warriors' presence made her feel more at ease. They would protect her and Violet should something happen.

Violet yawned. She tugged on one of her long golden curls, pulling it straight, then releasing it to watch it spring back to its original shape.

The others waited. And waited. "How long will this miracle take?" Rhiannon asked, growing restless.

"He was almost dead," Orrin said, stretching his legs before him as he lounged on a bench that he'd dragged near the fire.

When the man did not revive right away, they had arranged for a pallet to be brought for his bed. He lay silently against the heather-stuffed ticking. Despite the fact that the grayness had vanished from his face and his bleeding had stopped, Rhiannon was amazed the man yet lived.

She shifted her gaze from the man to Orrin. "Have you seen healings before?"

"Only a few that Lady Lockhart performed while traveling with her husband."

"What happened?"

Orrin repositioned his long legs once again. "Much the

same as this. At first nothing happened. Later, the person would wake up and be as they were before they were injured or sick."

"Is there no memory of the healing?"

"Oh, they remember." Orrin shuddered. "Two of the people I witnessed said they experienced excruciating pain while awake."

Rhiannon returned her gaze to Rhys. "Then 'tis best he sleeps." She brought her fingers up, her turn to gently tug on Violet's curl. The girl squirmed on Rhiannon's lap. "Perhaps it is also best if you head upstairs to change your clothing before supper."

Violet grabbed her curls in a playful attempt to keep them out of Rhiannon's reach. "Why do I always have to change my clothes?"

"Because you are a lady, and because I believe Mistress Faulkner has completed another dress for you to wear."

Violet released her hair and pouted. "But you never change."

Now that Violet had grown more settled in the castle, signs of her true intelligence had blossomed. Rhiannon pursed her lips while she considered how to respond. How could she explain the fact that she was not a lady in title in such a way that Violet would understand? She decided the best way to explain such a thing was to not explain at all. Tousling the child's golden curls, she said, "That's because I have only one dress."

Instantly Violet's playfulness vanished. "That is my fault." She turned and buried her face in Rhiannon's chest. "I wouldn't let you wear my mummy's dresses."

"Nay," Rhiannon said, bringing the girl's tear-filled gaze to her face. "It is not your fault. Your mother's dresses belong to you. When you get older you can choose to wear them or not. Had I known it was her gown when I put it on, I never would have done it."

Violet sniffed.

"Would you like to help me make us each a new dress tomorrow?"

The girl's face brightened. "Should we use your bed curtains or mine?"

Rhiannon chuckled, relieved that the girl's mood had shifted so quickly. "Before we attack the bed curtains again, go ask Mistress Faulkner if she has any more stored fabric."

Violet nodded, then darted up the stairs, followed by Hamish and Travis.

"Why did you really send her away?" Orrin's brows arched.

A heavy mantle of grimness settled over Rhiannon. "We need to move the man somewhere less public. If the Charm Stone's healing fails, I don't want Lady Violet to witness his death. She's been so happy as of late. What if he dies, and she thinks it's her fault? Her nightmares have finally just started fading."

"Just as Camden's are becoming more regular," Orrin said with a frown.

"He has nightmares?" Rhiannon asked.

Orrin nodded. "He used to have them often when we were enslaved in the Holy Land."

"He told me about that time." She shook her head. "I still cannot believe that you both—"

"We both learned to survive," he said, cutting off whatever sympathy she might have offered. "Stay with Rhys while I gather a few men to transfer him. With the other warriors gone, we've extra pallets in the rooms above the stable." He stood. "There are guards at the door. You should be safe here for the short time I will be gone."

Rhiannon watched him go, leaving her alone with Rhys in the great hall. The flames in the fireplace licked greedily at the logs. A crackle and hiss pressed against the silence. Why had Orrin told her such a private detail about Camden's life? The information seemed a little too convenient. What did Orrin have to gain from her knowing about Camden's nightmares? She released an exasperated sigh. Nothing.

Before she could consider other possibilities, the door to the great hall creaked open. Rhiannon could feel a presence, but could not see who was there. "Orrin?" she asked.

Silence.

Camden? She shot to her feet, her heart thundering in her chest. Had he returned so soon?

A dark shadow fell across the entrance to the great hall. "Not Orrin, my dear."

She could feel the blood drain from her face as she beheld Bishop Berwick in the doorway. "How did you get past the guards?"

"Holy men can do many things that regular mortals cannot." As he came into the light, she could see he was dressed in the dark brown robes of a monk.

That voice. She could not stop the chill that raced down her spine as recognition flared. That voice had ordered her to be burned alive. "You are no holy man."

"Your opinion of me matters not." His face contorted with disgust, then quickly shifted to benign superiority. "I am on a mission for the Church and I will not be distracted from my purpose."

"It would be impossible for you to slip past the guards at the gate, the wall breach, or even the door to the keep without help. Who helped you?"

He ignored her. "I've heard rumors of witchcraft being performed here this day." He continued to stride forward, until he stood an arm's length from her. "The Church will have none of it. Such behaviors are punishable by death."

"There has been no witchcraft practiced today or any other day."

He held out his hand with its gold insignia ring for her to kiss. When she remained where she stood, irritation clouded his face.

"What do you want?" Where was Orrin? Where was anyone?

"I've come for the girl and the Stone. My sources assure me Lady Violet did indeed attempt witchcraft to try to bring a man back from the dead." His gaze dropped to the pallet on which Rhys lay.

Frustration and rage rose within Rhiannon, but she fought desperately to control her temper. "I will never hand the child over to you for punishment or anything else."

"No one is here to save you this time." He moved past her toward the stairs. Determination gleamed in his eyes.

"I don't need anyone to save me or Lady Violet." Lightning swift, she grasped an iron skillet from the cooking bench near the hearth. She lunged for him and swung the pan with all her might. It hit the side of his head with a resounding thump. The man's eyes flared. He swayed on his feet, then fell to the ground.

"Stay away from Violet," Rhiannon breathed as the man crumpled at her feet. A trickle of blood flowed from his forehead down across his face. The door of the great hall flew open, hitting the wall opposite with a thud, and Orrin charged into the room with a group of warriors. "Mistress Rhiannon?"

"It's all right. I took care of him."

Orrin raced forward. "How did he slip past the guards?"

Now that the danger had passed, Rhiannon set the pan down on the bench as a fatigue overwhelmed her. She staggered slightly as her gaze moved to the stairs, where Violet stood with her small bow and an arrow.

"I came to protect you, but you knocked him out before I could shoot," Violet said, moving to Rhiannon's side.

Rhiannon grasped the child to her in an emotion-filled embrace. "What a brave little girl you are."

Violet wiggled away. Setting her bow against the wall, she headed for the bishop.

"Lady Violet, what are you doing?" Rhiannon asked, suddenly terrified. She reached out, trying to stop the girl.

Violet stepped around Rhiannon's grasp, moving to kneel beside the holy man.

The bishop's eyes flickered open and his gaze clung to Violet. "There you are," he said in a silky tone.

"If you promise not to attack this castle again, I will heal you."

Violet frowned at the man as she held her hand out to Rhiannon. "May I have the Stone, please?"

Rhiannon bolted to her side. "Lady Violet, no!" She grabbed the little girl's hand and partially carried, partially dragged her up the stairs. The bishop only had hearsay to accuse Violet of witchcraft. He needed no direct proof. "Orrin, get rid of that man before he does something horrible to us all."

"Aye, milady."

She could hear Orrin and the other warriors escorting the bishop out from the chamber as she raced up the stairs with Violet in her arms.

"You can't harm me," the bishop's voice floated up the stairs.

"I would damn my immortal soul for a chance to do so," Orrin ground out.

"Do it, and you'll regret it. If word of my demise gets to the Church council, you'll be a man with a bounty on his head."

"You ever come back here again and I *will* kill you," she heard Orrin say before the rest of the conversation faded away.

The bishop wasn't going to win. She wouldn't let him

win, spies or no spies. The bishop might be a powerful man, but nothing he could do to any of them would be as horrific as what he'd already put all of them through.

Could it?

Later that evening, Bishop Berwick stood in the doorway of his mother's bedchamber and rubbed the egg-sized lump at his temple. Damn the Ruthven girl. No one assaulted his person and lived.

He pushed his anger aside as his focus shifted to the woman lying in the bed. The yellow candlelight in the room cast an eerie glow across his mother's sunken features. Death would claim her if something drastic didn't happen soon.

When prayer had failed him, he'd turned to other things—terrible things, he knew. But what else was a devoted son to do? He'd tried everything he could think of to get that Stone away from the Lockharts.

"How is she?" he asked the young maid at his mother's bedside.

"I had to give her juice of the poppy. It was the only thing that quieted her. Should I try to wake her? Would you like to sit with her for a while?"

"Nay," he said with more force than he had intended. In an effort to block the scent of her decaying flesh, he brought a square of linen up to cover his nose and mouth. "I've paid you handsomely to see to her needs." He turned away, not wanting to stay in the presence of death any longer than necessary.

What would it take to get that healing Stone away from the Lockharts? He had truly despaired at ever possessing that Stone until he'd seen his spy lying on the floor in the great hall. Perhaps divine intervention would serve him yet. The bishop allowed himself an indulgent smile.

The scoundrel may have survived stabbing and drowning,

but Rys's illness appeared to be the same that wracked his own mother's soul. Perhaps this was God's ultimate revenge. Perhaps the sickness would spread to Lockhart Castle. And then they would have no choice but to bring the Stone out of hiding.

With the Stone, he could cure his mother. Just like a goldsmith needed fire to separate the base metal from the pure gold, he needed that Stone to help him purify the souls of his flock. A man who could do that would surely impress the Church council. A man of miracles would be the only choice for the next Archbishop of Glasgow.

There was one more thing he could do to sway Camden Lockhart to do his bidding. He hurried to the elaborate desk in his chambers and pulled out a clean sheet of linen.

The Church council had not arrived at his earlier summons. This time they would come. They would want to know about the act of witchcraft performed by Lady Violet Lockhart. The girl was only a child. His hand paused above the paper, before writing the word *witchcraft,* but his thoughts drifted back to his mother and he knew what he had to do. Through means fair or foul, he would see that the Charm Stone came to him.

After writing his message, he sealed it with a waxed impression of his insignia ring. His clerk would see to its delivery.

Within a matter of days, all hell would break loose over the Lockhart clan. The thought brought a smile of utter satisfaction to the bishop's lips.

Chapter Nineteen

hree days later, the breach in the wall had been fixed. The new stones appeared almost pink in an otherwise sea of gray. Rhiannon stared out the bedchamber window at the wall, then beyond, toward the south.

A small sigh escaped her. She was grateful the repairs to the wall were complete. But what she really wanted was to see a familiar head of dark hair ride over that rise, safe and whole. She could want no greater gift this day, the day of her birth, than to have Camden return. *For Violet's sake,* she amended in her thoughts.

Violet seemed to grow in confidence every day. But a wedge had come between them since Rhiannon refused to allow her to heal the bishop after she'd struck him on the head. Rhiannon looked over at where Violet was quietly playing, and tried to hold in a sigh of sadness.

"Can I go visit the horses?" the girl asked. "Orrin said he'd show me the new foal that was born last week."

"Do you want some company?" Rhiannon offered, even though she feared the girl's answer.

Violet stood and without meeting Rhiannon's eyes, headed for the door. "Orrin will protect me." A moment later she was gone.

A sharp pang knifed through her. Violet was pulling away. Each day she grew more distant. Soon, the child would have no need of her at all. Perhaps it was time for her to leave.

And go where? She had no home, no family she wanted to return to. Mother Agnes had made it clear she was not suited for a life in the abbey. Rhiannon went to her bed-chamber and took in the opulent furnishings. Never again would she experience any of the finery that had been hers, however temporarily. She sat on the bed and pulled out the Charm Stone from the small pocket inside her gown.

She'd been afraid to return the Stone to its hiding place in the chapel for fear Violet would retrieve it again. Until Camden returned, she had decided it was best to keep its location unknown to everyone, Violet included.

Despite the bishop's injury and the warning he'd been given never to return, she was uneasy knowing he had taken a house on the outskirts of the nearby village. He wouldn't give up his quest to obtain the Stone. He desired its power too much. But what would he do next to get it?

The scents of hay and horse filled the air as Rhiannon opened the heavy wooden door to the stable. She wanted to check on Rhys to see if the Stone had indeed performed a miracle.

"Orrin," she called when she stepped inside. Late morning sun permeated the stable's usual gloom, painting the world around her in a sea of gold.

"If ye be wantin' Master Orrin, he ain't here," called a lean and wiry stable boy from the stall on her right. He poked his head around the wood, eyeing her with curiosity.

"Do you know where Rhys is?"

The boy gave her a crooked smile as he stepped all the way out of the stall. "He be out in the lists with Master Orrin."

"In the lists?"

"Come, I'll show ye." He leaned a long-handled scoop against the wall. He strode toward her. "That Rhys lay dyin', then he just opened his eyes, sat up, and wanted to go a sparrin'."

"He's well then?" Rhiannon asked, overcome with

emotion that the Stone had worked after all. Tears misted her eyes as she fell into step beside the boy. He led her through the stables to the back door that exited into the lists.

"He seems better than ever." At the open doorway he stopped and pointed toward two men in the center of the field. They faced each other, swords extended, watching, waiting for the other to make the first move.

The sharp clang of steel shattered the silence as Rhys attacked, his advance vigorous. Orrin easily avoided the blade, blocked it with his own. Satisfaction rode Orrin's features as he pressed his own attack. "Damn good to see you well, Rhys."

Rhys brought his sword down, sliding to the hilt. "If I were any better, I'd best you this day."

Orrin easily disengaged. "You wish."

"It is good to see that you have not all been at your leisure while I've been off battling for king and country," Camden called from the far side of the lists.

Rhiannon's heart jumped as she recognized his voice. He and his men walked their horses into the lists.

"Camden," she whispered. His hair was pulled back away from his face, and his chin sported several days' beard growth. His eyes, so normally clear and piercing, were heavily smudged with dark shadows of weariness.

His eyes found hers. Warmth flared. He handed the reins of his horse to a stable boy and proceeded toward her.

She raised a hand to smooth the escaping tendrils of her hair away from her face. Her cheeks flushed when she remembered the last time her hair had been in wild disarray with him. Heat coiled through her belly and between her thighs like silken ribbons, pulling her toward him.

"Did you fare well in battle?" she asked when he stood but a handsbreadth away, close enough to touch if she only reached for him. But did she dare be so bold?

"I've returned with all the men. The English have fled."

Relief flooded her at the discovery that he'd been fighting the English and not her family. She reached for his sleeve only to have him turn away. "The castle wall is repaired. I hope that means things were uneventful during my absence."

She pulled her hand back and tucked it in the folds of her gown. Her gaze connected with Orrin's. Surely he would report on what had happened while Camden was away, yet he remained strangely silent.

The humor in Camden's face faded. "Will no one tell me the news?"

"Bishop Berwick came to call," Orrin said.

"Lady Violet used the Stone to heal Rhys," Rhiannon said at the same time. She held her tongue, hoping Orrin would proceed. He did. In a rush, he told Camden what had happened.

Camden stood utterly motionless. Any warmth that she might have imagined in his eyes faded. The morning air fairly crackled with tension.

Once, his gaze shifted to Rhys as the story unfolded, before it returned to hers. He stared, hard. Only his clenched jaw betrayed the control it took to keep his anger in check. But she could see it, feel it, as though their time apart had heightened her awareness of him.

When Orrin told him about the Stone, his expression became grim, unreadable. "Where is the Stone?" he asked, his voice rough.

She dug the Stone out of her pocket and held the amulet out to him.

"You had the Stone with you?"

"Only to keep it safe while you were gone."

"By allowing Lady Violet to use the Stone you put her in grave danger. Everyone at the castle saw Rhys's healing." Camden's face darkened. "I trusted you with my niece, with," he hesitated before adding, "everything." He stared down at the Stone in his hand.

Pain twisted in Rhiannon's chest. Every decision she'd made while he was gone had been to protect Violet. She'd done everything she could think of to help the little girl. So why was he so angry at her? She straightened her back as a sudden realization struck her. "Are you upset with me or are you upset because you weren't here to protect Lady Violet yourself?"

He flinched at her words, and she knew she'd hit upon the truth.

She darted a glance at Orrin. He dropped his gaze, suddenly intent on studying his boots. "When you and Orrin were in the Holy Land the two of you only had each other, I realize that. But your life is different now." She waved a hand at the crowd who had gathered in the lists. "Look around you, at the men and women of this castle who would sacrifice anything to help you battle the bishop and win."

He scowled at her. "I fight my battles alone."

"Then perhaps it's time for you to change." She lifted her chin. "I know a thing or two about trying to change. It's hard, especially when people around you think that it's impossible."

His scowl deepened. "That's unfair."

She shook her head. "No, you're being unfair to me and to everyone else in this castle who cares about you."

A flicker of surprise crossed his face. "You care about me?"

If she were honest she would admit her emotions had progressed far beyond caring and into love. She drew a breath to tell him when a prickle of awareness drew her gaze from him to all the castle's residents who hung upon their words. Heat filled her cheeks and the words died on her tongue. "Excuse me, milord." She turned and headed back toward the keep.

Several moments later Rhiannon shut the door of her bedchamber behind her. She leaned against the wood, trying to steady herself. Her breath came in short, sharp bursts not because she'd run through the castle to get to the chamber, but because of the magnitude of what she'd almost revealed.

Her physical response to his presence had been immediate. She'd felt her breasts swell and the heat that had moved through her body in mindless, melting waves. She had wanted to touch him, to greet his return home in a very different sort of way.

She inhaled sharply and clenched her fists at her sides. She wanted to touch him still, even though he'd greeted her with only bitterness and anger.

"Rhiannon."

A shock of desire moved through her.

"Open the door." His voice sounded thick.

"I can't," she whispered, praying her voice wouldn't betray her emotions.

"You can't or you won't?"

Silence followed.

He'd gone. Rhiannon leaned back against the door, grateful that he'd gone, and disappointed all the same.

A moment later he stood in the door that separated her room from Violet's. She could see the tension in his body as he slowly moved toward her.

"Camden."

"We need to finish what we started below in the lists."

Chapter Twenty

Rhiannon straightened away from the door. Remorse filled him at the pain in her eyes. He'd hurt her yet again. If anyone was to blame for Violet's use of the Stone, it was he. He'd felt a presence behind him in the chapel the other day. He should have followed his instincts and hidden the Stone someplace else.

And yet he had·turned his anger against Rhiannon. He knew she had acted in Violet's best interest, allowing the girl to use the Stone one time, then keeping it from her so that she did not endanger herself. It was what he would have done.

Not only had she been right in her actions with Violet, she had put into words something he had been avoiding for three years now. He was no longer a prisoner in the Holy Land. He no longer had to fight his battles alone. Rhiannon had proven her own honesty over and over again. It was time to give a little of that back. He stopped a handsbreath from her.

High color glowed on her cheeks, and golden hair spilled over her shoulders. Her blue dress concealed her body, but he needed no image to recall the soft and supple curves beneath her garments.

He had tried not to think of her over the past four days, and for the most part he had been successful. Battle tended to take one's focus, all of it. Only when he closed his eyes as the battle died during the night did his willpower fail him. If he had hoped to exorcise her from his blood upon his return, or sought to use the days away to regain his perspective, there, too, he had failed miserably.

He was drowning in the scent of her hair, the sight of her, and if she did not stop looking at him that way, he might be tempted to recall even more.

Camden tensed, his whole body fighting his desire to take her in his arms. "I don't want to be alone anymore."

Her amber eyes flared. "You aren't alone."

"I feel . . . uncertain."

"About?"

"Everything around me is changing."

She cast her eyes downward. "That's not always a bad thing."

"Nay. But it is unsettling. I've never felt like this before. I don't like feeling one moment that I can fly, and the next moment like I want to smash something."

Rhiannon looked up. Confusion lingered in her gaze. "That sounds dreadful."

"It is, but it's not." He groaned. "I'm not good with words. Let me show you what I mean."

A flicker of apprehension crossed her face. "How?"

He brought his fingers up to the delicate curve of her cheek. "Give me from now until dawn to show you."

She smiled tentatively. "Until dawn."

Camden had asked her for one hour to prepare for their evening together. Rhiannon paced the length of her bedchamber, waiting for Camden to come.

She paused at the window to look out at the drifts of snow that dotted the land and rested her head against the cool glass. She waited with her head pressed against the chilled glass for what seemed like hours before a soft knock came on the door. Rhiannon straightened.

The maid, Rosy, peeked her head inside the chamber.

"The master asked me to help ye dress. In this." She entered the room carrying a large box that she set on the bed. "Go ahead, open it."

Rhiannon found herself drawn to the box until she stood beside it. Possessed by a force outside herself, she smoothed her fingers over the edge of the large box. With a sudden rush of joy, she lifted the lid to reveal several yards of frothy fabric in the color of the sky on a clear spring morning.

Carefully, she lifted the edges of the cloth and the fabric took the form of a dress. The fitted bodice came to a V in the front, and a much lower V in the back that flared out from there to flow to the ground in waves of ruffles and lace. Tiny seed pearls were sewn into groupings of threes, dotting the entire dress. The iridescent decorations warmed beneath her touch. It was the most beautiful gown she had ever seen.

"He wants me to wear this?"

The maid nodded. "He had it made for ye after the mishap with Lady Lockhart's gown. Let's put it on. The entire staff is waitin' belowstairs to see ye in yer gown."

"You all want to see me?" she asked, stunned. "Why? Why would your opinion of me shift at all? I have not changed."

"Nay." The maid dropped her gaze to the floor. "But ye showed all of us that ye would willingly put others' safety above yer own. Ye saved Lord Lockhart from an attacker. Ye helped Charlotte survive her childbirth. Ye protected Lady Violet when we were attacked and ye were taken in return. Ye are appreciated." Rosy removed the dress from the box, then draped it across the bed, revealing its full beauty and elegance. "Let me help ye dress."

Rhiannon stared at the dress as her mind reeled from the maid's forthright comments. She would have to agree that the household's behavior toward her had shifted. There were subtle signs: a cautious smile, an offered bowl of pottage at the midday meal, a fresh basin of water near the bed upon awaking, a warm fire in the hearth each night.

At first she'd let those things pass as necessities that Camden had insisted upon. But the kindness had continued while he'd been gone. An extra warm blanket on her bed one night, the lavender soap that had appeared by her washbasin, and most notable of all, no one hissed at her or spat on her as she passed them in the halls. Had they truly started to accept her? Despite who she was?

And if so, what did it all mean for her future? A warm glow flowed through her. "Let's get this dress on. Shall we?" She would find no answers to her questions standing in this room.

In no time at all with Rosy's help, the silken fabric draped across her breasts, her hips, her thighs, fitting her to perfection. The fabric was foreign to her. She had never seen its equal. Had Camden brought it back with him from the Holy Land like so many of the furnishings of his castle?

"Ye look enchantin', milady," Rosy said as she stepped back to admire Rhiannon in the gown.

"I feel enchanted."

"I'll see ye belowstairs with the others." Rosy bobbed a curtsy, then left the chamber.

Rhiannon let her fingers glide through the sea of light blue silk and lace, and a smile came to her lips. The dress wrapped her in a cocoon of comfort and confidence until a knock sounded on the door and Camden entered.

He took a step into the chamber, then stopped. The intensity of his gaze made her uneasy, causing a tight stricture in her chest. "You look magnificent," he said, his voice thick. A heartbeat later, he continued toward her, taking her hands in his.

"Are you ready?"

He took her arm and guided her from the chamber

down the stairs. At the bottom of the stairs, the entire staff crowded into the great hall to watch them. Murmurs of excitement floated about the hall.

At the bottom of the stairs, Mistress Faulkner awaited them. She held out a fur cloak to Camden, who took it and placed the heavy warmth about Rhiannon's shoulders before adding a second cloak around his own. "One last thing," he said, accepting a silken band from Mistress Faulkner. "I must place this over your eyes."

"A blindfold?" She tensed at the memory of the last time her vision had been taken from her.

He must have seen the tension in her body because he added, "A temporary measure." His blue eyes glinted with mischief. At her sharp nod, he tied the band around her eyes. "Now we proceed."

Holding her tight, he led her out the front door of the keep and onto the castle grounds. Evening air brushed against her cheeks, and she nestled into the heavy cloak about her shoulders. It was long enough to brush against her legs, and she was grateful for the extra warmth. He led her along for a spell before stopping and gently removing the blindfold.

It took a moment for her eyes to adjust to the fading light of day, and when they did, she felt the breath leave her lungs. She froze, taking in the scene. After that first stunning impact, she felt a rush of overwhelming rightness. As if everything in her life had led her to this moment.

She moved slowly into the scene. A hundred candles glittered in the darkening evening air, on the ground and higher up, on a semicircular stone wall at the edge of the castle's fish pond. A thick sheet of ice covered the pond that glistened and sparkled beneath the glow of the flames.

It was as she remembered from the night so long ago with her mother. The night he'd asked her to share her memories with him. "You did this for me?"

The sheer beauty of the moment robbed her of speech. She reached out to one of the clusters of candles near her, her hand hovering over the soft golden light. The flame was warm beneath her palm, as warm as the look in Camden's blue eyes.

"Do you like it?"

"It's beautiful." Thickness tightened her throat.

"Aye, 'tis beautiful," he said, not looking at the scene before them but at her face. He took a step closer, drawing her body against his. They were isolated in a cocoon of intimacy, out of view from the rest of the castle. "Will you glide with me?"

She nodded, not trusting her voice. He drew her over to a bench nearby and slipped pattens on her feet, then slipped into his own. He drew her up against his body, shifting his cloak so that her body pressed against his before he wrapped his cloak about them both. Then, slowly, carefully, he guided her about the ice.

The night air brushed against her cheeks as they glided from one end of the ice to the other, their bodies moving as one. She could feel her breasts swell, her pulse accelerate at his nearness. The heat of his body wrapped around her in a cocoon of warmth and arousal.

His lips caressed her temple, brushed the sensitive place just behind her ear. She drew a sharp breath. "Why did you do this?" she asked, needing to understand his motives before she couldn't think anymore, before his nearness clouded her brain.

"I want to remind you of a happier time."

He moved to kiss her neck. She pulled back despite the fact her knees felt weak and rubbery beneath her. "I need to know something."

"What?"

"You know who I am. That used to bother you. Does it still?"

The glow of the candlelight illuminated only one side of his face, leaving the other in darkness. Mysterious. She'd seen his ruthless side when she'd first arrived at the castle. She'd also seen his gentler side, more times than she cared to admit. But who was this man, truly?

"I used to think I knew who you were, and I was swept away by you anyway." He paused. "Does that make sense?"

"Aye," she breathed. Of all the things he had said tonight, that made the most sense, yet unsettled her at the same time. It was what she'd always wanted. Someone to look past her name, and into her heart and mind. To look at the person she was meant to be.

He gave her a cautious smile. "Will you let me find out all there is to know about you?"

Could she willingly make herself any more vulnerable to this man? She lowered her gaze to the candles burning brightly against the black of night. The price of such a deed would be her very soul. But her reward could also be lifelong happiness. Was it worth the risk?

She brought her gaze back to his. She held out her hands. "Skate with me."

He smiled as he grasped her fingers with his own. An odd air of protectiveness charged Camden's movements as he gently guided her into the center of the ice. He twirled her around, slowly, allowing them both to glide across the slippery surface.

The breeze caressed her suddenly heated cheeks. Warmth stirred within her as her gaze met his in the candlelight. He exuded confidence, intelligence, and sexuality. It was his sexuality that reached out to her now as she became acutely aware of the strength of his hands holding hers with such exquisite care, the way his thighs tensed then relaxed against the soft fabric of his tartan as he used his strength to keep them spinning in a breathless circle.

Then as if he, too, had suddenly become aware of her exploration, their movements ceased. The world slowed back into stillness. Desire flared in the depths of his eyes.

She couldn't look away. She couldn't breathe.

"Rhiannon." The word was a caress.

She trembled as an echo of his desire rippled through her.

"I want to touch you."

Her heart was pounding so hard, she was certain he could hear it.

He brushed her throat with the back of his fingers, and a primal shudder moved through her. Her nipples hardened again, pushing against the sheer linen of her chemise.

He pulled her to him. "Tell me you want this." His voice was raw as he held his desire in check. She could see the effort his restraint was costing him in the pulse that thrummed in his jaw, the way the muscles of his chest bunched beneath the thin fabric of his shirt.

"I cannot resist you." She could smell him, that familiar scent of musk, of mint, of maleness. He slipped his hand beneath her cloak. He slid his hands up her arms, across her shoulders, then back down, taking the bodice of her gown and her chemise along with them. The dress fell to her waist, exposing her breasts.

His lips lowered to her breast, and his mouth closed on her nipple. Heat flashed through her, and the muscles of her stomach clenched.

His hands grasped her breast, caressing her gently. He nipped at the tender peak, gently rolling her sensitive flesh between his teeth.

Her spine arched, and she cried out. She was intensely conscious of him pulling her dress and undergarments down to her ankles. He followed with his hands the path the fabric had taken down the length of her body, leaving her for a moment to toss his cloak over the ice. He fell to his knees atop the thick fur of his cloak, exploring her bare buttocks in his palms as he buried his face in the tight curls surrounding her womanhood. His tongue slipped inside.

Her fingers reached out, blindly digging into his hair as he continued his assault. She arched backwards, the sensations almost too intense to bear.

The air swirled around her, but she hardly noticed, so warmed was she by heat—the warmth of his hands caressing her as he stroked the molten heat inside her. She could hear the harsh sounds of her own breathing echo in the night air.

They were exposed—to the night, to the elements, to each other.

His teeth closed gently on the small nub of her, nibbled, then pulled, stroking her, teasing her, until she felt as though she would incinerate right there in his arms. She peaked, erupted, as sensation after sensation rode through her, carried her.

In the next moment, he pulled her down until she was nestled in the warmth of his fur cloak. He moved over her, parted her thighs, and plunged deep inside.

Again sensation after sensation rippled through her with an intensity that consumed. And she wanted nothing more than to merge into one with him.

He thrust shallowly, then deeply, not letting her get used to the rhythm.

She nestled against the furs, her breath coming in halting gasps.

"Do you feel me?" He drew out and plunged deep, thick, hot.

She felt every inch of him, but she wanted more. She lunged forward, trying to take more of him.

He withdrew until he was barely inside her. "Is it good?"

She strained to keep him with her, inside her. "I want all of you."

He plunged deep into her with a force as primal as the night that enveloped them. She arched up from the ground and gave a low cry of satisfaction. She met each thrust with her own.

He cupped her buttocks in his palms and lifted her deeper into each thrust. "Rhiannon . . . give me—" He spoke through gritted teeth, his nostrils flaring with each harsh breath. "I want more." He moved desperately, his hips thrusting.

Her head thrashed back and forth at the erotic caress of his words, his texture inside her, his passion. Frantic cries filled the air as tension coiled tighter and tighter with each stroke of his body. Sensation streaked through her, building, spiraling. Her senses sharpened, sending shards of sensations: darkness, light, earth, snow, musk, Camden.

He thrust again, and she climaxed, the tension exploding with a force that sent a fiery release through her. An instant later she could feel him spasm again and again within her, spilling his seed into her body.

He collapsed on top of her, his breathing harsh and strained. They lay there in silence for several moments.

The stars seemed to twinkle with all the satisfaction that rode through her body. And even though Rhiannon had never felt happier, fear niggled at the edges of her awareness. No matter how much she had wanted to possess Camden tonight, she knew in her heart it was a mistake. She should never have let this happen. All her defenses were down, and she lay exposed and vulnerable before him. No matter how much he professed to wanting to know the real her, in the end he would hurt her. She expected it. He wouldn't mean to, but it would happen.

It always happened.

But for now, in the aftermath of their lovemaking and shielded by his arms, she would allow the fantasy to continue. Because, for the first time in her life, instead of feeling lonely, confused, and downtrodden, she felt very much alive.

Chapter Twenty-one

Camden pulled the furs snug around their bodies as he lay still, his breathing slow and steady. Satisfaction like he'd never known before drugged his limbs. He closed his eyes. Only for a moment would he sleep. Then he'd carry Rhiannon inside and plant her firmly and forever in his bed. The fur of his cloak cushioned his skin. Rhiannon's body, nestled against his side, warmed his spirit. Sleep beckoned with an irresistible allure. . . .

The night sky surrounded him in a veil of black—trapping him, condemning him as surely as the holy man had by tossing him in the dungeon.

He dug his fingers into the thick clay walls. He looked for a purchase to climb his way out. Perhaps when he got to the top he could find a way to unfasten the wooden door. He had to escape the nightmare and make his way back home. He missed his family. He missed everything about Scotland, a place so different from where he found himself now.

And Orrin, his one last connection to his homeland. . . . Camden had to protect Orrin. The holy man had already tried to poison Orrin's mind and make him do things that could cost him his mortal soul.

Camden gazed into the preternatural nothingness, praying for a glimpse of a ledge, a rock, anything that might help get him out of this pit of hell. His eyes strained to pierce the darkness.

The darkness pressed in on his lungs. Made it difficult to breathe. It was like being in a coffin. He'd blocked thoughts of death since he'd been stolen from his homeland's shores. He'd been forced to fight the bloodiest of battles in the holy man's crusade.

He'd killed countless men, both Christian and Islamic, but he'd never been afraid until this one isolating moment.

He clawed at the earth on all sides of the pit, finding only a smooth, slick surface. He would find a way. He would get free if he had to dig through the wall; eventually he'd escape.

Like David going forth to fight Goliath, he would face great odds. He scratched at the dirt, coming away with handful after handful. He would get out. He would protect Orrin. He would return home to keep those he loved safe.

He growled into the darkness. Digging. Digging. The footholds he created never seemed to take him higher, until finally he could see the trapdoor and the slightest glimmer of light.

He pressed into the light, digging faster. His body ached, his lungs burned. It didn't matter. Only freedom mattered now.

He thrust the trapdoor aside and broke through into the light of day, crawling out, gasping for clean air to fill his lungs. Blinded by the sudden brightness, he squinted as he collapsed back against the cool, soft earth. Something soft cradled his head, something warm that smelled of lavender. He craned his neck to look behind him, only to gaze at Rhiannon's face, her features etched with pain, with terror.

She was dead.

He'd failed to protect her from the talons of death.

The talons of death. . . .

"No!" Camden sat bolt upright. Darkness surrounded him. He froze. Was he back inside the dungeon? He'd escaped, long ago. His heart thrummed in his chest.

Where was he? The scene he'd arranged for Rhiannon gradually took shape. The tallow candles had burned low, their flames sputtering in the remnants of the suet, and snow flurries had left a light dusting across the furs that cocooned them in warmth.

Rhiannon stirred at his side. "What's wrong, Camden? What is it? A nightmare?"

He scooped her into his arms. "I am well."

"Are you truly?"

"I am merely wondering," he said, smiling down at her, "if I should try to further my attempts at seduction."

She arched a brow. "You've been very thorough already."

He pressed a kiss to her forehead, relieved that he'd only had a nightmare. He nestled against her hair, drawing in the scent that was so uniquely her own. Death would not claim her, not yet. He would do everything in his power to see that she lived to a ripe old age.

As the beat of his heart normalized, he gently lifted her in his arms, then walked to a bench nestled among the hay and candles. He wrapped a fur cloak about her shoulders, shielding her from the cold. "Sit here for a moment."

Wisps of their warm breath curled in the air. Silence surrounded them. He dressed quickly, then returned to her side with her clothing and slowly dressed her. And despite his efforts to take comfort in the flesh-and-blood woman who breathed beneath his fingertips, he continued to see her pain-filled visage in his mind.

How could he protect her from death? How could he protect anyone?

The Charm Stone.

It could keep Rhiannon and all of his people safe from illness. He grasped on to the thought like a lifeline. He would have to trust that the Stone could help him banish the image of Rhiannon's death from his nightmares.

But would it keep her safe from the truth about what he had done to her brothers? And what he might have done to her had his assassin succeeded? Camden stumbled in placing her gown over her head, enveloping Rhiannon in a sea of fabric. She laughed and tried to find her way out while he simply watched. Could she discover the truth about the assassin he'd hired? Should he just tell her? Would she hate him less if he did?

Her head poked out from under all the fabric. "Some help you are," she teased, and the moment to tell her the truth passed.

He turned away and picked up her shoes, sliding them onto her delicate feet. When he had finished dressing her, he fastened her cloak about her shoulders. "Thank you," he said.

"For what?" she asked, startled.

"For the best memory of my life." He smiled at her crookedly. His body throbbed to life once more at the thought of the passion they had shared. He could never get enough of her. "I intend to take you inside and further my seduction."

She stared at him, stunned. Good. He liked having her a little off-balance. With a chuckle of satisfaction, he lifted her into his arms once more and carried her back to the keep. A soft kick opened the bedchamber door.

Orrin stood just inside the doorway.

"Orrin." Camden set Rhiannon on her feet.

Orrin's troubled gaze shifted between Camden and Rhiannon. "I waited for your return. I did not wish to interrupt you."

"What's wrong?" Camden frowned.

"The gatekeeper and the two warriors who were first with Rhys when he arrived have both fallen ill. What could it mean?"

Camden's frown increased. "I had intended to speak with Rhys further." He allowed his words to trail off. He had meant to talk to the man the moment he'd arrived home, but he'd been distracted by Rhiannon.

"Go to Rhys now while I attend to the men who have fallen ill," Rhiannon said, removing her cloak to set it on the edge of the bed. "I may be able to make them more comfortable until you or Lady Violet can heal them with the Charm Stone."

Camden strode to his wardrobe. He opened the door and withdrew a tall black boot. He turned the boot over and placed his hand at the opening. The Charm Stone tumbled into his hand. "Take this." He held the Stone out to Orrin. "Go wake Lady Violet and bring her, along with the Stone, to Rhiannon and the men."

Orrin accepted the precious amulet. He paused, staring at the Stone. Something that looked like indecision crossed his face before he clamped his fingers shut and hurried from the chamber.

"This is not how I wanted the night to end," Camden said, wrapping her in his arms once more.

She melted into his embrace. "The night is young still." Rhiannon smiled as she pulled out of his arms and with a sigh of satisfaction left the room.

His mind shifting from Rhiannon to the troubles Rhys had caused him and his people, Camden strode down the hallway and the stairs to the great hall, where Orrin reported he'd last seen the man.

Rhys sat near the hearth, alone. He carefully sipped from a mug of steaming liquid. At Camden's arrival, he set the mug down on the long table before him and dropped his gaze to the wooden surface, unwilling to meet Camden's questioning gaze. "Lord Lockhart, I beg forgiveness."

"Have you told us all of it? Everything you did to assist the bishop?"

Rhys nodded, his expression a mixture of remorse and pain.

Regardless, Camden could not stop the anger that surged through him. This man had spied for Bishop Berwick, breached his outer defenses at the castle, and helped the assassin he'd hired to kidnap Rhiannon. "Why would you betray your own people?"

The man flinched at Camden's tone. "At first I thought 'twas ye who'd betrayed us all."

"How?" Camden asked, startled by the man's accusation.

"The Ruthven girl," he explained. "Ye protected her. It angered me at first until I saw past my own rage." He shook his head slowly, a look of awe on his face. "She would've allowed herself tae be burned tae death rather than betray either ye or Lady Violet."

Camden's anger dissipated. "Then why, Rhys? Was it revenge that drove your actions?" As he said the words, Camden's heart stumbled. He could ask himself the same question and be found guilty.

"Revenge wasn't the reason. The bishop threatened my son's life."

Camden tamped down his anger at the thought that any holy man could use a child in his schemes. "The man has proven he'll do anything to get what he wants."

"Even try tae murder me," Rhys said.

"You survived."

"Only because of ye Lockharts and the Charm Stone. I'll be forever grateful."

"Then help us now by telling me who else was trying to kill us. You could not have brought a cannon to our walls on your own."

Rhys nodded. "Bishop Berwick financed the attack. He wanted us tae take both Rhiannon and Lady Violet, but we couldn't find the little girl."

Camden smiled grimly, knowing their failure was thanks to Rhiannon's quick thinking and skill with a bow.

"I don't think the man meant tae harm the wee one. He seemed desperate tae take her unharmed. He wants her for somethin'. For some skill she possesses."

"He wants her for her power over the Charm Stone." Camden pressed his lips together into a hard line. The man would never get either Violet or the Stone while he still lived.

"She's a miracle worker." Rhys pulled up the edge of

his linen shirt to reveal a pale thin line across the flesh at his side.

Camden inspected the man's side. Hardly a trace of his wounds remained. It was a miracle. "But why is he so desperate for Violet?" And suddenly it all made sense. "He cannot use the Stone without a Lockhart. And Violet's youth would allow him to manipulate her into doing all that he asked."

Rhys's eyes went wide. "A man of God who could do miracles would be seen as divine."

"Damn the man," Camden cursed, suddenly wondering if the Ruthvens had truly been responsible for Clara's and James's deaths. Or had he just assumed that they were based on the circumstances the bishop had laid before him?

He thought back to when he'd first arrived at Lee Castle and found James there. He'd been so filled with grief that he had just assumed that the Ruthvens had been the ones to betray James to the English. He'd found the Ruthvens' crest on the sword in James's body. He realized now the bishop could have easily stolen the sword and done the deed himself.

And Clara. Pain tightened Camden's chest at the thought that she had died alone, without her family to at least try to save her. Had he known, he would have moved Heaven and Earth to keep her from the noose. And again, he had just assumed the Ruthvens had betrayed her. But he'd had no proof. And without reasoning it through and thinking of all the other possibilities, Camden had acted.

What else was the bishop capable of doing to get the Charm Stone?

"I must go." Camden raced down the hallway to where Rhiannon and Violet would be attending the other ill men. A dark omen of doom followed him as he hurried through the shadowed half-light of the hallways. What horrors had he unleashed upon his people because of his own mistakes?

Outside the chamber where the sick men lay, Camden paused. He had no reason to suspect anything. And yet the sense of danger refused to go away.

He opened the door and stepped inside.

"No!" Rhiannon said sharply, bringing his steps to a halt. "Don't come any closer."

"What's wrong?" Camden asked, his gaze raking the three men stretched out on pallets near the hearth. His heart thundered in his chest. Had he been right to assume the worst?

"How is Rhys?" she asked, a hint of panic in her voice.

"He's almost as good as new." Camden took another step closer.

Rhiannon's gaze shot to his. "Stop!" Her face was pale, and her eyes glittered with fear. She reached over to the gatekeeper and gently lifted his bare arm. "They have all been complaining that their arms are sore and their thirst is great."

From the doorway, he stared at the red, puss-filled boil beneath the gatekeeper's arm. Talons of fear gripped him, chilling him to the core. The vision of Rhiannon's lifeless body in his dream passed before his mind's eye. He forced the image away. "Is that what I think it is?"

"I cannot be certain. I have never seen it before. But I heard tales from my mother." She moved over to one of the two warriors, and pulled the blanket up to reveal his inner thigh. A black boil rested there the size of a small rock.

"Heaven help us." Camden had heard stories as well, of large boils that appeared red at first, then black. The color of death. *The plague.*

"What can we do?"

He had never felt more helpless. "Who has come near these men?"

"There's no way to be certain. We are all at risk." Rhiannon slumped back on her heels. "Pray to God we are wrong."

A chill wracked him. "We will know one way or the other very soon. The plague kills quickly." His gaze scanned the small chamber. "Orrin and Lady Violet should have been here by now."

"It's a good thing they aren't." Rhiannon straightened. "Lady Violet must not enter this chamber. Perhaps she ought to be sent away for a time?"

He shook his head. "If we don't know who is at risk, we might be sending her off to her death. Or that might be exactly what the bishop hopes we would do so that he can snatch her easily without anyone to protect her. Nay, 'tis best she stays here, where we would know if something happens to her."

"Could she use the Charm Stone to treat water? I can give the men the charmed water in her stead."

He nodded as he backed out of the door. "I will go see if I can find her and Orrin." Just outside the door, he paused. "I don't want to leave you behind."

"I am here already." She gave him a grim smile. "I might as well stay and try to make these men more comfortable."

He nodded. "I shall return shortly with help." He shut the door, leaving Rhiannon behind in the clutches of a beast that might very well destroy them all.

Chapter Twenty-two

A message?" Bishop Berwick asked as he snatched the linen sheet from his clerk's hand. The man bowed once, twice, then a third time as he backed toward the doorway, then out of the chamber. The bishop smiled at the thought that he was perceived as powerful and dangerous. But his pride shifted in the next heartbeat to intrigue as he turned the message over to reveal the seal of the Church council.

Quickly he broke the wax and scanned the missive's contents. He read the letter twice, then tossed it into the hearth, allowing the flames to devour it. The Council would arrive on his doorstep in less than a day. Before they would agree to charge a child with witchcraft, they wanted proof.

He would give them proof all right. He smiled as he returned to his desk and pulled out another sheet of linen and wrote a dire warning to the Lockharts. Lady Violet would be charged with witchcraft. He would see it. Then, somehow, he would convince the Council to allow the girl to be reformed by him. He didn't want to hang a child, but he wouldn't let the Lockharts know that. Once complete, he set the missive at the top of his desk and turned to stare into the flames.

He withdrew a square of linen from the folds of his gown as a wave of heat swamped him. He stepped back, away from the hearth. The fire seemed more intense today than it had yesterday. He blotted the perspiration that dotted his brow.

But succeed he would once he finally got the girl and the Stone away from the Lockharts.

His thoughts shifted to his mother's disease-ravaged body in the room down the hall. "How can You torment my mother with illness?" he asked the powers above, then flinched at the sign of his own weakness. He knew God brought illness to his home to remind him of man's fragility.

Sickness brought pain and burning. And just as nothing purifies gold like fire, nothing cleanses the soul like illness.

He wiped more perspiration from his brow and released a bittersweet sigh. He suffered the same fate as his mother. The remedy had always been patience and fortitude. "I will not fail You," he whispered to his master. "I will possess that Stone, and with the little girl's help I will once again be in Your favor."

He moved away from the fire. It was time to set his plan in motion. "Billings!" The bishop shouted for his chamberlain, as he adjusted the collar of his gown to allow for more airflow.

A moment later, his pale-faced servant arrived in the doorway. "Your Grace."

"See that my horse is brought around to the front door. Ask the warriors I hired to meet me there, fully armed, in less than a quarter hour. You will remain here and prepare the chamber next to Mother's for our future guest."

"Aye, Your Grace." He bowed once more before leaving.

The bishop leaned back against the wall of his study and crossed his arms over his chest, suddenly feeling the need for support in order to remain upright.

He'd be seen as a man of miracles before the day was through.

The warrior who'd had black boils covering his body died less than a quarter of an hour later. In the moments after Camden had left Rhiannon, the man had experienced such agony that she was grateful when death finally took him. She closed the man's pain-filled eyes one last time before she sat back, numbed by the experience.

How had this monstrous plague ended up here? Would they all be destroyed? Or was it too much to hope that the Charm Stone could save them all? She had seen its healing powers with Rhys's wounds, Charlotte's baby, and her own burns.

Rhiannon closed her eyes, fighting back both terror and tears as she said a prayer that the Charm Stone would provide a cure for them soon—before anyone else died.

Orrin arrived at the cottage just as the bishop's horse was starting forward, leading a contingent of armed men.

"Stop!" he cried, and wheeled his horse in front of the procession of soldiers. "I have what you want, Bishop." Orrin might be betraying his best friend, but he hoped to avoid further bloodshed at Lee Castle.

The bishop stepped down from his horse, and Orrin dismounted as well. "You are dismissed for now," the bishop told his army.

"Come," the bishop commanded with a wave of his hand, moving back to the cottage. He seemed to weave a little as he walked. Orrin frowned. The man appeared drunk, yet his eyes remained clear and he did not smell of mead or ale.

Bishop Berwick led them to a dainty, feminine chamber. He appeared out of place in the room, in his stark green robes and mitered hat.

Once they were alone, the bishop turned to Orrin, his cheeks flushed with excitement. "Where is the Stone?"

Orrin hesitated. Could he do this?

He forced away the pain that tightened his chest. Giving the bishop the Stone was the only way to guarantee that Camden and those he loved stayed safe. His friend had lost too much in the past few weeks. Orrin would not stand by and watch the torture continue.

He held the Stone out to the bishop. "I'll have you swear on the insignia of your office that you will never harm Camden Lockhart or any of his relations ever again."

"You have my word as a guardian of the Church." The bishop snatched the Stone away. An odd light filled the bishop's eyes as he stared into the bloodred Stone at the center of the coin. "How does it work?"

Orrin explained the simple process of preparing the healing water with the Stone.

"That's it?" The bishop frowned. He withdrew a square of linen from his robes and dabbed at his brow. "I do not need the girl to perform the deed?"

"Nay," Orrin replied, knowing it was a lie. He might be willing to sacrifice the Charm Stone, but he would never hand that child over to the bishop. As soon as he returned to the castle, he would persuade Camden to send Lady Violet far away, out of the bishop's reach before the man realized he needed her. "And now that you possess the Stone, you will leave the child alone."

"I swear it," the bishop said distractedly.

Silence filled the chamber, and Orrin could practically hear the mental cogs turning in the bishop's head as he gazed upon the Stone, as though possessed by a force outside himself.

"I'll hold you to your promise," Orrin vowed as he left the chamber. He had to return to Lee Castle, and confess to Camden what he had done and why. Even though his motives were pure, the knot in his chest still felt a lot like betrayal.

The bishop wasted no time in using the Stone to prepare a cup of water for his mother. The sooner she got better, the sooner he could spread the word of a miracle.

Should he call all the servants to him? Miracles needed an audience for believability. The bishop tucked the Charm Stone inside the folds of his robes and hurried to his mother's chamber. At the door he hesitated. What if the Stone's magic did not work?

Perhaps it was best to administer this miracle without a crowd. His mother's maid would be with him. That would be enough for now. And when it did work, he could cure anyone of whatever ailed them. At the thought, he laughed, bringing the maid's attention to the door.

He was invincible.

Open boils now dotted his mother's face, arms, and body. The Stone had better work, and quickly.

He moved to the bedside. "Allow me to sit beside her," he asked the young maid at his mother's bedside.

The girl staggered away from the bedside and the bishop noted for the first time that she had grown pale and her eyes appeared glassy. Perhaps he had best prepare a mug of tonic for her after his mother was healed.

He teased the liquid between his mother's lips. Unsettling thoughts tugged at his mind. The use of the Stone was so simple. He dipped the amulet into the liquid three times, then swirled it to the right. No magic words, no incantations. *No witchcraft*. The unwelcome thought took root in his brain and refused to go away.

Lady Clara Lockhart had done nothing to deserve the end he had given her. Her daughter would have fallen into the same trap once the Church council arrived. Except he'd made a promise to Lockhart's man Orrin to retract his charge of witchcraft and let the young girl go free. He'd made that promise, but it was one he had no intention of keeping.

The bishop scowled down at his mother's withered body. How long ago was it now that Robert the Bruce had knighted Sir Simon Lockhart for his loyal service while he himself was granted nothing for his service? Fifty years, maybe more?

The slight had eaten at his soul for years as he'd had to endure his mother's censure. Only by advancing within the Church had she found him worthy of her attentions once again.

Yet for him the bitterness remained. Until he'd joined forces with Malcolm Ruthven. A man who had just as much hatred for the Lockharts. Together, they had nearly brought that family to its knees.

Only Lord Camden Lockhart and Lady Violet remained. The bishop clasped the Charm Stone in his palm, allowing the cool metal of the coin to warm in his hand. The Stone was his, along with its miraculous powers.

Warmth flowed from the bishop's hand up his arm and throughout the rest of his body. He swayed slightly in the chair beside his mother's bed. He gripped the bedding to steady himself, then tucked the Stone safely away in the folds of his robe. Revenge was a powerful elixir, draining him of strength at his moment of triumph.

Everything was in place for the Church council to finish what he had set in motion. Soon Lord Camden Lockhart and Lady Violet would pay for the slight Berwick had received at the hand of Camden's sire. Another wave of exhaustion suddenly overtook him. Beads of moisture formed at his temples and the room swayed before his eyes.

He grasped the doorjamb, steadying himself. He needed to rest. He took a hesitant step toward a chair when the room whirled, blurred before his eyes. He swayed, then hurtled into a dark abyss.

"Violet, where's Orrin?" Camden asked when he found his niece in her chamber, playing happily alongside a servant's child. A maid sat quietly in the corner of the room, sewing as she kept an eye on the two girls.

"Look, Uncle Camden, Mistress Faulkner made me a doll," Violet said with animation as she held up a wooden figure dressed in muslin and lace.

"That's very nice," he said distractedly. "Orrin didn't come to get you?"

His niece paused in making the doll dance. The joy in her eyes dimmed. "Why would he come to get me? Is something wrong?"

Camden forced a smile. "Nothing to worry about. We were merely checking up on you. I can see that you are enjoying time with your new friend."

He waited until she returned to her play before he motioned for the maid to draw near. She set her needle aside and came forward. Camden held up his hand, halting her progress, before she reached the door. In a low voice he said, "Keep the girls in this room."

Her eyes widened, but she nodded. "As you wish, milord."

His frown deepened at her words. Nothing in his life was presently "as he wished." Suddenly the nursery was too warm, the laughter of the girls too loud, and the walls a little too close.

Needing escape, he left the chamber and headed out of the keep. He had to find Orrin and the Stone.

An hour later Orrin slammed the door to the great hall behind him. He was breathing heavily, his chest rising and falling as he leaned back against the door. Dear God in heaven, he hoped he had done the right thing.

Camden would be furious. But Camden's anger he could handle. The pain and agony that the bishop continued to cause all of them he had no tolerance for.

Orrin withdrew from his sporran the letter that had prompted his rash actions. The missive was addressed to Camden, but Orrin had broken the bishop's seal and read its contents. He closed his eyes. It was the bishop's threat, come true. The bold writing blazed across his mind.

An accusation of witchcraft. Lady Violet would be taken by him. Tried as a witch. Hanged.

"Orrin."

Orrin opened his eyes to see Camden striding toward him. He clutched the missive in his hand. He would put the very foundation of his friendship with Camden to the test this day.

He had done what he knew Camden would never do. His friend was more likely to fight those who challenged him. But even the mighty Lord Camden Lockhart could not take on the entire Church and win.

Orrin straightened grimly.

"Where have you been?" Camden asked. Relief filled his eyes.

The relief would fade in a heartbeat. "I've been to see Bishop Berwick."

"Whatever for?"

Orrin swallowed his fear and thrust the letter into Camden's hand. "Because the man threatened to hang your niece as a witch."

Camden stared at him, his eyes wild in his white face.

"I knew you would never allow Lady Violet to hang, so I offered the bishop a compromise."

Camden's eyes darkened. "What kind of compromise?"

Orrin felt his blood run cold beneath Camden's sharp appraisal. "I gave him the Charm Stone."

Camden's gaze shifted to disbelief. "The Stone is gone?"

"Aye." Orrin couldn't stand to see the hurt, the betrayal so clearly stamped upon his friend's features. "And now that he has the Stone, we must hurry to get Lady Violet away from here before he discovers that the Stone needs a Lockhart to release its magic."

"I expected loyalty from you, Orrin." Camden's voice

was low, and as sharp as steel. "Above everyone else, I had expected you to stand by me."

"I wanted to help you. Without the Stone there was no further reason for the bishop to press his accusations. I did not want Lady Violet to die like her mother. The bishop promised to leave you and Violet alone."

Camden frowned. "You expect honesty from the man who hanged an innocent woman?"

Orrin's eyes widened with horror. "What have I done?" he said, mostly to himself.

"Without that Stone, we are doomed." Camden's harsh words echoed in the chamber, bringing all eyes to the two of them.

"Why? What's happened in my absence?"

Camden grasped Orrin by the arm and dragged him off to a less public corner. "The plague has spread to Lee Castle. It is only a matter of time before it consumes us all unless we use the Stone to heal ourselves."

"Plague." Fear tightened Orrin's gut. "Are you certain?"

"Aye."

Disgust at his rash action pulsed through Orrin. "I'll get the Stone back. I will go back to the bishop's house and retrieve the Stone if it's the last thing I do."

"Nay, Orrin," Camden said fiercely. "We are in this together, as we always have been."

Orrin looked at his friend with a spiraling despair. "I really did think I was helping you."

A flicker of deep pain crossed Camden's face. "I know that, you fool."

"Can you ever forgive me?"

"We have yet another battle to fight to get back what rightfully belongs to the Lockharts. Are you with me?"

Orrin's nod was fierce. "To the end."

"Let's hope it doesn't go that far. But we must retrieve the Stone, and soon."

Orrin straightened. "I can have the men ready for battle in under an hour."

Camden nodded. "I will join you then."

Chapter Twenty-three

Mistress Faulkner and four other women were in the chamber with Rhiannon when Camden returned. Rhiannon still wore the blue silk gown he had given her only a few hours past. She appeared as lovely as a cornflower in the soft summer sunshine instead of surrounded by a sea of death.

Three pallets lay against the far wall with linen sheets pulled up over the heads of those who lay dead. On the opposite side of the room, four more pallets had been set up, three occupied by moaning female servants and one by his steward.

Rhiannon dabbed at the fevered forehead of one of the women. "I am so sorry I called you Mistress Plague," the redheaded maid, Sophia, moaned. "My sharp tongue has brought a curse upon this household."

"Shh," Rhiannon soothed as she smiled down at the woman. "You did no such thing. God's mercy will see you through this. And I do forgive you for any unkindness."

The young woman clutched Rhiannon's hand. "'Tis more than I deserve."

The woman on the opposite pallet reached over and clasped Rhiannon's arm. "Please, you must send for a priest." She closed her eyes tightly for an instant before opening them again. "I'd like to take confession before I die."

Tears shimmered in Rhiannon's eyes as she gently stroked the woman's purple and black spotted flesh with a cool towel she'd dipped in a pail of water near the bedside.

'We sent a message on to Glasgow not long ago, asking for someone to come. We've had no response yet."

"No one will come," the woman moaned.

"Even if they don't, I am certain that God will accept you or anyone here without last rites. The Church itself has made such reparations during earlier outbreaks of the plague where priests were not available."

Rhiannon sat back on her heels, wobbling slightly. Camden could see the dark smudges of exhaustion beneath her eyes, and yet she hardly took a moment to rest before rinsing her towel in the bucket and dabbing it over the black suppurations that covered the woman's body.

"Rhiannon," Camden called softly as he moved away from the doorway and into the chamber until he stood by Rhiannon's side.

"Don't come in here," she pleaded.

"I am already at risk." He stood before her, wanting more than anything to wipe the exhaustion from her face.

"Is there no way to stop this tragedy? Three have already died, and many more have fallen. I've had reports of warriors, servants, these women, and their children becoming ill. And that's just here at the castle. We have no idea how far the plague has reached. Can we not use the Stone to save them?"

"The bishop has the Stone."

"What?" Rhiannon gazed at him in shock. "How?"

"There's no time to explain." Camden reached for Rhiannon's hand, for the towel that dabbed futilely at the woman's body. He wanted her to understand what he was saying before he left. He did not want her to think he was abandoning her. "The men and I go to war against the bishop. We will return with all due haste."

"You are leaving?"

"I will return." His tone was fierce.

She nodded. "I understand."

Did she truly understand that he would never run from even this danger if it meant keeping her safe? He frowned at the glazed expression that fell across her face. Numbness had crept into her soul, protecting her mind from the complete horror of death and devastation that surrounded her.

Camden leaned forward and kissed her forehead. "I will be back for you," he whispered with all the passion in his heart.

A spark of animation came back into her face. "I will be here."

He accepted her promise as he bolted out the door, urgency spurring him on. They had to hurry before the devouring beast consumed them all.

Rhiannon pushed past her growing fatigue and carried a tray laden with bread and cheese up the stairs from the kitchen to Violet's room. At the door of the chamber she paused, praying that the sickness had not spread to the young girl's chamber.

After knocking softly, Rhiannon pushed the door open and remained at the entrance. At the sight of Violet playing with her newfound friend, Rhiannon released the breath she hadn't realized she'd been holding.

Violet was safe.

Violet glanced up at Rhiannon and smiled, before she caught herself and arranged her features into a sour expression. "Why are you here?" she asked.

Undeterred, Rhiannon barely stepped into the room to set the heavy tray on a table near the door. "I brought all of you some food, and I ask a favor."

The maid set her sewing aside and rose from her chair.

"Stop," Rhiannon commanded. "Please, come no nearer to me."

The maid's face paled. "Why, milady?"

Rhiannon swallowed roughly. "Plague has hit the castle."

The maid gasped.

The children froze in their play. Even they knew the implications of that terrible word.

After a long pause, Violet said, "I can help. If you will only bring me the Stone."

"I would if I could." Rhiannon felt her shoulders dip as she explained what had happened.

"I was mad at you at first, for taking the Stone from me." The shield of aloofness around Violet dissolved as her eyes filled with tears. "I'm not mad anymore. I tried to protect you."

Rhiannon stared at the little girl, baffled. "What do you mean?"

Violet set her doll on the floor and rose, heading for Rhiannon. "I thought that if I—"

"Stop. I beg you. Come no closer. I could not live with myself if you became ill because of me."

The girl froze. Fear, stark and vivid, glittered in her eyes. "I thought that if I allowed myself to care about you, that you would be taken from me like my daddy and my mum. So I started pretending I didn't care."

Rhiannon felt a rush of sympathy at the child's logic and how she'd tried to protect herself from further loss. "I'm not going anywhere, sweetheart."

"How can you say that? The plague . . ."

"I am not going anywhere," Rhiannon said with such conviction she almost made herself believe the words were the truth. "Our lives were brought together for a reason."

Violet nodded. "Because God knew I'd need a mother."

An odd kind of peace settled over Rhiannon at the young girl's words. "Promise to stay in this room? All of you?" She searched each of their faces for agreement.

"We promise," Violet stated for them all.

Convinced that they would do as she asked, Rhiannon returned to care for the sick and dying.

Camden cupped his hands around his mouth and blew his hoary breath to warm his fingers as he waited for his men to surround the bishop's house. He wanted all exits covered before they attacked the bishop and his men. The bishop would surrender the Stone before the battle was through.

Dawn began to lift the gloom of night and give shape and substance to the bricked walls of the bishop's borrowed home. Tension knotted the muscles of Camden's back and neck as he waited in the cold that seemed to soak through his heavy layers of clothing to scratch wet, icy fingers up and down his spine. He was well-armed for this attack, with two daggers strapped to his chest, a claymore against his back, and his curved sword strapped to his side. All within reach and deadly, should the bishop choose not to cooperate.

It did not take long for his men, twenty-five heavily armed warriors, to surround the house. They waited in the growing light of day for the order to strike.

They were loyal, every single one of them—loyal to him not because of his politics or his religion or even his wealth, but because they were family. Their dedication even Orrin's, warmed his spirit as he drew his curved sword and signaled for the charge to begin.

On his signal, half the warriors charged into the house while the other half waited outside for men who might try to escape. The bishop's forces were small but powerful. That they'd been stripped of their cannon gave Camden a measure of comfort as he dismounted and charged through the door his warriors had just knocked off its hinges.

In less than ten minutes, the bishop's men had been shredded by Scottish steel. Some men lay dying, surrounded by their own blood while others lived, cursing, moaning, their faces gritty masks of fear.

Camden led the charge into the inner chambers of the house. The servants cowered as they drew near, waving Camden's men through the corridor. They stopped abruptly at the sight of the bishop himself, sprawled on the floor in the middle of the hall.

Inside the nearest chamber, a young woman lay upon the floor as well, her face and neck covered with a red rash. The plague had struck here, too.

"Go get some horses from their stable," Camden ordered the warriors who had followed him into the room. "We'll take those who are living back to Lee Castle."

"What about the plague?" Orrin asked. "We are all exposed. Our only hope now is to find the Stone and pray its magic works on us all." Camden knelt beside the bishop's body.

"Help me turn him over."

Together, they rolled the holy man onto his back and saw the red rash that dominated the bishop's neck and face, evidence that he had fallen to the plague. "No one, not even he, deserves to suffer such an illness," Camden said. "He'll die soon without our help."

Orrin thrust his hands boldly into the folds of the man's priestly robe. "The Stone has to be here somewhere."

"Move away from him," a female voice called from behind Camden. "You aren't going anywhere with my son."

Camden twisted, looked across his shoulder at an old woman. Her shoulders were hunched and her body appeared almost skeletal beneath her linen night rail. In age-spotted hands she held a slim dagger, aimed directly at Camden's back. Her gnarled fingers had turned white beneath the force of her grip. But the woman was old, and by the look of her sallow and spotted skin, none too healthy. Several dark black spots appeared as shadows on her torso beneath her thin linen night rail. But one of the open wounds on her neck appeared as thought it had started to heal.

"Mistress Berwick?" Camden asked calmly as he remained hunched next to the bishop's body. "Both you and your son have the plague. He will most likely die soon unless we take him back with us to our castle for treatment."

"He will be fine," she said. Her hand shook under the strain of holding the weapon erect. "The man is holy."

Camden glanced at Orrin, then slowly turned to face her. He hoped his movements would distract her as Orrin continued to search through the bishop's clothing for the Stone.

"Even holy men can fall beneath the gauntlet of the plague."

The woman turned a pasty white. "He is a man of miracles. He will heal himself. He healed me."

Camden shook his head. "The only miracle here is that you are both still alive." He slid closer. "Your son did not heal you, milady. But something did. You appear to be one of the rare people who has fallen to the plague, then lived."

The old woman frowned. "What could you know of healings? You are no man of the Church."

Camden stepped closer. "Nay, I am not. But I do know about healing people. I can make you completely well, like the young girl you used to be."

The dagger wobbled in her hands. "My son is the miracle worker. Not you." Her gaze dropped to the bishop's body. "Get away—"

Camden leapt at her, knocking the dagger from her

hands. It tumbled to the floor. A heartbeat later he caught the woman in his arms, steadying her.

"Leave my son alone," she wailed.

"I found it," Orrin announced, in a triumphant voice. He clutched the Stone in his hand, allowing it to dangle from its silver chain.

The older woman twisted in Camden's arms, fighting him with more vigor than he had expected, further proof that she was indeed recovering from the dreaded disease. He set her free, not wanting to cause her harm.

She ceased her writhing and dropped to the floor beside her son. "Wake up, Harold." She pushed against his shoulder. "Show these men that you are mighty, indeed."

"He's ill, milady." Orrin tried to reason with her.

She turned a wild-eyed gaze upon him. "A holy man's body is too pure to host illness."

"We are wasting precious time." Camden frowned at the woman. "Either we treat them all here and leave them behind, or we take them with us—willing or not."

Orrin stood over the bishop's body. "If we leave them behind we could make better time on our return to Lee Castle."

Camden did not like the idea of abandoning them, with only the old woman to care for them. But what other choice did he have if he was to see to the needs of his own people? He reached for the dagger the old woman had dropped and tucked it into his belt. "Give me the Stone, and draw some water. The sooner we treat them, the sooner we can leave."

Orrin tossed the Stone to Camden. It arced across the room, the bloodred Stone glistening as it moved through the air. Camden palmed the Stone. Gratitude moved through him at the return of his family's legacy.

He brushed his finger over the Stone in the center of

the coin. It warmed beneath his touch, as if the Stone somehow knew a Lockhart was in its presence.

Orrin returned with a pail of water and a wooden cup. He placed the pail before Camden. "There's been enough death. It's time for healing."

"Leave my son alone." The older woman batted at them with her gnarled hand.

Camden took the mug from Orrin and scooped up a portion of water. He quickly treated the liquid, then tossed Orrin a speaking glance. Orrin nodded slightly, and grasped the woman's shoulders as Camden tipped her head back and forced the water past her lips.

She sputtered, but eventually stopped struggling, until they'd given her the entire cup. They carried her to the bed and set her there to rest, bringing the bedsheets over her body. She seemed to drift off to sleep.

Leaving the woman to her slumber, Camden returned to the pail and drew another mug of water. Once again, he dipped the Charm Stone in the liquid three times, then swirled the amulet to the right. "Help me with the bishop. Lift his head while I pour the liquid down his throat."

Between the two of them, they swiftly treated the bishop and the maid while the old woman continued to sleep.

"Let's hope this works," Orrin said as he and Camden carried the bodies of the bishop, then the maid, and placed them on the room's only bed next to the bishop's mother.

"Rhys's healing proves the Stone can cure the plague." Because if it did not . . . the possibility was too horrible to imagine. Camden strode to the bucket and treated the remaining water with the Stone. "Before we leave, every warrior and every servant needs to drink this water."

Orrin nodded as he accepted the bucket and gathered the men. No one put up a fight. They seemed eager to drink anything that might keep them safe from the horrifying illness.

When the task was complete, Camden returned to his horse and gave the signal for them to ride out. Now that the Stone had been returned to its rightful owner, they had to return to Lee Castle before it was too late.

Chapter Twenty-four

Rhiannon was too tired to feel anything. *Not pain.* The strain in her shoulders and back had turned to numbness hours ago. *Not grief.* She'd been forced to submerge her emotions—both sympathy and horror—as the castle's residents collapsed in illness and death all around her. She had no time to grieve the dead when the living needed her help. *Not fear.* She had managed to ignore the ache that had settled under her arms, but she could not dismiss the red rash that had crept across her throat and chest with alarming speed. She'd fallen victim to the plague herself. Hours marked her presence upon this earth.

The light of dawn filtered through the front door of the keep. She had moved from the bedchamber above to the great hall hours ago as more and more residents became ill. She had thrown open the door to the keep, praying that the slight, cool breeze would carry away the stench of death that hung over the castle like a shroud. A huge fire in the hearth kept the residents warm.

Rhiannon leaned her head back against the cold stone of the castle's hall. She needed to rest, only for a moment. She could feel the tears of exhaustion and grief behind her eyes, but she buried her emotions deep inside, afraid that if she gave vent to anything she would be consumed by an overwhelming tide. Nay, it was best not to feel anything at all.

The only other person who could help was Rhys. She had asked him to take care of the dead. Since he was now healthy and strong, he could carry their bodies into the hall and line them against the wall without injury to himself. And in between carrying the dead, the man built a massive burial pyre so they could burn the bodies. Which was where he was now, leaving her alone.

No footsteps sounded anywhere in the hall as the servants, scullery maids, pages, warriors, and grooms had either fallen ill or run away in terror. She didn't blame those who'd left. There was a time when she might have run herself. But not any longer.

She could not change who she was, and finally she accepted that she did not want to. Her family might be known as criminals and thieves to most of the Scottish people. But she suddenly realized that she was shaped by her family's reputation not to do bad, but to do good—to be more than a Ruthven had ever been before. Strong, dependable, and honest.

She was all those things and more.

Strengthened by her thoughts, Rhiannon pushed away from the wall, ready to continue the battle against her unseen enemy. "I will fight you to the end," she said, allowing her conviction to resonate throughout the hall.

In order to sustain the fight, she needed fresh water. The cistern in the courtyard had been used dry. If she wanted water, she would have to fetch it from the well. Alone.

A sense of desolation swept over her, but she forced it away. Water. She had to get water. Straightening, she stepped out the door of the keep, through the courtyard to the stable where she hitched two horses to a cart. Beads of sweat broke out on her forehead, but she brushed them aside with the sleeve of her dress and pressed on.

She gathered as many buckets from the stable as she could find, and after placing them in the back of the cart, she stepped into the driver's seat. With a flip of the reins, she headed out.

The task of drawing the buckets of water from the well grew steadily more difficult with each bucket she filled. Even in the cold, sweat ran down her face and soaked through her blue gown as she struggled to lift the heavy buckets into the wagon. Over and over again she filled the buckets, until finally the task was complete.

"I never realized water was so heavy." Rhiannon leaned against the side of the cart, her breath coming in halting gasps. Now all she had to do was drive the water back up to the castle and repeat the process again, unloading what she had gathered. She swiped at her face with the back of her hand, then climbed into the driver's seat.

By midday, the task of retrieving water was complete. And Rhiannon found herself once again kneeling beside the castle's residents, wiping their brows of fever and cleansing their wounds.

What was keeping Camden? What she wouldn't give right now to feel the strength of his hand wrapped around her own. Had he deserted her as well as the others?

She clamped her mind shut at the thought. Camden would never desert her. She repeated the mantra over and over again as she continued her work.

He would never desert her.

She was so busy with her ministrations she did not hear anyone approach until a hand gently clasped her shoulder. She turned to see Violet standing beside her.

"Get back to your chamber," Rhiannon gasped, as fear twisted her heart.

Violet shook her head. "I want to help."

"Nay," Rhiannon cried, feeling a nauseating despair creep over her. But Violet would not be deterred. And Rhiannon no longer had the energy to fight her.

With a sigh of defeat, Rhiannon nodded. Perhaps it was for the best. Someone would have to take over the care of the sick and dying when the inevitable happened to her.

The gates to the castle stood open.

Sheer black fright swept through Camden at the absolute silence. No one and nothing stirred beneath the light of the midday sun.

He jumped from his horse and raced across the courtyard toward the doors of the keep, which were also open. The stench of rotting flesh assaulted his senses as he burst into the great hall.

He searched the room, desperate to find Rhiannon. His gaze tripped across the rows of bodies hidden beneath shrouds of white linen. *"Merciful heavens."* His voice was raw. He thrust his hand into his sporran. His fingers clutched what he'd hoped would be his people's salvation. But the plague had devoured them faster than he'd ever imagined possible.

The knot in his chest eased as his gaze slid to Rhiannon and Violet, sitting beside Mistress Faulkner. Rhiannon bathed the woman's forehead with a cloth, then returned her rag to the water only to swipe at her forehead once again.

"Rhiannon," he shouted as he moved across the chamber to her side.

She continued to dip, then swiped as though she had not heard him. She stared off in the distance at something he could not see. Her expression remained blank, devoid of all emotion. Her beautiful blue gown was torn and filthy, her hair a wild tangle of knots.

She kept dipping her cloth, then swiping.

"Violet, why are you down here?" His voice filled with agony.

"I wanted to help."

"You are so very much like your mother." He gave her

what he hoped was a comforting smile before he turned to Rhiannon.

"Rhiannon, can you hear me?" He dropped to his knees beside her. "Are you well? *Dear God,* answer me."

Her gaze finally focused on his face. "Camden?"

Relief lightened his chest. "Aye, my love."

"Camden!" Her eyes widened with horror, her faculties suddenly restored. "Get away from me!" She scooted away from him, frantic. "Plague. I'll kill you. Go away."

Violet offered him a ragged smile. "She's been ill for several hours, Uncle Camden. I did not know what to do."

He stood and grasped Rhiannon in his arms. She struggled desperately to free herself. He drew her closer, tucking her head beneath his chin. "Shh, my love. Help is on the way."

When she stopped struggling, collapsing against his chest, Camden held out the Charm Stone to Violet. "Will you treat the water while I hold Rhiannon?"

She bit down on her lip. "The cistern is dry and the well is so far away. We've used all these buckets of water. There is nothing in the castle left to drink."

"The ale," he said softly over Rhiannon's head. "Use the ale."

Violet nodded. Before she could turn toward the storeroom, Orrin and the other warriors who'd ridden out with them entered with several casks of ale.

"When I saw that the cistern was dry, I knew you would need something to use as a tonic. I figured the ale was the quickest choice."

"Aye," Camden agreed. "Set the casks down here." It took four men to carry each of the big casks that they set down near where he held Rhiannon so fiercely.

"Help Lady Violet by drawing the ale into those buckets," Camden ordered the returned warriors. "Once the ale is treated with the Stone, each of you should drink before you treat the others." At Orrin's puzzled expression, he added, "It will not help to have any of you fall ill."

Orrin nodded, then handed Camden a mug of the treated ale. "When that is done, what should we do with the dead?"

Camden closed his eyes. The image of twenty or more bodies in the hall was there right behind his eyelids. He blew out a heavy breath. There had to be others, he deduced from how rapidly the illness had spread from Rhys to everyone else. "Set them in the courtyard for now. The Stone can do nothing for those who have already died."

Orrin nodded.

"And, Orrin, I shall also need you to find the others who have left the castle in fear. Send a contingent of men out to round them up. They must be treated or the chain of death could continue unchecked."

"Agreed," he said. A moment later, he and the others set to work.

Camden drank the contents of the mug, then cradled Rhiannon in his arms, unwilling to release her. He turned to Violet and dipped the wooden mug into the ale she had just treated. "Drink."

The girl put the cup to her lips. When she was finished, she pursed her lips into a frown. "Your ale tastes terrible."

He laughed. "Duly noted. I will try to meet your standards in the future."

She smiled, then giggled, the sound a balm to his heart. Violet had suffered so much, yet she was strong, a survivor, just like Rhiannon, and just like him.

His gaze shifted to the woman in his arms. "Will you be all right," he asked his niece, "if I take Rhiannon upstairs to her chamber? She needs to rest."

"I agree," Violet said. "She wouldn't allow me to help her until a short while ago."

He scooped Rhiannon up in his arms, then stood. He

grabbed the handle of a pail of healing ale that Violet had just prepared before carrying Rhiannon up the stairs to her chamber.

He settled her gently upon the crimson damask that covered the bed and drew a cup of ale from the bucket. "Rhiannon, you must drink." When she didn't respond, he shook her gently. No response. Determined that she should live, he lifted her head to the cup and pressed the liquid through her lips.

She swallowed convulsively as he encouraged her to take the entire contents of the cup. He would leave nothing to chance. Not where this woman was concerned. He returned her head to the pillow and with tenderness stroked her hair.

He slowly unlaced her dress until he could slide it up over her head. Her chemise followed, until she lay bare before his eyes. Camden felt his throat grow heavy and thick at the sight of the egg-size boils that marked the skin beneath her arms, and the red rash that dotted her neck.

The woman before him was as brave as any warrior he had taken with him into battle. Her body was marred by disease, her mind battered by the fatigue and suffering. He saw not her battered and ravaged body, but under her rash the delicate peach skin of her cheeks, her halo of golden hair, and the gentleness in her soul. And he knew that he loved her no matter what her lineage.

He'd always known love would be a passionate and powerful emotion, but he'd had no idea that it would also leave his nerves raw, his stomach churning, and his spirits so high he felt as though he could fly.

He immediately sobered. Would he get the chance to tell her he loved her? Wretchedness moved through him, and he did something he hadn't done for the last ten years. He prayed.

Please, don't take her from me when I've only just realized what a gift You have given to me.

Humbled by his own sense of desperation, he left her briefly to retrieve a clean length of linen. He dipped the linen in the bucket of ale, then with a gentle caress, bathed each deep purple boil.

As though by magic, each boil slowly vanished, leaving her flesh unmarked.

He dipped the cloth over and over again as he had seen her doing when he'd arrived at the castle, treating her entire body. "Thank you," he said, his throat aching under the intensity of his gratitude. He had never expected his prayers to be answered so swiftly. Perhaps it was not God who had deserted him all those years ago, but he who had abandoned his faith.

"Forgive me," he whispered.

"I forgive you," Rhiannon whispered in return.

Darkness surrounded him, lurking, waiting to close in. Camden tensed in the grips of a dream. His chamber faded, the walls of the keep vanished, and he was back in the Holy Land, standing on the rocky shoreline of a foreign land on the day of his release.

He and Orrin had survived the horrors of bondage and war. And yet now that they were free to return home with the wealth they had acquired, home seemed more like the foreign land.

Silence surrounded him, the kind of silence that comes upon you at sea just before a storm. For seven years he had lived in a world of torment and pain. Only Orrin could understand what each life claimed had done to his soul.

The darkness crept closer as he thought back to all the things he had done to survive. Yet now at this moment of judgment, could he live with those choices, could he move past them? Or should he allow the darkness to overtake him, to swallow what remained of his life?

Or he could allow himself to live. To fight for those things that were worth risking his very soul for—the protection of family, of country, of those he loved.

Memories of battles swirled in his head. They tumbled over each other, melded together and separated yet again. So many battles. So much death.

Camden pressed against the barriers of his mind until he stood not on foreign soil, but on the fertile shores of Scotland.

Home.

What kind of honor justified war and destruction? Was protecting those you loved enough?

The dream shifted to Lee Castle, to the family who awaited him there. The emptiness inside him vanished, filled now with hope and love. He knew that the battle he struggled with now was his most important of all—and the most difficult. The prize was the future, and the possession of his soul.

He breathed in a deep, heather-scented breath of Scottish air, held it, allowing it to flow down to his center, to the place of his despair. Slowly, breath by breath, he found himself healing. His thoughts focused, crystallized. There were things worth fighting for, worth killing or dying for. All a man could do was choose his battles carefully and follow the path his heart told him was right.

Camden startled awake. He stared into the afternoon light and pulled the woman beside him more firmly against his body. For the first time since his return to Scotland he felt his burdens lighten.

Because now he knew what path was right for him.

Chapter Twenty-five

The stench of rotting flesh had faded, replace by a minty, musky odor. Rhiannon opened her eyes. Where was she?

A sea of red surrounded her head. Golden light chased the darkness from the room, reminding her of spring—of life, of renewal, and of the glorious breezes that rippled across the fields of heather, carrying the scent of the sea. A tangy saltiness touched her tongue, and she shifted her gaze to see Camden bending over her.

"Welcome back." He soothed a damp cloth over her temples. She drew a deep breath, savoring the deliciousness of his scent, holding it in her memory for what remained of her days.

Or hours . . .

"Plague!" She bolted upright.

With a gentle hand he caught her shoulder, stroked her arm. "It's gone."

She stared at him, startled. "How long have I been in here with you?"

"Only a few short hours." His hands drifted down her arms to settle at her waist. "And you were quite talkative."

Rhiannon stared down at her chest, her arms. The red rash and the large purple and black spots were gone. "What did I tell you?" she asked, grateful she had been healed, but unsettled by her loose tongue. She could remember nothing.

"You told me about your mother. And you mentioned a few things about your father. But most important, you told me that you loved me."

Silence descended between them and she heard the crackle of flames in the grate and smelled the musky sweetness of burning peat. She was safe, and well. "Did I really say that?"

He nodded, and for the first time she saw a fragile vulnerability in the warmth of his eyes. "Was it a feverish imagining or the truth?"

Rhiannon did not want to hide her thoughts or her emotions any longer. The plague outbreak had taught her one thing: Life was short. And she was no longer afraid to reach for what she wanted.

"I have always told you the truth. I fell in love with you in the cottage that day."

His fingers stroked the curve of her cheek. "I love you. With my body if you will have it, my heart if you will trust it, my soul if you will take it into your safekeeping."

Rhiannon choked back tears at the touching words of the Celtic prayer. The scent of him, the feel of him, the taste of him combined to send her senses spinning, reeling out of control. His words echoed in her mind. *He loved her.*

Camden shifted to sit beside her. "I feared I'd lost you." He put a hand behind her head and lowered her to the pillow, his mouth following her down, kissing her with tenderness and passion.

He pulled back to study her face a long moment later. "Why did you not leave when you saw the plague?"

"I loved you, Violet—and even your people—too much to leave you without help."

His expression clouded. "My people were not always kind to you."

The love swelled in her heart and she could not resist stealing a tender kiss from his lips. "Nay, they were not. But you were, once you chose to accept me." She traced the cleft in his chin with her finger. Her hands rippled down his neck, to his chest, to his waist to release the yards

of tartan from around his waist before she grasped the ends
of his shirt and tugged it over his head.

She sighed appreciatively as her hands slipped over the
hardened planes of his chest. She scooted up and leaned
forward, allowing her hair to brush across his skin, teasing
his nipples to erectness.

Her mouth gently closed around the hard bud and she
sampled it with slow, swirling probes of her tongue. At his
groan of pleasure she slid further down his body, allowing
her lips to explore the flat surface of his belly, and to nip
playfully at the rigid steel of his muscles.

"What a seductress you are." He pulled her back up
along the ridges of his chest and twined his hands in the
long strands of her hair, forcing her head to arch gently
back. "Shall I seduce you as you have me?" His mouth
came down to plunder the creamy skin of her throat, the
top of her breasts. She relished the feel of his hands upon
her flesh, exploring her mysteries, revealing her need. She
wanted his heat. She wanted his strength. She wanted to
feel healthy and whole again.

Her lips boldly caressed his, her tongue greedily wanting
to know the taste and feel of him.

He dragged her into his arms, pulling her tight against
the hollow of his hips. She felt the hardness of his arousal
against her. With urgent hands, he pushed her chemise off
her shoulders and lowered his head to her exposed breasts.
He taunted first one, then the other.

A hot shiver went through her. She arched her back
again, thrusting her breasts forward. On a moan of pure
pleasure, she coiled her hands in his hair, freeing it from
the leather queue at his nape, curling her fingers around his
neck, urging him on.

With a deep-throated groan, he pulled back and pushed
her linen chemise down past the rounded softness of her
hips. He followed the garment down, his hands on her

thighs, his thumbs stroking the golden thatch of downy curls, parting her flesh, probing her intimately with his tongue.

She cried out as pleasure gripped her and pushed shamelessly, eagerly as sensation after sensation burned through her. Her body felt weak, drugged as she looked down at his dark head.

"Please." It was all she could say as an all-consuming heat moved through her.

He settled between her thighs. "Are you well enough for this?" he asked, his voice raw, his eyes as dark as midnight.

"Oh, yes." Her voice broke with emotion.

He plunged deep, reaching the quick of her.

Instead of stroking her need, he remained still, as he lavished her neck, her ears, her collarbone with a volley of tender erotic kisses.

She clutched his shoulders, feeling the sweet frustration and tension mounting within her as he manipulated her body to a fever pitch. She felt as though she had to move or she would shatter into pieces. She began to shake as tremor after tremor pulsed through her with unfulfilled need. "Camden." His name was a cry of desperation that set him into motion.

His rhythm was hard, wild, swift, and tumultuous as he filled her again and again with a desperate hunger that was as out of control as her own.

Her head thrashed back and forth on the pillow as she tried to keep from crying out at the intensity of the passion shuddering through every muscle, every nerve of her body. He was shaking too, she realized dimly, as she brought her hands down to his hips and met each thrust with an eagerness she did not know she possessed.

His breathing was harsh; he shivered and quaked uncontrollably as an urgency born of blood and fire overtook them both. He moved hard, faster, deeper until he cried out and threw his head back, his neck arching, his body going rigid.

In that moment their pleasure peaked, exploded in a fiery release that robbed her of both reason and sanity. He plunged once more, as deep as life and breath itself as they soared together into a place of sheer ecstasy.

They lay there limp, unable to move even the tiniest muscle, entwined in each other's arms for several silent moments, until their breathing steadied and the cool moisture of the room caressed their heated flesh.

"I love you," he whispered as he placed a kiss upon her temple.

"Why?" she asked with a touch of wonderment. "After everything my family put you through, how could you—"

He put a finger to her lips. "The past is just that. Let's leave it behind and start anew."

She nodded. A warm glow rippled through her at the thought of a new beginning.

He met her gaze, his eyes warm and sincere. "Marry me? Stay with Violet and me forever."

"Violet?" She startled. "Is she well? She didn't—"

"Violet is fine. She is eager to see you when you feel up to it."

Relieved, Rhiannon reached out and took his hands. She laced her fingers through his. "Will Violet agree to our marriage?"

He nodded. "She is very much in favor of your remaining here."

"Then, yes. I will marry you."

"On the morrow. I would claim you today, but this day must be for the dead."

She searched his taut gaze. "Why such haste?"

"I love you, isn't that reason enough?"

The past day and many hours of pain had shown her over and over again to embrace the moment. Life was too precious to waste when you never knew when it would end. "Aye, love is reason enough. But where will we find a priest? I sent a summons to Glasgow, but no one has come. I would not trust the bishop to help us."

A smile returned to his face. "Hush, my love. We will work it all out, you'll see."

"But—"

He silenced her with a kiss. "Is that the only way I can keep you quiet?"

She ceased her anxious questioning and smiled. "I can think of less pleasurable ways to spend our time."

"Agreed." He stood and gazed down at her ragged clothes. "We should burn all the clothing, bedding, and blankets that anyone who was sickened by the plague used. That includes your dress. Just to be safe."

She nodded. "I will miss it because you gave it to me, but I understand."

Rhiannon moved to the wardrobe to retrieve the green gown Mistress Faulkner had made for her. She quickly dressed, watching in fascination as he laid his tartan on the floor, folding it with quick precise movements before he lay upon it, belting the fabric around his waist, then stood.

Her gaze lingered on his well-muscled body appreciatively. "Suddenly I find the idea of marrying you on the morrow very appealing. Shall we?" She motioned for the door.

On his deep-throated chuckle, they headed to the great hall. Once there, Rhiannon's mood immediately sobered as her gaze fell upon the rows of shrouded bodies lining the wall. A raw and primitive grief overwhelmed her. She released an anguished sob.

Camden came to stand behind her, pulling her back against his chest. "So many lost." He shook his head.

"For a moment upstairs, I almost forgot."

He kissed the top of her head before moving away to join Orrin, who crouched beside the bodies.

"Twenty-two are dead," Orrin said, his gaze anguished. "In a matter of hours . . ."

"How many were spared because of the Charm Stone? We have to focus on that."

Orrin nodded. "The men rounded up several people in the surrounding hillsides and brought them back here to be treated. I am fairly certain we have contained the illness."

Camden clapped Orrin on the back as he shifted his gaze to Rhiannon. "That's good news."

"'Tis about time something good came to this castle," Orrin stated, his tone relieved.

"Then you should also know that Rhiannon has agreed to marry me." The smile in his eyes when he looked back to Rhiannon contained a sensuous flame that brought heat to her cheeks.

A slow smile lit Orrin's weary face. "It's about time the two of you stopped fighting and realized you were meant for each other. When?"

Camden's expression sobered. "We have much to do here to set things right. I will need everyone who is able to help build a funeral pyre for the twenty-two who have died. We must show them our respect before continuing on with our lives."

Orrin nodded his agreement. "Rhys has already built a pyre on the hillside to the west of the castle."

Camden nodded. "Very well then." He turned back to Rhiannon. "Will you see to Lady Violet? The last I saw her, she was in the kitchen with Mistress Faulkner."

"Mistress Faulkner lives?" Relieved tears came to Rhiannon's eyes. She quickly turned away and headed out the door of the keep and to the kitchen building beyond.

As Camden watched her go, his emotions shifted from elation to dread. "Do I tell her, Orrin?"

Orrin's gaze snapped back to Camden's. "Tell her what?"

"That I set out to have her murdered? That I was responsible for her nearly burning at the stake? That I am the one who may have killed her brothers?"

A deep frown cut across Orrin's face. "For centuries marriages have been founded on lies."

"I made a vow that I would never lie to her," Camden replied in a low, tormented voice.

"Only you and I and the assassin know the truth. The assassin is dead by your own hand. And I vow never to tell anyone." Orrin shook his head. "Your secret is safe."

Camden knew he could trust Orrin. What his friend had done with the Stone had been out of a desire to help, not maliciousness.

There was no way for her to find out about what he had done. Even so, a deep feeling of unease rippled through him. Could he live the rest of his life knowing that he had deliberately withheld that information? Should he tell her and risk losing her?

He had one day to decide. Before they married, he would have to reconcile his deeds in his own heart.

The bishop opened his eyes to see the faces of seven men hovering over him. Had he died? Was this his last reckoning before his fate was decided? He stared up into each face, praying as he did that they could see only the goodness in his heart, and not the villainy that had taken root inside him since he'd been passed over for recognition by Robert the Bruce.

"He's awake," a voice from above said softly.

"Why doesn't he speak? Is he damaged in some way?" another voice asked.

"Get away from the bed, all of you." He recognized that voice. His mother. He suddenly noted the golden light of the setting sun. So he wasn't in heaven after all.

He struggled to sit up as consciousness burned through the haze in his mind. The Stone. He fumbled in the deep folds of his robes, but came up empty.

One of the gray-haired men frowned at him. "Is he still feverish?"

His mother hobbled to his bedside and shooed the men back. The bishop stared in awe at her neck, her face. The rash had vanished. The boils were gone, and a curious spark missing for years had returned to her gray eyes. "He's fine." Her gaze pierced his with a warning. "You had a fever, nothing more. Now get up and greet the Church council properly."

"The Church council?" His plan. His revenge. They had arrived. He leaned against the headboard of the bed, felt the bite of the elaborately carved wood against his back.

He reached out and touched the wrinkled skin that lined his mother's face. "You are better."

Her gaze narrowed on his face. She sniffed as though insulted. "Only by some miracle did I escape the abuse of that madman."

He knitted his brows, confused. "You what?"

She turned away from the bed, addressing the men who hovered nearby. "My Harold suffered under his assault as I did myself. Can you not see that?"

The oldest of the men stepped forward. A heavy frown creased his deeply lined face. "We have heard your story. Now we need to understand your son's. Bishop Berwick, tell us what has happened here. And why would you place the burden of witchcraft on a supposedly young and innocent child?"

Unease crept up the bishop's spine as he took in the severe faces of the seven men who surrounded his bed. What had his mother told them? "I—"

"Just tell them, Harold, that Lord Lockhart burst into our home, killed our warriors, and threatened to murder us unless you revoked your charge of witchcraft against the Lockhart child."

That was not what had happened. He paused as his brain scrambled to find a way to make this situation work in his favor. And then he found it. He straightened, pushed the covers away from his legs and sat up, swinging his legs over his bedside. "Why don't we all go ask Lockhart for his version of the truth?" Or at least whatever version of the truth would place the Charm Stone back in his own possession and dangle Lockhart from the hangman's noose.

He would have that Stone. He would have everything that was his due.

Chapter Twenty-six

The glow of the flames changed the night sky into a vignette of red and orange. The huge funeral pyre had been made to hold all twenty-two bodies. The wood beneath was also piled with the bedding and clothing and anything that could be fouled by the disease that had wracked their home.

Camden gave a final blessing in the tongue of the ancients. The pain of sorrow burned in his chest as he stared at the macabre, obscene beauty of his people returning to their Maker. Acrid wisps of smoke drifted around the living who had gathered upon the hillside to send their kin on their way. They had all worked the rest of the day through to make their home secure once more.

On one side of him, Rhiannon gently took his arm in a protective clasp. Violet stood on the other side, holding his hand. The two women he had never known he wanted in his life, yet they made him feel things he had always dreamed of but never dared to hope for all those years ago while he had been a prisoner in a faraway land. He wanted to know all the things that love was meant to be. He wanted children, to be a father, to give Violet everything she might miss by not ever truly knowing her own parents.

He wanted to fully live whatever time he had left upon this earth, with a clear conscience and a clean heart.

He had to tell Rhiannon the truth. And then he had to convince her to stay with him. The task would not be easy, but it was necessary, he knew that now. "Rhiannon, I must speak with you when we return to the castle."

Her brow knitted. "Is everything all right?"

"It will be very soon." His tone held all the resolution he longed for in his soul. By this evening, he prayed all would be as it should be.

"You're trembling." Camden tightened his arm around Rhiannon's shoulders as they walked back into the great hall.

She gave him a small smile. "I suppose I am."

"Why? Do you fear returning to the castle after all you've endured here?"

She shook her head. "Nay. If anything, the plague has proved to me I have strength I didn't know I possessed."

He frowned. "Then what frightens you so?"

"It's not my fear, but yours that worries me." She looked up into his eyes and he saw the vulnerability he had seen there upon their first meeting. "I heard the fear in your voice outside. You wished to speak with me?"

He offered her a solemn nod. "You are very observant."

She came to a stop in the middle of the hall as the others filed in around them. "Tell me now."

"Rhiannon—"

"Visitors at the gate." One of the guards raced into the great hall, his breathing hard, his face flushed. "They are asking for Lord Lockhart." His eyes widened. "There are eight men and one woman."

Camden released a soft imprecation at the untimely interruption.

" 'Tis the Church council, the Bishop Berwick, and his mother."

Camden set his lips grimly. His gaze lingered on Rhiannon's face for a moment before he moved past her. "We'll talk later. Go upstairs with Lady Violet. That man means to make more trouble. As if he hasn't done enough already."

Camden hurried through the sea of people streaming

back inside the keep. At the door, he came face-to-face with Bishop Berwick. "Who let you in?"

"The gates were open." The bishop gave Camden a black look. "We took that as an invitation. The Council and I would like a word with you."

The bishop pushed past him and into the hall. Behind him came seven older men in ornate green robes with bands of gold trimming their sleeves. Each one gave Camden a condemning look as they walked past. A foreshadow of things to come?

And behind the men, walking bent over a cane, hobbled Bishop Berwick's mother. "Mistress Berwick," Camden greeted her with a chill in his voice. The glint in her soft gray eyes told him she was up to something.

Once inside, the men headed for the dais. They sat behind the long table, facing the rest of the room. His people, curious to know why the bishop had called upon them yet again, this time without his warriors, lined the chamber's wall. Their restless chatter created a soft hum that hovered over the room.

"Lord Camden Lockhart," the oldest councilman stated, with a hint of censure in his tone. "The Church council has come here this evening on a serious matter involving you, the Mistress Berwick, and your young niece, Lady Violet."

A sudden chill washed over Camden. "What about Lady Violet?"

"We will get to her. First, however, we must deal with the matter of you assaulting Mistress Berwick in her own house. These are times of war," the old man continued, looking down at Camden from beneath his bushy gray brows, "but cruelty to women will not be tolerated by the Church council."

"She claims I assaulted her?" Camden shifted his gaze to the bishop, who stood beside his mother. A flush reddened the bishop's cheeks. Camden bit back the stinging retort that seared his tongue. His arguments would do him no good. It was the woman's word against his. His men could vouch for his behavior, but their loyalties would be questioned, and he had no desire to bring further pain to anyone else under his protection.

"When we arrived at the Bishop Berwick's home earlier this evening, we found Mistress Berwick lying prostrate on the bed over her son's body. She claims you injured them both out of revenge."

"And why would I feel the need to seek revenge against these two?" Camden asked, so startled by the allegations that he reacted with a stunned, harsh laugh.

The man glanced at the bishop and his mother before continuing. "Because the bishop challenged you about the proper care of your niece along with your niece's caretaker, a woman of questionable character."

Everyone in the room gasped, except Camden. Instead, anger singed the corners of his control. Praise the saints that Rhiannon and Violet were safely upstairs and unable to hear such bitter claims against them. "You can question my character all you like. But you will leave Mistress Rhiannon and Lady Violet out of this."

Camden strode toward the table where the Church council sat. "All of this is not because of my niece or her companion, but because of the bishop's greed to possess the Lockhart family's treasure."

Again the chamber filled with excited voices, gasps of horror and intrigue.

Bishop Berwick moved forward to meet Camden in front of the table. "If you know what is good for you, you will hand over that 'treasure,'" he said for Camden's ears alone. An evil smile spread across his thin lips.

"Never," Camden growled quietly.

The bishop's cheeks darkened in anger.

As Camden turned to the council, he caught sight of

Rhiannon and Violet standing on the bottom step, watching the proceedings. He nodded at them, oddly comforted by Rhiannon's presence, despite what she might have heard the bishop say about her. "I can state, without any reservation, that I have never been deliberately cruel to a female before."

"Never?" the bishop drawled.

"Never."

"Was it kindness then that prompted you to hire an assassin to kill all of the Ruthvens, including Mistress Rhiannon Ruthven?"

Hushed silence filled the chamber. Not a sound could be heard expect the pulse of Camden's own heartbeat in his ears. He shifted his gaze toward the stairs, to the pale look of devastation on Rhiannon's face. He stood stock-still, his face expressionless, his fists balled at his sides. *Dear heaven above, how could the bishop know that?*

A sneer cut across the bishop's face. "Do you deny it?"

"No." A cacophony of chatter filled the chamber. He could care less what everyone else thought. He only cared about Rhiannon. "There is an explanation."

She stepped from the stairs fully into the chamber. "Rhiannon." His voice was thick and low as he strode toward her. "I was about to tell you the truth myself."

She lowered her lashes, hiding her eyes from him. "Did you succeed in killing my brothers?"

"Aye."

"You were responsible for the attack in the horse cart?"

"Aye."

"At the cottage?" her voice trembled, as did her hands.

"I tried to break off the attacks then." It was too little, too late, he knew.

She clamped her arms around her waist as though holding herself together. "You were responsible for those men who took me away and tried to burn me?"

He could hear the desperation in his own voice, but he

didn't care. He looked back at the stairs, to the little girl who hid there in the shadows. He had to own up to all of it if they were to ever have a future together, the three of them. "Ultimately, aye."

"I feel like such a fool to have trusted you." Rhiannon closed her eyes. "How could I be so naive to let you manipulate me like that?" She opened her eyes to reveal a shimmer of tears. "What else have you lied to me about?"

He took a step closer and touched her arms. "I didn't lie about my feelings for you. My desire for you was more than sincere."

"Don't." She flinched back, holding her hands out to stop his advance. Her eyes blazed at him from within her pale face. "You don't have to pretend you care for me any longer."

"I do care for you, my love. More than anything." He took another step closer. He held out the Charm Stone to her. "You know how much this Stone means to the Lockharts. But you mean more." He pressed the Stone into her hand. "Give it to the bishop or keep it for Violet."

She stared down at the Stone in her hand. "This Stone is a blessing."

"You decide its fate."

She shook her head. "Only you and Lady Violet can use the Stone, so why offer it to that madman?"

"Only a Lockhart can use the Stone?" Anger laced the bishop's voice as his gaze shot to Orrin. "You lied to me."

Rhiannon held the Stone back out for Camden to take. "The Charm Stone means everything to you."

"You mean more," he repeated. "The assassin is dead. He cannot hurt you any longer. I shall watch over you and Lady Violet, forever. All that I am, all that I have, are yours."

Tears fell onto Rhiannon's cheeks now, trailing down her face.

"I have found my faith once again because of you—

faith in myself, and faith in us." Camden paused. "I'm asking you, Rhiannon, to have faith in me."

A suffocating sensation tightened his throat as the silence lengthened between them.

"What are the three of you talking about? The council should be involved." The oldest member of the council stepped forward, his mouth set in annoyance.

The bishop put out his hand. "Quickly and quietly, give me the Stone," he whispered low enough for only Rhiannon and Camden to hear.

The tears in Rhiannon's eyes vanished, replaced with fury. "You brought the plague here." She took a step forward, forcing the bishop back.

"The plague?" The councilman stopped his progression toward them and his eyes widened in terror.

"Keep your voice down." The bishop darted a gaze back at the council members. "I'm warning you."

"Twenty-two people are dead because of you," she said in a voice clear enough for all to hear.

"No!" The bishop backed farther away from Rhiannon. "The woman, she lies."

"She speaks the truth." Rhys stepped out of the crowd.

The bishop's eyes went wide and his face paled. "You're alive."

"Because of this." Rhiannon held the Charm Stone from its short silver chain for all to see. "The legendary Charm Stone."

"The source of witchcraft," another one of the council members gasped.

The oldest councilman stood before Rhiannon. His brows turned down in a frown. "Have you used this Stone, milady? Have you performed acts of witchcraft?"

Camden felt his muscles clench. His thoughts flashed back to Clara, to the helplessness he had felt at not having been there to help her when this very same Council had found her guilty of the same crime. He gripped the hilt of his sword, determined to fight his way past the Church council if necessary to keep Rhiannon safe.

"Why is it that if I use the Stone to heal people it would be seen as witchcraft to you? Yet if the bishop uses the same Stone it would be seen as a miracle?"

The councilman frowned. "Milady, perhaps the issue is too complex for you to understand."

"I understand all I need to. This Stone saved my life and the lives of all the others who you see before you now," Rhiannon continued. "After each use of the Stone both Lady Clara and Lady Violet made the sign of the cross over the body of the person they had treated. To me that shows a certain respect for the divinity of healing by the Creator, not witchcraft."

"If you need further proof of the Stone's goodness, its powers healed me from the plague and a deadly knife wound," Rhys said from the crowd.

The man from the council reached out and touched the silver coin housing the Stone, hesitantly. "What do you mean, it has healed you?"

Rhys stepped up beside the older councilman. "I was close to death when I arrived at the gates of Lee Castle a few days ago. That man," he pointed to Bishop Berwick, "exposed me to the plague that his mother had contracted. Without knowing I was ill, I came here and unfortunately spread the sickness to innocents." Rhys pulled aside the tail of his tartan and lifted his shirt to expose his chest. The councilman narrowed his gaze on Rhys's chest. "I was near death, and yet I lived. Without a mark from either the plague or the knife upon my body."

"Nay." The bishop came forward and snatched the Charm Stone from Rhiannon's fingers. "Liars. They are all liars, who shall be punished." He spun around, his eyes wild, heading for the stairs. Before Camden realized where the bishop was headed, he'd grabbed Violet from the shadows and hauled her into the chamber.

Camden drew his sword and charged, stopping an arm's length away from the bishop, his blade jabbed at the bishop's throat. "Let her go. I've had enough of you and your accusations."

The bishop moved his free hand into the folds of his robes. A flash of silver warned of a dagger.

"Do not draw your weapon," Camden said coolly. "I'd like nothing better than an excuse to slit your throat."

"You'll regret this," the bishop snarled.

"Why should we regret setting things to rights?" Rhiannon asked, pulling Violet into the safety of her arms before lifting the Charm Stone from the bishop's hand.

The bishop growled, then twisted toward the Council, careful to avoid thrusting himself into Camden's blade. "This little girl is the witch here, not that woman," he tossed a bitter glance Rhiannon's way.

The chamber exploded in an uproar. The members of the council at the table turned to speak to each other. But Camden kept his eyes firmly on the bishop. "You've been exposed. Your plans for the Stone will never come to fruition."

"You're wrong." He shook his head. "It's my fate to become the next Archbishop of Glasgow. The Council will side with me. You will suffer because of my mother's accusations against you. And that little girl will hang, just like her mother."

Violet clutched Rhiannon's skirt in her hands, burying herself in the green fabric. "Don't let them hang me," Violet gasped.

"You will not hang, Lady Violet," Rhiannon reassured her, stroking her golden curls. "Members of the Council. Please, hear me out."

The room settled into silence.

"Can someone bring me a mug of ale from the barrel near the hearth?" One of the young women she'd helped survive the plague brought her a mug filled with ale. "Thank you, Mary Anne."

The young woman curtsied. "Milady."

Rhiannon embraced Violet. "One more time, will you treat the ale?"

At Violet's nod, they approached the councilmen at the head table. The oldest councilman followed behind them. "The Charm Stone brings the wondrous gift of healing." Rhiannon set the mug on the table and handed the Charm Stone to Violet.

"Lord Camden Lockhart explained to me that only those who are Lockharts through marriage or by blood can use the Stone." At Rhiannon's nod, Violet dipped the coin into the red liquid three times, then swirled it to the right.

As Violet treated the ale, Rhiannon prayed that without someone saying an incantation, the Council could not rule Violet's actions as witchcraft.

Violet withdrew the coin and dried it on her dress. "The ale, when it is consumed by someone ill, will help that person to heal." Violet extended the mug toward the councilman near them, then handed the Stone back to Rhiannon.

He merely frowned into the mug. "How do I know the ale is safe to drink? How do I know I won't get the plague from drinking the liquid?"

Rhiannon took back the mug and took a sip herself.

Still he remained silent, scowling at the mug she'd returned to him. Rhiannon splayed her hand in a gesture encompassing the room. "All of these people drank from the treated ale. Now all are healed. Have you known anyone to survive the plague before?"

The councilman grasped the mug and sniffed the contents. "Very few are lucky enough to survive the disease."

He brought the mug to his lips and drank. He frowned at the contents. "The ale tastes like any other."

One of the councilmen at the table stood. "Bishop Berwick, what kind of madness have you involved us in? What we witnessed was not witchcraft. No incantation was said. Witchcraft involves incantations and curses. The Charm Stone calls upon God's mercy. Would you have us deny His miracles?"

"No, that's not it. She—" the bishop objected, then stopped short at the prick of Camden's blade.

The other men of the council stood. "We've heard enough here today."

"What about the man's abuse of me?" the bishop's mother cried over the roar of voices that filled the room once more.

The oldest councilman turned to the woman. "Domestic matters are not our concern. We gave you our ear because of the seriousness of the charges you made against the man. And of those your son made against his niece." He narrowed his gaze on the woman. "Show me one bruise the man inflicted upon you and I will charge him with this crime."

The woman sputtered. "Well, I . . . give me a moment," she said, pushing back the sleeve of her brown homespun gown.

The councilman shook his head. "We are done here." He turned to address the room. "All the charges are dropped against the Lockharts. You will retain possession of the Charm Stone. And should the people of this land ever need its healing properties, may we call upon you?"

Camden lowered his sword. "It would be an honor, sir."

The councilman turned a black look on the bishop. "As for you and your mother," he said, signaling for the other members of the council to come forward and restrain the two by the arms. "I have decided to transfer your services to a needy parish on a remote isle in the Hebrides. You leave on the morrow."

"The Hebrides?" the bishop gasped. "We will perish that far from civilization."

"Or find penance," the councilman said.

"No! We must stay and fight," the old woman cried. "You will be named archbishop, Harold. It is your destiny!" She was still protesting as she and her son were hauled out of the castle.

With the threat of the bishop gone, Camden sheathed his sword. He offered the councilmen a respectful bow before he turned to Rhiannon.

Slowly, he drew closer until he took her hands in his own. "Can you forgive me for what I did to your brothers?"

A flicker of pain crossed her face. "That they are dead saddens me. No one deserves to die so violently."

"I regret—"

She brought her finger to his lips, silencing him. "No regrets. You told me once before that we should concentrate on the here and now."

He held her gaze, hoping she could read all the love and sincerity in his eyes. "Stay with me. Marry me on the morrow as we'd planned. The future is ours if we take it. If you can forgive me . . . ?"

Chapter Twenty-seven

He asked for her forgiveness.

Rhiannon's eyes stung with tears as she brought her gaze to his. Mother Agnes had said to fill her heart with forgiveness. Had the abbess known, somehow, what would transpire between herself and Camden?

She startled at the tenderness in his warm blue eyes. "I should be angry with you."

"Furious," he admitted.

She kept her expression neutral, not allowing him past her guard. Not yet. She had to be certain. "As a Ruthven I have grown up with nothing but pain and devastation in my life. For a short while, I had hoped you would offer me something different, something more."

He opened his mouth to speak but she silenced him with a finger to his lips.

"I came to you in one of the darkest moments of my life." She looked about the hall at the castle residents who lingered there, some talking with the members of the Church council, some watching her and Camden with pensive looks on their faces.

She offered them an encouraging smile before returning her gaze to his. "I never imagined becoming married when I came to you. Later, it did not seem reasonable that you could love me, a Ruthven, your enemy."

"And now?" he asked, his gaze filled with hope and possibility.

"I've learned that good things can come from bad." She held her hand out to Violet who flew to her side.

"I cannot imagine living a single day without your sweet smile to greet me," she said to the little girl.

Violet hugged her legs all the harder before she scowled at her uncle.

Rhiannon forced back a chuckle. Poor Camden. He didn't stand a chance against the two of them.

"And what of me? Will both of you allow me into your lives?"

Violet pursed her lips. "As long as you don't cheat any of us again."

"Cheat you?"

Violet nodded. "Don't cheat me of a mother. Don't cheat Rhiannon of a husband. And don't cheat yourself of a wife."

Camden shook his head, dazedly. "I'm so glad we cleared that up."

Violet nodded, then grabbed his leg, pulling Camden up against Rhiannon. "Please say you'll marry him?" Violet pleaded.

Rhiannon's breath caught at the sensation of his body pressed so intimately against her own. "I'll marry him."

"You will?" Camden breathed. The smile in his eyes contained a sensuous flame that warmed her to her soul.

"I bring nothing into this marriage but myself and my notorious last name."

"Milady, I vowed to give you all that I have. My surname included."

Rhiannon smiled, hiding none of her pleasure. She had wanted nothing more than to change her last name only a few weeks ago. But now she understood that a person's worth was not determined by their last name. She reached for Camden's hands, lacing her fingers through his. "I accept."

"My lady, my love." He leaned forward and brushed his

lips against her temple. "I will spend my life protecting you, and making amends for the pain I caused you."

With joy rising where there had once been emptiness, Rhiannon replied, "And as your warrior's lady I look forward to it. Exactly when will these 'amends' begin?" she asked in a sultry tone. She meant to comment further, when he pressed his lips to hers, interrupting her words and her thoughts with the most overwhelming kiss of her life.

Chapter Twenty-eight

R hiannon stood on the battlements where she and Camden had first made love and drew a deep breath of the fragrant morning air perfumed with newly blooming heather. Camden had asked her to wait up here for a signal of the bagpipes to come to him.

The tranquility of the morning calmed her sudden nervousness. She was not nervous to marry the man she loved. Nay, she knew that the rest of their days would be filled with joy. They had both suffered so much already, her with her family, and him while being held prisoner in the Holy Land away from those he loved.

Rhiannon lifted her chin, allowing a whisper of the breeze to tug at her thick cascade of hair. She wore it loose about her shoulders as he liked best. The staff, dressed in bright plaids, brought the grounds of the inner bailey alive with their joyous dancing and lilting voices. Yesterday's tragedy was but a memory on this day that she and Camden would marry.

Camden.

He waited across the courtyard for her to join him. The sound of the bagpipes rose above the din of voices, calling her forward toward her groom. As though he knew she had started her journey toward him, Camden looked up and a slow, sensual smile came to his lips. Rhiannon forgot to breathe as she drank in the sight of him.

He wore his plaid of green and blue and red cloth over a crisp white shirt that did nothing to hide his bold masculinity. He was powerful, forceful, yet gentle. And he belonged to her from this day forth.

With the bagpipes soaring, she continued to drift toward him down the stairway, through the castle and out of the keep. As she neared, he clapped his hands, twice. Instantly, the warriors forming a makeshift aisle drew their swords and held them in an arch for her to pass beneath. Rhiannon's breath caught in her throat as Camden took her hand, smiling into her eyes. "You are breathtaking, my love."

"As are you, my husband." Rhiannon was glad she had decided to wear the Lockhart plaid as her wedding gown. It was her family plaid now.

At the end of the row of swords, Violet waited for them, wearing a new dress made from Lockhart plaid as well. Rhiannon held out her hand. There were no longer shadows in the girl's eyes, only joy. Camden took Violet's other hand and walked with the two women toward the eldest Church councilman, who had offered to return this morning to perform the wedding ceremony. When they stopped, Rhiannon released Camden's hand and knelt before Violet. "Before your uncle and I marry, there is something I must ask of you."

"What?" Violet grew serious.

"Will you, Lady Violet Lockhart, accept me as your mother? I cannot replace the mother who bore you, but I will promise to love you as she would have loved you all of your days."

Violet's face brightened and she threw her arms around Rhiannon's shoulders. "Nothing would make me happier."

Rhiannon ruffled the little girl's curls. "Then we will be a family, the three of us."

Violet released Rhiannon. "Hurry and marry each other so I can have a new mummy and daddy."

Rhiannon stood and placed her hand in Camden's larger

one. She stood proudly before him as they took their marriage vows. At last they were pronounced man and wife. The sound of the bagpipes rose and swelled over the thunder of cheer and applause from the crowd.

"Before we seal our vows with a kiss," Camden said in a suddenly somber tone. "I have something I must give you." He stepped back to where Orrin stood, and accepted two narrow wooden boxes, one longer than the other, from his hands. When he joined her once more, Camden held the objects out to her. "My gifts."

With hesitant fingers, she lifted the lid of the longer box, and tears misted in her eyes. "Camden," she whispered brokenly. Inside the box lay a newly milled bow and six arrows.

"For the woman who can protect herself, though her husband hopes she never will need to do so."

Then she opened the second box. Inside lay the Charm Stone.

He picked up the Stone and held it out to her. "Now that you are a Lockhart, you have the power to use it," he said.

She accepted his gift, twining it in her fingers. "Thank you." Filled with overwhelming joy, she slid her arms around Camden's neck. "But I have nothing to give you in return."

With a possessive hand at the small of her back, he pressed her closer. "You have given me two gifts I never expected." At her startled gaze, he brought his lips to hers and kissed her with a reverence that touched her very soul. After what seemed like an eternity he broke the kiss but did not release her.

"And what is that?" She looked up at him with her heart in her eyes.

"Freedom and love." He cradled her against his chest. "For a warrior who once had neither of those things, they are the most precious gifts of all."

*   *   *

And from her vantage point, still holding on to Rhiannon's skirt and her uncle's leg, Violet looked up. Not at her new mother and father, but at the Charm Stone that dangled from Rhiannon's fingers. The red Stone at the center of the coin seemed to glow with happiness beneath the warmth of their affection.

Warmed by their love and the happiness within, Violet smiled. The Charm Stone's magic had certainly worked to heal two wounded hearts.

Afterword

In the final book in this series of Scottish Stones of Destiny, I set the story around a famous Scottish amulet called the Lee Penny. For the purposes of the story, I renamed the amulet The Charm Stone.

The Lee Penny was obtained by the Locard family during the Crusades in 1330. After the death of Robert the Bruce, king of Scotland in 1329, his friend Lord James of Douglas set out to take the dead king's heart to the Holy Land, making the pilgrimage that the king was not able to undertake in his lifetime.

While making their way through Spain, Douglas and his band of knights battled with the Saracens. Douglas died on the battlefield, but the king's heart in its silver casket was rescued by Sir Simon Locard of Lee, who brought it back to Scotland for burial. After that event, the family changed their clan name to Lockhart to reflect the service they had done for their king.

It was during this same battle that Sir Simon Locard imprisoned a wealthy emir. The emir's aged mother came to pay his ransom, and in the course of counting out the money, a pebble inserted in a coin fell out of the lady's purse. She was in such a hurry to retrieve it that the Scottish knight realized it must be valuable and insisted that the amulet be added to the ransom. The lady reluctantly agreed and explained what virtues the Stone possessed.

The stone was a medical talisman believed to drive away fever and stop bleeding. The amulet was used frequently in the same manner described in the book, according to tradition. In 1629 the Lee Penny helped cure sick oxen, but as a result a young woman was burned at the stake for witchcraft for using the Stone. There are records of an accusation of witchcraft against Sir Thomas Lockhart during the Reformation, but the Church Synod at Glasgow merely reproved Sir Thomas and advised him to cease using the Stone.

During the reign of Charles I, the citizens of Newcastle, England, requested the use of the Lee Penny to cure a cattle plague. In order to guarantee the stone's return, Sir James Lockhart required a bond of 6,000 pounds. The penny was used, and the plague abated.

Many cures for both animals and humans, directly related to the use of the Lee Penny, are recorded through the middle of the nineteenth century.

The Lee Penny is the most widely know of all the Scottish amulets thanks to Sir Walter Scott's *The Talisman,* which also features the mystical Stone.

I hope you've enjoyed learning more about three important treasures of Scotland through the pages of *The Warrior Trainer, Warrior's Bride,* and *Warrior's Lady.*

Alissa Johnson

"A joyous book from a bright star." —Kathe Robin, *RT BOOKreviews*

As Luck Would Have It

A WOMAN OF THE WORLD...

After years of wild adventures overseas, Miss Sophie Everton is in no hurry to return home to the boring strictures of the ton. But she's determined to reclaim her family's fortune—even if she has to become a spy for the Prince Regent to do it.

A MAN ON A MISSION...

Before she can get her first assignment, she lands right in the lap of the dark and dashing Duke of Rockeforte. She's faced hungry tigers that didn't look nearly as predatory. Somehow the blasted man manages to foil her at every turn—and make her pulse thrum with something more than just the thrill of danger.

AND THE FICKLE FINGER OF FATE

To make a true love match, they'll have to learn to trust in each other...and, of course, a little bit of luck.

ISBN 13: 978-0-8439-6155-3

SHIRL HENKE

"…mesmerizes readers with the most powerful, sensual and memorable historical romances yet!"
—*Romantic Times BOOKreviews*

Sky Brewster's heart cries out for justice, and she will not be satisfied until she sees her husband's murderer dead at her feet. To get the job done, she'll leave her Sioux people to make a devil's bargain with a man whose talent as an assassin is surpassed only by his skills at seduction.

Max Stanhope is an infamous English bounty hunter who always delivers—dead or alive. But now he must take a wife to claim his birthright. When his newest client turns out to be as delectable as she is passionate, he figures he'll mix business with pleasure.

The beautiful widow and the Limey make a deal: her hand in marriage for his special skills. But an old Cheyenne medicine man has seen the Great Spirit's grand design, and True Dreamer knows Sky Eyes of the Sioux is destined to love the…

PALE MOON STALKER

ISBN 13: 978-0-8439-6112-6

Connie Mason

Wulfric the Ruthless had sworn vengeance on the Danish raiders for killing his young wife. But when he laid eyes on Reyna the Dane, all he could see was a woman of extraordinary beauty. She was his thrall, gifted to him by his brother to warm his bed. Could the beautiful healer also ease the fire burning in his heart?

When Reyna first caught sight of Wulf, she thought he was the man she'd vowed to hate forever. But Wulf's golden body and seductive kisses awoke very different feelings within her. As one Northern night blended into another, she realized he was no longer her enemy but her beloved…

Viking Warrior

ISBN 13: 978-0-8439-5746-4

DAWN MacTAVISH

The battle that won Robert Mack his scars was lost in the cradle, and thus the third Laird of Berwickshire wore his silver helm not for personal protection but the sake of others. While the right side of his face was untouched—handsome, even—the left lay in ruin. No man could look upon him without fear. Nor could any woman. Such a life was worse than any prison, so Robert set out for Paris and the great healer Nostradamus.

The powerful young Scot reached a land in conflict. With a boy on its throne and her people at war, all of France was shadows, intrigue and blood. All except for Violette Cherier, a blind flower girl with honey-colored hair, as beautiful and fragile as her namesake. Soon enough, what at first seemed Robert's unwise act of kindness proved sage. The fires of civil war were rising, and Violette was the only one who could free the…

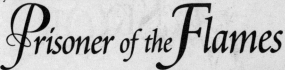

Prisoner of the Flames

ISBN 13: 978-0-8439-5982-6

☐ **YES!**

Sign me up for the Historical Romance Book Club and send my FREE BOOKS! If I choose to stay in the club, I will pay only $8.50* each month, a savings of $6.48!

NAME: _____

ADDRESS: _____

TELEPHONE: _____

EMAIL: _____

☐ I want to pay by credit card.

☐ **VISA**   ☐ **MasterCard**   ☐ **DISCOVER**

ACCOUNT #: _____

EXPIRATION DATE: _____

SIGNATURE: _____

Mail this page along with $2.00 shipping and handling to:
Historical Romance Book Club
PO Box 6640
Wayne, PA 19087
Or fax (must include credit card information) to:
610-995-9274
You can also sign up online at **www.dorchesterpub.com**.
*Plus $2.00 for shipping. Offer open to residents of the U.S. and Canada only. Canadian residents please call 1-800-481-9191 for pricing information.
If under 18, a parent or guardian must sign. Terms, prices and conditions subject to change. Subscription subject to acceptance. Dorchester Publishing reserves the right to reject any order or cancel any subscription.